volume three
murder in the light of day
right and wrong are relative

lar e hale

All rights reserved. No part of this book shall be reproduced or transmitted in any form or by any means electronic, mechanical, magnetic, photographic, including photocopying, recording or by any information storage and retrieval system, without prior written permission of the publisher. No patent liability is assumed with respect to the use of information contained herein. Although every precaution has been taken in the preparation of this book, the publisher and author assume no responsibility for errors or omissions. Neither is liability assumed for damages resulting from the use of the information contained herein.

Copyright 2021

ISBN-13: 9798612816959

This is a work of fiction. Characters and incidences are the product of the author's imagination and are used fictitiously.

Published June 2021 by lar e hale

acknowledgements

I'd like to thank my beta-reader, JoAnna. She is excited to read what I send her and always gives helpful feedback. I especially like when she says something is 'Really good!'

I'd also like to give my editor heaping wheelbarrows of thanks and gratitude. If not for her patience and support, I wouldn't have written a single page, let alone a best-selling series of award winning books.

Okay, that last is a rumor I am spreading, but my regard and appreciation for her is heartfelt and true. Thanks, J.

Books by Lar E Hale

The Murder Series

making a case for murder
doing what has to be done

when murder becomes mayhem
some people need to die

murder in the light of day
right and wrong are relative

what goes around

When Gregg came to, his arms were pulled behind him and tied to a tree, his mouth crammed with tighty-whities, his screams muffled and fruitless. How she'd managed to haul and fasten him to the tall spruce was a mystery, but the sharp glint of a knife in the moonlight was as plain as day.

~

She tossed his manhood, such as it was, into the brush, cut the rope holding him in place, and then kicked the log he'd been standing on from underneath him. She heard the noose catch, not bothering to look, and left him dangling in the wind. If he held his hands together tightly to keep from sliding down the trunk of the spruce, there was a chance he could stop what was happening.

It was more than he'd given her sister when he and his friends raped her over and over.

With the quiet sounds of night critters came the *calm*, and her thoughts turned toward her dad, as they always did.

chapter one year ago

"What am I going to do, Dax?"

Tasha's eyes glistened through the teary mist as a small coalescence fell and began its downward journey. I wanted to wipe it away but feared the moment would be adversely affected in the attempt, as if touching her would burst the bubble of her affection after I'd said yes to her questions.

Did I kill Mary's father? Did I kill those men last night?

I only meant to eliminate two who'd sent two others to harm her and my recently adopted daughter. However, due to unforeseen complications I had to dispatch a few more, which happens sometimes when murder becomes mayhem.

As for Mary's father, he needed to die from the get-go.

"If you're not being rhetorical, I have an answer."

"Oh, I don't doubt it," Tasha said, struggling between a suspended disbelief and an exhaustion ready to devour her. "You seem to have one for just about everything – including justifiable homicide."

"So you agree it was justified?"

"I didn't... That's not what I..."

"I know," I said, holding up my hand. "Sorry. It must be difficult to hear the truth, let alone come to terms with it. But if you could do so in the next few minutes before Mary gets home, that would be great."

She was accustomed to his use of humor in stressful situations, but his smile, and the way he looked at her, were things she never grew tired of. Or thought she ever would. Tasha was in love for the first time in her life and wondered if she'd fallen too far into its depth to climb out.

"Does Mary know?" she asked.

"About her father, yes."

"What about Anatovich and his men?"

"No."

Which, if not entirely accurate, was at least factual. I never discussed those kinds of things with Mary, but I was fairly certain she knew exactly what I'd done.

Tasha yawned a thirty-one hour fatigue. She needed to be asleep if she wasn't already. Surely this was all a dream.

"Would you mind if I lay down in your bed for a bit?"

"Have I ever?"

He smiled again, and she should have left but instead asked a question she didn't really want answered.

"Have there been others, Dax?"

"Are you asking as a detective or a fiancé?"

"Yes," she said, troubled but too tired to think clearly.

In the span of a second, trusted truisms filled my mind – *no sense closing the stable door after the horse done bolted, in for a penny in for a pound, what the hell might as well* – when what I'd rather do is lie my ass off.

But that ship had already sailed.

"Do you remember what Arnold told Jamie Lee Curtis in the movie *True Lies* when she asked a similar question?"

~~

Jeri Ryan pulled out of the Taylor's driveway long after Tasha helped her interview the little girls. The parents of two had come from Ohio and Arizona to reclaim their stolen daughters, and Leigha, the third, had been reunited with her family in the early hours after midnight.

The man, as they called him, left the ladies at the Taylor home in Wewahitchka on his way to the Florida Keys, or so he'd said. According to them, he saved their lives by killing the degenerate that made them do despicable things.

The monster was Dimitri Anatovich, head of a sex trade organization Jeri had been building a case against, and he'd sent someone to persuade her to drop it.

When she refused, her life was threatened. When she still refused, the thug showed a picture of a battered Tasha and threatened to kill *her*. Even then, and as much as she loved her best friend, she'd been prepared to let them both die rather than submit – until he called the men who held Tasha hostage and discovered they also had Mary.

Jeri capitulated. She had to.

Anthony Ferrelli eventually left her house, went to see Anatovich, and got his malevolent ass handed to him by *the man*. Or so she hoped.

She was waiting for conformation that he was dead. He needed to be because not only had Ferrelli threatened to kill Tasha and Mary if the case wasn't dropped, but he held their lives over her head unless she did as she was told – starting with, "Take off your shirt."

The ringtone saved her from thinking about the rest.

"This is Ryan."

"Director, it's Donald."

Jeri was too tired to correct her assistant, as she always did, by saying she was a *Deputy*-Director.

"What do you have for me?"

"The good news is the low-life scumbags are still dead, both Anatovich and Ferrelli have been fingerprint verified, and we've found evidence linking others to his operation."

She took a long, extended breath and released it slowly. Ferrelli was done. Gone. Finito.

Halle-fucking-lujah.

"And the bad news?" she asked.

He hesitated, and Jeri braced herself.

"Donald?"

"Cadaver dogs sounded at multiple spots in the woods on Anatovich's property. I'm afraid this may turn out to be a major dumping ground. We're bringing in the necessary equipment for excavation."

The thought of frightened children being used for sex before being disposed of like garbage infuriated her. Thank goodness *the man* found the three Wewa girls before they were thrown away as well.

"Do we have anything more on our killer?" she asked.

"There's video of him leaving with the girls, but most of his face is turned away from the camera, as if he knew it was there. We're dusting for fingerprints, but he was wearing gloves so don't expect much. Looks like a professional hit."

3

Jeri nodded to herself. Seven men were killed by a man who went there to do so, and she wasn't at all mad about it. Not even a little bit, despite her FBI sensibilities.

"Thanks, Donald. Send the video to the lab, see if the facial-recognition peeps can do anything with it. And let me know if you dig up anything else."

After a few seconds of silence, she apologized.

"I didn't mean it like that."

"I know, Ma'am. And I will.'

"I'll be back sometime tomorrow afternoon," Jeri said, intending to stay the night with Tasha and her *family*.

"Do you want me to cancel the morning meeting then?"

"Shoot, I forgot all about it. No. Some are coming from out of town. I'll head to the airport now and fly back. What time is the conference?"

"Eight AM, sharp."

"Who the hell is responsible for that?"

"You are, Director," Donald said with a grin. His boss believed that the early bird caught the most reprehensible criminal worms and brooked no complaints to the contrary. 'Get up, get out, and get em' was her mantra.

"Donald, I'm not a Director. I'm a *Deputy*-Dir . . ."

~~

The sound of phaser-fire emanated from Tash's phone, and I plucked it from her bag to turn down the volume but decided to answer instead.

"Hello, Jeri."

"Dax? Why are you . . . What's wrong? Is Tasha okay?"

"She's fine, just taking a nap. I don't usually mess with her cell, but the phaser ringtone must be set to kill because it was loud enough to wake the dead."

They were steeped in Star Trek lore and lexicon going back to their police academy days nearly two decades ago. Jeri and Tasha were full-on Trekkies in every meaning of the term, whereas I was more a Trekker myself.

"Did you need me to get her for you?"

"No," Jeri said, "don't wake her. She needs the rest."

"So do you. You still coming over, staying the night?"

"That's why I called. There's a meeting I need to attend first thing in the morning. With all that's happened over the last twenty-some hours, it plain slipped my mind."

"Well, considering what you've been through, I think you are allowed a momentary lapse. Are you alright?"

"I, like Gloria Gaynor, will survive."

"It's too bad you can't make it. You could sing that song in all its glory and we could *doo-wop* as your Pips."

I smiled when she told me the Pips belonged to Gladys, not Gloria. I knew that of course, but her derisive laughter was worth the rebuke.

"You're a funny boy, Dax."

"But not as funny as you?"

"You got that right. Tell Tasha I'll call her later?"

"Will do."

"Alright then. Take good care of our girl and I'll see y'all in a few days."

"I will. Stay safe."

Mary pulled up into the clearing, and I shut off Tasha's phone before stepping outside.

"Hey, girl. How'd you do?" I asked, grabbing the kayak from the bed of the truck.

"I went, I saw, I conquered," she said with a twinkle. "Those fish didn't stand a chance. Take a look."

She lifted the cooler lid. Plastic bags of filleted fish lay on a bed of ice. Flounder, speckled trout, and ... Pompano?

"Wow. A little late in the season for this guy, isn't it? Where'd you find him?" I was more than a little impressed. She was becoming quite the fisherman. Not as proficient as Tasha but starting to challenge my position as second-best.

The little shit.

"There's a hole where a few delinquents like to go and hang out instead of staying in school with their classmates. Unfortunately for them, they got caught playing *hooky*."

I grinned and cocked my head when she said, *Dammit*. "No, I got it. It was clever."

"It's not as good as it was in my head coming up the driveway. Turned out to be more 'ha-ha' than 'ha-ha-ha.'"

"Well, I think you made a valiant effort to incorporate a migrating *school* of fish and catching a straggler with a hook. I'm sure it would've been better if you had more time."

"Oh, ha," she said, and we grinned at her accumulation of the number of *ha's* she'd been shooting for.

Mary asked about Tasha as we rinsed off the kayak and sprayed salt air and water from the rods and reels.

"She's laying down," I said. "Probably asleep by now. She was one tired puppy."

"Where did she go so early this morning?"

Maybe it was a look in my eye or my reluctance to reply, but Mary's expression changed from sanguine to serious.

"What's wrong, Dax?"

~~

Tasha, as played by Jamie Lee Curtis, asked her secret agent husband if he had ever killed anyone as they sat tied to rickety chairs waiting to be tortured by terrorists.

"Yeah," Dax said, slurring his Schwarzenegger accent as the *truth serum* began to take effect. "But they were all bad."

She cracked up, even before he raised and lowered his eyebrows. Tasha had heard many of his parodies, including a spot-on Clint Eastwood, but the peculiarity of Arnold's voice coming from Dax's face was hilarious, and she laughed so hard it woke her.

The room was dark, save for the light leaking beneath the bedroom door, and she stretched long and deep as Dax's offbeat impersonation tarried in her thoughts.

Perhaps it had all been a bad dream – she hadn't been attacked, Mary hadn't killed the men who held them captive, and Dax hadn't murdered anyone.

That illusion vanished the moment her cheek brushed against the pillow. One of the men struck her with the butt of a gun after she'd been bound with duct tape. And if Jeri hadn't complied, they would've killed her. Mary, too, after she showed up for their sleepover.

But Dax had seen to it that Anatovich would never send anybody to harm anyone ever again, hadn't he?

Questions like how he knew who Dimitri was or where to find him gave way to more serious concerns.

Dax was a killer. And Mary?

Before she could come to grips with the possibility, the door slid open after a couple of soft knocks. Mary closed it behind her, walked to the bed, and took a seat on its edge. She sat quietly and peered through the darkness, waiting for her eyes to adjust. When the bruised cheekbone became more visible, Tasha saw a flash of anger spark, followed by tenderness and apprehension.

"So. You know about my father."

"Dax told me *he* killed him."

Mary tilted her head at Tasha's inflection.

"You think he's covering for me?"

"It's something he would do, don't you think?"

Dax had been teaching Mary to defend herself since he found her in the woods, and Tasha attributed what she'd done last night to her training. But the way those men were eliminated with such cool efficiency was disturbing, made more so by Dax's revelation. Maybe he was protecting her?

"Truth is," Mary said, "it didn't occur to me at the time – to kill my father. After being bound, gagged, and raped repeatedly, you'd think that would have been a no-brainer, especially given what I had to do to get him to untie me."

Tasha saw her relive the horror of that experience and placed a hand on her arm to give comfort.

"But I was nearly destroyed by the time I escaped, and all I wanted was to get out of that house and go kill myself. And if anyone other than Dax had found me, I would have."

"Why do you think that is?" Tasha asked. "Why him?"

Mary paused, remembering the sorrow on his face after seeing a video her father had made and placed on her phone to humiliate, threaten, and guarantee her silence. Dax didn't know how much his tears had touched her heart, but it was what he said afterward that brought her back to life.

"He didn't talk me off the ledge by saying it would all be okay. Instead, he said something that, all of a sudden, made it possible to imagine it *could* be."

"What?"

"'*I'm going to kill him.*'"

Tasha blanched, and Mary's heart filled with empathy as she laid next to her, head propped by hand and elbow.

"I know. It sounds jarring out of context, but you can't know the depth of what it meant. The man who'd terrorized me would be gone from my life forever. I no longer needed to die because that son of a bitch would never hurt me again – in person, in the press, at trial, from prison, or with videos of what I did to survive. I'd be free to live. Dax saved me in the only way I could have been."

Tasha smoothed the strands of hair behind Mary's ear. It was difficult to refute the reality that her father's death was the best way to overcome his evil. And Dax's love and support had been critical in restoring what was lost, made her strong, confident, capable.

Unsettling as it was, and in spite of adamant objections from the cop inside of her, Tasha thought she might maybe, someday, come to accept Dax killing the man who'd brutally molested Mary.

But what about the men last night?

"Would you rather they had killed us instead?" Mary said with patient incredulity. "Like I told you before, if those men didn't want to die, they shouldn't have come to kill you. They got what they got and that's that."

Tasha didn't realize she had said her thought out loud. And while those weren't the men she'd been thinking about, her remarks and fierce affection brought a new perspective.

Would she have acted any differently if they had come for Mary? Or Dax?

"I understand, but we cannot make our own decisions about who lives and dies. The law is there to protect us from anarchy. Don't you see that, hon?"

"Yes, of course. But the rules only apply if abided by. When people like my father and those men disregard them, it's necessary to treat their contempt like the malignancy it is. A surgeon doesn't toss cancer in jail, hoping it won't kill again. She excises every last bit so the body can thrive. Men like that don't change, Tash, and they don't deserve more consideration than is fair. They lived to harm others. And now they don't."

Tasha closed her eyes as the words resonated, the crisp articulation seemingly spoken by an adult.

Mary was mature well beyond her years with opinions formed by horrific experience, thoughtful deliberation, and intelligent discourse. It wasn't easy to dismiss her as an idealistic teenager because Tasha found merit in what she said, despite its unlawful premise.

The law and what's right are often at odds, she mused. The sin of slavery destroyed millions of lives and was legally enforced for centuries. But it was always wrong.

Maybe Mary's point of view was more an evolution of justice than its violation?

After a few minutes of quiet, Mary asked a question.

"Are you going to arrest him?"

"I don't know," Tasha said.

A minute later, she asked another.

"Are you still getting married on Saturday?"

"I . . . I don't know."

"Well, just so we're clear," Mary declared, "I'm keeping you as my mother whether you two get hitched or not."

"Oh, yeah?" Tasha said, a lump clogging her throat.

"You know what they say about a life saved – it belongs to the saver. And I'm not giving you back. Well, unless you reciprocate someday. Then we could make a trade, I guess."

Mary smiled and returned Tasha's hug, sealing the deal.

"Uh, Mom?"

"Yes?"

"I can't breathe."

"Oh. Sorry, hon."

They lay still until Mary spoke up.

"Tash?"

"Uh-huh?"

"If Dax is arrested I'll come forward, say it was me. And people will believe it because I'll make them. You need to know that."

Tasha didn't doubt her ability to convince a prosecutor or jury of her guilt. And then what? After hearing the sordid details of what that man did to his young daughter, would she even be charged? Or convicted if she was?

9

Probably not. And she probably knows it.

In addition to her premature wisdom, Mary was smart as a whip. She would have factored the variables, calculated the possible outcomes, and made her decision accordingly.

Did she know what Dax did to Anatovich and his men? If so, Tasha had a good idea of what she would say ... *They threatened his family, Tash. And he saved us like I saved you. By making sure that never happened again.*

But did Mary know how close to death he'd come?

~~

After adjusting the fan so it didn't appear obvious, I set the table. Sure, I could have knocked on the door and called out *dinner* instead of having it waft down the hall, but I was a little nervous about what they were talking about and did not want to become the focus of their conversation.

There were too many things they didn't know, details that, if asked for, might permanently alter our relationships. Perhaps irrevocably.

Maybe not with Mary. I think she was aware of what I'd been doing since her father and believed as I did – if you do evil, you need to die.

But Tasha might not be as understanding or forgiving. And I wasn't altogether certain she should be.

It bode well that they were wearing smiles when I saw them, but Tasha's diminished as soon as she saw me.

"Mary said Jeri had to get back to Atlanta?"

"She had a meeting she forgot about. Are you hungry?" I poured her a glass of her favorite wine, a Kendall-Jackson chardonnay, and handed it over.

"Yes. Thanks." Tasha took a long drink and then a chair at the dining room table.

Across from her, Mary crooked a finger at me.

"Garcon, I'd like some of what she's having, please."

She didn't have to smile the way she did to get her way, though it raised her cuteability quotient, because we'd long ago adopted an *Italiano* philosophy about *vino* with dinner. A little was fine, even healthy. It also deepened the bond between the girls by sharing Tasha's love for the *grapes of life*, as she put it.

I, on the other hand, preferred a much softer beverage. A Mountain Dew, Coca-Cola, or what I considered nectar of the Gods, A&W Rootbeer. Not in soda cans, however, but straight from the tap into plastic gallon jugs.

After pouring some wine into Mary's glass and topping off Tasha's, I lifted my frothy brew.

"To us."

We clinked our glasses with more solemnity than usual and took our time before pulling them back. For me, it was a sobering moment; I could have lost them last night.

I still could.

"Ready for the good stuff?" I asked.

"This *is* the good stuff," Tasha said, taking a huge sip.

Mary joined her in Kendall solidarity while I went into the kitchen. The buzzer was a minute from doing its thing, so I shut it down, pulled the pans from the oven, turned off the stove, and *Voila*, our surf and turf dinner was done.

Or rather its redneck equivalent, meatloaf and fish.

No, I'm not one, but I do appreciate many of their ways. Like the ingenious use of duct tape for what needs *fixin*.

"Hey, are you going to feed us or what?"

I told Mary to hold her horses. When I set the platters on the table, they began scooping food on their plates before I could say *Bon Appetit*. One thing about us, we didn't stand much on ceremony.

"Hey, Mare?" I asked as we crossed forks over a plump piece of pompano. After a brief skirmish, I yielded and took some trout instead. "Were you able to get hold of Isabel and tell her what happened?"

"Yes. She hadn't seen the news so her freakedoutness wasn't as bad as it could have been. But Watson . . ."

Tasha grinned at the made-up word; a new quirk Mary acquired from Dax. As she listened to their playful banter, she was struck by its normality in the wake of last night and contemplated the implication. Nine men were now dead, essentially executed by two of the people she loved most in the world. How could they laugh and behave so casually as if it were just another day?

Was there something wrong with them?

"Huh?" Tasha said.

"The three girls from last night," Mary repeated. "Dax said you and Aunt Jeri talked to them this morning. Are they going to be alright?"

"Yes. Well, they will be, I think. In time. I sure hope so." Tasha shrugged and thought about all they'd been through. "The *man* may have helped them there."

"How so?" I asked but wished I hadn't. The look in her eyes reminded me about the danger of thin ice – it was easy to fall through and drown in the cold, freezing water.

"He told them they did what they had to in order to stay alive, and they were never to blame themselves for any of it. Ever. He made them promise. The girls believed him."

I heard ice cracking under my feet as her gaze lingered, worried Mary might somehow become suspicious.

"It sounds like he's one of the good guys," Mary said and stuffed a hunk of meatloaf in her mouth.

"You mean, except for all the killing," Tasha remarked.

"Yup. Except for that."

Again, Tasha wondered if she was aware of what Dax did. And what her knowing might mean?

"Well, he certainly made an impression on them. They won't even give us a description; said they weren't going to help us catch him."

"Can't say as I blame them, Tash," Mary said. "After all, he saved their lives."

I tried to change the topic, but Tasha wouldn't budge.

"They're protective of him, for sure. Especially after they thought he was dead."

"Why would they think that?" Mary forked some fish, dipped it in some sauce, and brought it to her lips.

"He fell to the ground after being shot in the chest and lay still for a long time. One of the girls started to cry. We think he was wearing a bulletproof vest."

Mary's fork stopped mid-air and Tasha knew she knew. "Mare . . ."

"Tasha . . ." I said, and the yellow light lit.

I jumped up from the table, gratified to see Mary do the same. We turned off most of the interior lights and joined Tasha by the window with our guns drawn.

Someone or something must have tripped the *halfway down the driveway* alarm. They had to be on foot because the gate alarm would have flashed if breached by a vehicle.

"Do you see anything?" Tasha asked me.

"Not yet."

Mary and I often played *what if* scenarios as part of her training, so we were ready for most anything. Even those who'd come to kill her for killing them.

"Mare. Cover the back door," I said.

She moved quickly and positioned herself accordingly.

I turned off the motion sensor lights and the remaining alarms, preferring to draw the threat in rather than chase it away. So I could kill it.

"There," Tasha said.

"I see him. Hmm. Why isn't he skulking?"

"It's Dom," she said.

Dominic was her partner in the police department, and she moved to let him in.

"Hold up, Tash. Let him come to the door. Mare, how's it looking?"

"Clear."

"Hang there until all's well, okay?"

"Copy that."

Tasha was intrigued by their contingency planning and operational cohesion. They were a tight unit, ready to meet unknown danger - with deadly force if need be.

But her admiration gave way to anxiety.

"We still good, girl?" I asked after making sure Dominic hadn't been followed. Mary said *yup*, and I nodded at Tasha just as Dom raised a fist to knock. She opened the door and said, "Hey."

Dominic noted they were armed and tried to ease the tension with humor. "Y'all expecting Jehovah's Witnesses?"

"Well, you know how tenacious they can get," I said and shook his hand. "How are you doing?"

"I'm good, Dax. Didn't mean to traipse up your drive in the dark, but I couldn't reach Tasha on her phone."

"Shoot. That's my fault," I said, explaining why.

"What's up?" she asked Dom and flicked on the light.

"A man called this afternoon and left a cryptic message for you but didn't leave a name or number."

"What did he say?"

"*Tell her I'm dying.*" Dominic handed her a pink post-it. "I traced the call to a small town in Oklahoma."

Tasha knew who it was before she took the note.

"It's my father."

"Geez, Tash. I'm sorry."

She looked at Mary who shook her head, answering the unasked question of whether she'd shared with Dax what Tasha had shared with her.

"It's alright. We've been estranged for a long time."

Dominic gave his condolences after a moment and then turned to leave.

"Wait, I'm heading out, so I'll run you back to your car," Tasha told him and grabbed her handbag.

"You sure you don't want to finish dinner first?" I asked, afraid of her leaving with so much unresolved between us.

She gave Mary a kiss and a squeeze before answering.

"I need to be alone, Dax. I have a lot to think about."

Tasha hugged me and declared her love without saying a word, expressing hopes and fears through arms reluctant to let go.

It felt an awful lot like she was saying goodbye.

chapter two

Jeri arrived at the FBI's Atlanta field office two hours before her early bird meeting. A search for buried remains would begin soon, starting with ground penetrating radar. She wanted to hope nothing would be found but couldn't, knowing it was likely in vain.

Men like Anatovich were animals who preyed on kids, feeding on them until their bones were stripped clean. They were the worst kind of evil, and, as Deputy-Director of the human trafficking division, she saw far too many like him.

Why the hell is that? Was there a pedophilia pandemic? Some nature-nurture issue that needed more pinheaded pinpointing? Perhaps it was due to . . .

She shook her head and opened the folder on her desk, refusing to go down *that* rabbit hole again this morning. After reading the preliminary reports, Jeri plugged the flash drive into her computer and brought up the video.

Donald was right; their killer knew about the camera. His head was down and turned aside, leaving just a sliver of face to work with. She'd seen the lab make an identification with less – but not often.

Something about the video made her thoughts itch and it wasn't until the fourth viewing that Jeri figured out why. When the killer stepped outside followed by the three girls, they were all holding hands. It was natural for him to take hold of the one in front to keep them close together as he led them from the house. But what subliminally stroked her was the way he moved his thumb back and forth across the back of her hand.

Gently. Soothingly. Affectionately.

He cared for those girls, personally or generally, and a sense of awareness arose. Jeri had seen that gesture before.

In fact, she thought the whole thing felt familiar but couldn't for the life of her recall how or why. And the harder she tried the faster the reason ran away, changing a game of hide and seek into one of tag. *You're it.*

It was like that sometimes, and she'd learned to ignore that mischievous imp until it got bored and gave her what she was after without a fuss.

The phone on her desk buzzed with a text from Tasha and then rang in her hand before she could type a response. Her eyes closed before answering.

"Yes, Donald."

~~

Tim watched his partner fiddle with the vintage Bolo tie at his neck as he studied the pages of the binder for the umpteenth time in the last few days.

The umpteenthousandth over the last eleven months.

Brian Murphy compiled a loose-leaf folder of unsolved homicides that he believed to be the work of one individual. And whenever someone was killed, he scanned his murder book looking for similarities.

"So, what do you think?" Tim said with a grin and a sip. "Is it her? Is she the one?" They'd been talking about the girl over in St. Vincent and he took another swig of coffee as they eased into the early morning goings on.

"I think not. Teenage serial killers, while not unheard of, are so rare as to be almost non-existent. That girl's modus operandi is more self-defensive in nature than serial. Besides, most of these murders are far from home, and she's only had her driver's license a couple weeks."

"There you are then," Tim said whimsically. "She'd not dare drive to a murder without a license. Wouldn't be legal."

"I'm sure she would've been grounded long before her murders became a spree," Brian said in jest. However, there was an aspect of the St. Vincent killings he found interesting.

Her story was making the news merry-go-round again. After escaping horrific abuse, she'd been taken in by a local who'd later been shot in the back by an unknown uncle who tried to take her to an isolated cabin in the woods in order to pick up where her depraved father left off.

But Mary Stewart-Palmer didn't let that happen. When it was all over, she'd put three bullets in his skull as he lay on the ground after shoving an ink pen into his eye. And two nights ago, she managed to disarm one of the men who had taken her detective friend hostage, put a couple in *his* head, then killed the guy whose gun was on the detective's temple.

And yes, he was also shot in the head. Twice.

Murphy reckoned someone must have taught that girl the value of a permanently solved problem. The detective?

Maybe, but law enforcement didn't usually train to kill so . . . definitively. No, it was probably the new dad.

Good on him, as the Aussies say, he thought.

~~

Tasha got out of the car and yawned and stretched for what seemed like minutes. Too tired to drive and not in any hurry to get there, she thought a walk on the beach might do her some good. After stowing her purse in the trunk, she stuck the cell in her pocket, slipped off her shoes, and let the sugary sand have its way with her toes.

As she ambled along the water, her thoughts were of another shore she'd expected to walk this weekend.

Before leaving town, she'd called her captain and told him exactly what she texted Jeri – her father was dying, she was going to see him, and the wedding would have to wait.

He conveyed his sympathies, said *take all the time you need*, and assured her the tarpon would still be there when she got back.

That last was said to lift her spirits, or so she'd thought. But as it was a nuptial-fishing event he might have meant it.

The affair was to be held on a nearby spit of sandbar called Bird Island behind a real island called St. Vincent that sat beside a deep channel connecting the Gulf of Mexico to Apalachicola Bay. It was where she'd said *I love you* for the first time on a starry night in front of a crackling fire just before she told Dax something else.

Tasha stopped and pulled the phone from her backside. He'd sent a text earlier, but she hadn't texted back.

His morning messages were usually light, funny, or a clumsy but endearing effort to be sexy, and she would send a response that tickled or teased them both. But today he was sparse and tentative, which he'd never been before.

'*Hey*' was all it said. Because things had changed. How much she didn't know, but it scared her.

Taking this trip to Oklahoma could be a huge mistake, perhaps risking whatever chance they might have. But she needed to think, in depth and without distractions – like his kiss, his warm breath on the nape of her neck, his magical fingers tracing up and down her body . . .

When he answered the phone, she said, "Hey."

"You know, if you weren't so good-looking, I might take issue with you plagiarizing my work."

Tasha couldn't help but smile. "Work?"

"Well, yeah. It took a considerable amount of thought and effort to pen such a singular yet profound verse."

"Hmm. It's a bit brief for a verse, don't you think?"

"*Hey* is the foundation upon which meaningful prose is constructed. Such as *Hey there, Hey now, Hey you*, or even *Heyyy, Macarena*."

He wasn't making it any easier by being funny, but he probably knew that.

"Hey, Dax?"

"See that? You're a poet who don't know it. How about I come over and we plagiarize the heck out of each other?"

His chuckle made her tingle. She thought about how they were together, and the way he . . . pricked her prose. Dax was hungry in his appetite for her and generous with his attentions. Her pleasure was his desire, he would say, and she rejoiced, for lack of a better word, by reciprocating. Their attraction was powerful, giving, playful, nurturing. All-consuming and undeniable.

"I'm going to see my father," she said, with regret.

"Oh. Yes. Sorry. When are you leaving? Mary and I will take you to the airport."

"I'm not flying. I'm driving. And I've already left."

"I see."

She took the silence that followed as an understanding – they couldn't talk specifically about what he'd done over an unsecured phone, and his ability to influence what she did would be limited to what she allowed. Tasha sensed his concern but suspected it wasn't about going to jail.

It was about her. About them.

"Will you let anyone you invited to the wedding know? I've told Jeri and Dom, so they'll tell everyone else," she said.

"Is this only a postponement?"

The apprehension in his voice echoed her own.

"I don't know."

After another long stretch of quiet, she asked what she needed to know before the lengthy drive ahead.

"How many, Dax?" Tasha thought about clarifying, but he knew what she'd meant. And his answer was chilling.

"More than a few, less than a lot."

"I see," she said, but didn't. Not really. How could she?

"I'm sorry about your father, Tash. And for adding to your burden. Will you let us know when you get there?"

"Yes. If Mary's up, can I speak to her?"

"She is. Be safe and take care. I like you."

"Thanks. I like you, too, Dax."

What sounded casual was anything but, and her heart broke a little as she began to be afraid of losing them.

~

I knocked on Mary's door and handed her the phone, then went to make breakfast. After starting strips of bacon, I chopped pepper and onion, grated cheese and dumped it all into a bowl along with seven eggs, adding a splash of milk for taste and fluffiness.

As I whisked, I knew my life would never be the same. Of course, it had been that way since finding Mary, but this was different. And all my fault. I had no business falling in love with Tasha, given what I'd been doing, and absolutely no excuse for letting her love me back. I could have kept her at arm's length, should have stopped liking her so much.

After adding slices of mushroom to the mix, I poured the soon-to-be omelet in a skillet and turned the bacon with a fork, careful not to splatter the stove.

Woulda, shoulda, coulda never changed what *was*, so instead of supposing the past, I focused on what lay ahead.

The biggest problem was not the most obvious. What Tasha knew couldn't be proven because there wasn't any evidence, other than circumstantial. I'd been meticulous in my planning and execution. Well, except for the other night when the operation was more rushed than reasoned.

No, the real trouble was two-fold.

If I became an official suspect, Mary would be at risk of retaliation by those who'd want revenge. Which was ironic, as I had been doing something similar, sort of.

Except I really wasn't.

Right and wrong are relative. And ridding the world of as much evil as possible couldn't be any righter.

Second and perhaps more problematic – I loved Tasha. So much so, I was willing to give up my murdering ways even though it grieved me to let the wicked go unpunished. But she didn't know that, and it might not matter if she did.

"Guess we'll just have to wait and see," Mary said as she walked in and began to set the table.

I didn't respond as usual when she seemed to read my mind by asking if she was. Instead, I pretended not to hear, thinking she might slip up and inadvertently let me know.

"Oh, morning, hon. How'd you sleep?"

A twinkle in her eyes could have been awareness of my effort to uncover her secret. Or the beginnings of the classic *with my eyes closed* retort.

"Watson said to say, 'Hi,'" she said and winked.

"What? When?"

"Last night. In my dream." She smiled and reached into the fridge for our morning *dew*.

"Right," I said and folded the giant egg in half.

According to her, they shared a telepathic bond as well as each other's dreams. It was cute, but what if it were true? How cool would that be? And if she could mind-meld with Watson, she could conceivably do the same with me. Right?

"Right."

"Aha!" I exclaimed. "Caught you this time."

"Well, I wasn't being sneaky," she said, breaking off a piece of what she'd taken from the paper-toweled plate.

"Not that. The other thing. You said, 'Right.'"

"Uh, so did you." She took another bite of bacon and gave me a wide-eyed expression of innocent confusion.

"Yeah, in my mind. And you responded."

She tilted her head with furrows between her brows, but her eyes were beaming.

"You said it out loud when I told you about my dream. After getting the Mountain Dews."

"No, I ... Wait. Then why did you answer like I'd asked a question?"

"Did I?"

"So you're saying you were just mimicking me?"

"Am I?"

Mary took the spatula from my hand and rescued the omelet from the skillet before turning off the burner.

"Why?" I asked, and, as if doing the very thing I alleged, she correctly answered a *why* that could've meant anything.

"Because it's fun. And funny. And sometimes I like to keep you off-balance – don't ask me why because I'm not sure. Maybe it's a daughter thing. But riddle me this, Batman? If I *could* read your mind, would you really want to know? I mean, there must be things you'd rather not know I know. Right?"

Her Cheshire Cat smile, and the way she'd said *Right* like I had in my head, made me shake it in wonder.

I loved that kid like you wouldn't believe.

"Right," I said for symmetry's sake.

Halfway through breakfast, she asked if we could go to Tallahassee and bring Watson home.

"It'll save Isabel a trip, now that the wedding's on hold. Also, she'll be safe and out of danger should some bad guys come here looking for me. If any are left, that is," she said.

I told her it was a good idea. And without knowing the extent of Dimitri Anatovich's reach, even from the grave, it was a prudent move as well. It didn't make sense for anyone to come after Mary for killing two of their own, especially with the story plastered all over the news. But still ...

"Is it true what Tasha said last night about the man who saved those girls? Was he shot in the chest?"

I raised my head and saw her eyes boring into mine.

"First time I heard about it. Those girls were probably scared and might not be sure what they saw."

"That's not what I asked, Dax," she said with meaning. "Is it true?"

The cornerstone of our relationship was honesty. We didn't have to respond and could respectfully decline to do so without reproach. But if we answered, we didn't lie. Ever. And just as I had with Tasha, I told her the truth.

"Yes."

I put a hand over hers as she looked out the window to hide the shimmer in her eyes. She'd never asked so directly, and I couldn't *decline* because she had a right to know. This wasn't the first time I'd been shot.

My heart wrenched as she struggled to keep the worry from falling down her cheek.

"Would you mind not doing any gigs for a while? I'm not asking you to stop. Just take a break," she said.

Any lingering doubt I had about what she really knew dissolved when she looked at me. Mary wasn't referring to my playing guitar at local bars and other venues but rather its real purpose – to provide a legitimate reason to be in the area so I could do what had to be done.

What had long been in the shadows was now exposed to the light of day.

"Not at all, hon," I said, rubbing my thumb slowly across her hand. "I'd been going to cut back, anyway. Maybe quit."

"Really? Why?"

"I want us all to be a family, and it's not fair to ask Tasha to be okay with it. Or continue to deceive her."

"But how can you do that? Those sons of bitches need to be held accountable. All of them. It's important."

"I know. And I don't know." After a few seconds, Mary said she thought Tash knew it was me who killed Anatovich.

"She does." I expected a *how* or *why*, but she didn't ask. "And this trip to see her father is a lot of time for her to think about it without any input from me."

"What do you think she'll do when she's done?"

I shrugged my shoulders and took my plate to the sink. "Guess we'll just have to wait and see."

No sooner had the words left my mouth than I turned and caught her grinning at me.

"Isn't that what you said when you came in the kitchen? *We'll have to wait and see?* So, not only are you reading my mind but you're putting thoughts in my head as well?"

"Why, whatever do you mean?" she said and laughed.

~

After the dishes were all done, the makeshift device set, and the guns loaded, we drove up the driveway to the road. When the green gate swung closed behind us, I stopped and asked her to hand me the nine-millimeter in the glovebox.

"Maybe we can nip this now before someone gets hurt. Be ready to cover me with the Super if they get unruly."

"Roger that," Mary replied.

"How much time do I have?"

"Four minutes, thirty-seven seconds."

I was bombarded with questions the moment I stepped out of the truck, but the initial surge toward me halted when I clipped the holstered gun to my belt.

The Panama City media outlets were doing a fair job of keeping their mandated minimal distance. We'd come to a legal agreement about a year ago when I forced a news crew to the ground at gunpoint and then had them all arrested for trespassing and endangerment.

Back then, I'd been more concerned about her privacy. Now, it was about keeping Mary alive and well.

When the reporters started up again, I raised my hand.

"Listen, we appreciate your wanting to know if she's ok. She is. And I'm sure you're also concerned about her safety. Thank you. But those of you who have kids, or nieces and nephews you love, will understand my need to protect her. Not only from physical harm but emotional distress as well. And your being here makes it . . . Stop."

The camerawoman inching closer to the truck in order to get some footage of Mary through the windshield paused for a moment, and then continued. This worked well for me because of the opportunity to clarify the situation for those in attendance, and others in the viewing audience.

I pulled my gun and pointed it at her head. She stopped on a dime with the camera pointed toward me and I told her what I wanted everyone to hear.

"I'm afraid for my daughter's life. I'm telling you this so you know what will happen if you go anywhere near her. I'll shoot you dead. Right here, right now. I can't make it any clearer. Do you understand?"

It was hard to believe how quiet it got given how noisy it had been a few seconds ago, but, when she nodded, the news folk let out what sounded like a collective sigh of relief.

"Please step away from the vehicle, Miss," I said and thanked her when she skedaddled back to her newsie pals just as the *thirty-seconds to go* text vibrated in my pocket.

"Sorry if I've alarmed y'all, but I'm deadly serious about Mary's well-being. If you really care about her safety, not to mention your own, you'll heed the *Trespassers Will Be Shot* postings and leave us be. Do not come up to the house. And don't follow us around town. It makes us nervous."

Four, three, two, one... One... One... The explosion was louder than expected but helped drive home the point.

"Oh, and the property is mined. So please, be advised. Don't worry. That was probably just another armadillo."

I hopped in, started the truck, and drove away with one eye on the rearview.

"Well, that was fun. Hopefully, it'll do some good."

"Maybe," Mary said. "But where's mine? I didn't get to Super anybody."

"You had your fun at breakfast by acting like you didn't know what I was thinking."

Her chuckle said everything and nothing at all.

"I was a little concerned when you pulled out your gun. Would you have killed her?" she asked.

"No. She was just doing her job. But everyone needs to know I'm not playing around where you're concerned. And with any luck, the danger will disappear."

"A Dax a day keeps the bad guys away?"

"Something like that," I said as the *Live at Five* news van appeared larger in the side door mirror.

"And did you consider the unintended consequences of showing the world your deep and abiding love for me?"

"Such as?"

"Now a kidnapper knows you'll pay whatever they ask. Not very smart on your part."

I could see the sparkle in her eye as she pulled my leg.

"First, there's no question I like you. Quite a bit, even. But a deep and abiding love? Hmm. That might be a stretch. Second, I don't have much money, as far as you know. Once a kidnapper is made aware of that fact; he'll most likely give you back. Because you're such a little shit."

She raised her eyebrows with a pout and pained look, but I knew her too well to believe it.

"And third, maybe he'd take half the money I *do* have in exchange for taking you off my hands. Then I'd have enough left over to shop around for a little girl who'd at least tell me if she can or can't read my mind."

Mary cracked up and punched me in the arm.

"That really gets to you, doesn't it? The not knowing."

"Does not," I told her.

"Does to," she countered.

"Does . . . Alright, girl. Get ready to have your fun."

The newsies had made a big mistake by getting trapped between us and the vehicle behind them as we all came to a stop at a red light.

"Well they can't say you didn't warn them," Mary said as she pulled the Super-Duper squirt gun from the backseat filled with our special blend of water, sticky paint, and a tad of gasoline for *stank*.

"Careful not to spray anyone who might be smoking," I called out and grabbed the other Super to join her in making a colorful, gummy mess.

chapter three

The numbers that tumbled on the antiquated gas pump reminded Tasha of pear, orange, and cherry illustrations on a Las Vegas slot machine. She closed her eyes and pulled an imaginary one-arm bandit, watching her thoughts coalesce into words that spun around. When the wheels all stopped on *neither*, she exhaled. Dax wasn't a *sociopath*.

Or worse still, a *psychopath*.

She'd seen too much evidence of emotional attachment that couldn't be manufactured or ignored – and remorse for killing a woman who'd clobbered him with a crowbar that couldn't be feigned. What happened wasn't because he lacked genuine empathy for others but because he cared for them, misguided though it might be.

With that settled, she set the law aside for the moment and asked herself an objective question.

Did Mary's father deserve to die?

"Absolutely," she said, returning the nozzle to its place on the pump and taking her receipt before asking another.

Did Anatovich and others like him deserve the same?

"Yes. No question."

The man filling his car next to her raised an eyebrow. Tasha thought about explaining but hopped in her truck and drove away. She had more important things to worry about than a man she didn't know thinking she was crazy.

'Deserved or not isn't the issue before us today,' the law said in a prosecutorial tone. 'It's the right to . . .'

'We can address that later,' she said, attempting to shove it back with the other issues she'd pushed aside. But the matter of Mary's welfare asked for an expedited ruling on some of its concerns.

Is Dax a negative influence, a danger to her well-being? What about how he'd been training her?

Tasha imagined impartial opinions leaning forward to listen, but, before a judgement could be rendered, an errant voice from the peanut gallery section in her mind yelled out like so many others had all afternoon.

'If not for that training, you'd be dead. You both would.'

She could hear a murmur sweep through her thoughts and a gavel strike to restore order as her brain transformed into a *Witness for the Prosecution* courtroom.

It was true. Dax had saved their lives by teaching Mary how to save hers. And if she was being honest, the outcome might have been quite different if the roles were reversed, because *she* might have hesitated at a critical moment when the decision to kill needed to be made. Though she would've willingly given her life for Mary's without hesitation.

Just as Dax would.

'Why is it,' another voice from the peanut crowd asked, 'that a person who gives their life to save another's is hailed as noble, but someone who *takes* a life for the same reason is vilified?'

"That's a good question," Tasha said but was kept from further pondering by the ringing of her blue-toothed phone. After the judge declared a ten-minute recess in the cranial court, she tapped Jeri's name on the display.

"Hey, Seven. Wassup?"

"Is it my imagination, or has your English altered quite a bit since you've been with Dax?"

"Whatchu talkin' bout, Willis?"

"Thanks, girlfriend," Jeri chuckled. "I needed that."

"So, how bad is it?"

"Seventeen so far. Mostly girls. And we have barely scratched the surface."

"Jesus!" Tasha said, even though she wasn't what you'd call a 'believer.' How could she be? What God would allow something like this to happen?

"They were buried naked to facilitate decomposition. And to impede any attempts to identify the remains."

Jeri spoke in a just-the-facts tone of voice, but Tasha heard the crack in her voice and the anguish it conveyed.

"I'm so sorry, Seven."

"I know. Thanks. I'm on my way there now. Damn, it's horrific. You know what I keep thinking? Thank God *the man* got those three girls out of there in time."

"Yes, they were lucky," Tasha said, and then asked a question she'd later think unethical. "Anything on him yet?"

"No, nothing. And to tell the truth, I'm kind of hoping we don't find him. Would that be so wrong?"

Tasha knew her well enough to know the question was rhetorical, but she answered all the same.

"I don't know. Maybe not this time. In this case."

"Maybe. What about you?"

"Me?" Tasha said, fearful Jeri might know something.

"Your father."

"Oh."

"Am I wrong, or did you tell me a long time ago that he was already dead?"

"You're not wrong. And he's not dead, yet. Apparently."

Jeri didn't ask for more, and Tasha didn't give any, both knowing whatever needed to be said would be, in time.

"Alright, girl. I gotta go. Catchu later, gator."

"Gotta? Catchu?" Tasha asked. "Wassup witchu?"

"You see what's happened here? Dax has infected you, and you have now done the same thing to me. Whattahey?"

"That sounds more Native American than hip-hoppy. You sure you caught that from me?"

They laughed and left each other to the rest of their day.

~~

"I'll blow your head off if you come any closer," a voice said. "Now get your ass on out of here. While you still can."

Dominic stopped and smiled when the pump-action of a shotgun sounded. He stepped back before turning around, not wanting to trigger the *black eye* – an alarm that used squibs in the trees to simulate shotgun pellets and sprayed those who persisted with high-pressure, non-soluble paint.

It was a 'redneck security system,' Dax once called it. And he would add modifications whenever their names and faces were used to sell the news. As they were today.

The press had descended like vultures earlier and then complained when the subject of their attention took issue by planting explosives in his yard, spraying their vehicles, and threatening to kill them – all of it just fine with Dominic.

Dax was going to safeguard his kid, plain and simple. What was so hard to understand about that? He was well within his rights under the *Stand Your Ground* statute, and Dom advised the complainants to keep that in mind.

"We don't want anyone to get hurt so please, give them the same regard you'd want in a similar situation," he'd told them but knew they'd disregard the suggestion.

Oh well, he warned them. So had Dax.

Dominic looked around as he came to the road, pleased to see the shoulders free of news vans and looky-loos. The only vehicle in sight was one that had been in a vacant lot for the last two days. He drove over and ran the tag number.

When it came back as a rental from Georgia, he phoned the company for information. After thanking the agent for her help, he called in with a name and waited for a response.

He turned off the engine and opened the window, then the door. A sour smell took hold of his nose and led him to the rear of the rental car.

~~

When we arrived at an outdoor cafe near Florida State University, Watson made a beeline to Mary and Isabel to me.

"Dax! I'm so glad to see you," she said enthusiastically.

"Me too, Fluffy." I matched the exuberance of her hug and asked how she was doing.

"I'm good, thanks to you and Mary. And Watson. Sorry about Tasha's father. She must be heartbroken."

"Yes," I said but didn't really know for sure. We hadn't had a chance to talk about it.

Isabel left my arms for Mary's, and I grinned as Watson squeezed in between them. They rubbed and scratched him until he laid on the ground and offered up his belly, which added giggles to their laughter.

As we sat round the table eating an early dinner, Isabel looked at Mary in amazement as she listened to the story of *what happened* – the PG-13 rated version.

It was told in a way that captured the imagination while minimizing the dangerous reality.

"You're my hero," Isabel said with obvious admiration. Although more than a year older, she looked up to Mary.

"Mine, too." I raised my soda and Isabel followed suit. "To Maritello. Our very own Teenage Mutant Ninja Turtle."

Isabel giggled and said, "To Maritello!"

I smiled at Mary's discomfort. Although she was aware of her skills, she didn't like them to be too acknowledged. Praise made her blush. And I'd make it worse sometimes by telling her how cute that was. After which, she'd hit me.

As the girls talked amongst themselves, I took note of how jubilant Isabel was compared to the despondent young lady who stayed with us after she tried to kill herself. Her reasons were understandable but unacceptable to Mary who persuaded her she hadn't done anything wrong – those boys had. And in time, she began to believe in herself again.

"I don't suppose you've changed your mind about living with me on campus this semester?" Isabel asked.

"No. Sorry, Belle. I'm all signed up for online courses."

"Yeah. I know. It would be nice, is all. I miss you guys." And she did. Her mother didn't seem to like her at all, and her mother's boyfriend had liked her way too much.

"We're going to see a lot of each other, Fluffy," I told her. "So much so, you'll probably get sick of us."

"Well, you, yes. For sure," Mary said. "But not me. And not Watson," she added after he bit her ankle. "Damn, that hurt. You could've just nudged me, you know."

"What do you mean, me?" I replied. 'I'm her favorite. You two are just lucky to know me."

"Na-uh. No way. It's me. Ouch! Watson . . ."

"Y'all crack me up," Isabel said and laughed at us.

"Well, Mare, as the song says," I said, "we've got a long way to go, and a short time to get there."

We collected our trash along with some left by others who weren't so inclined and threw it in the can thirty feet away. I couldn't help thinking that a bullet in the butt would go a long way in adjusting the attitude of litterbugs.

After giving hugs to me and Mary, Isabel knelt and gave Watson a quick scratch and kiss. "Thanks for coming up and spending the week. It really helped get me back on track. Too bad you can't stay."

"Maybe he can?" I said, reaching into my shirt pocket. "Well, sort of."

A smile washed over her face as she stood and took the Golden Retriever charm from my hand.

"Oh, Dax, it's beautiful. And so thoughtful. Thank you. It looks just like him."

Isabel held it up for all to see before affixing it to the bracelet I'd given her when she became part of the family.

"See? Told you I was her favorite."

Watson just rolled his eyes, but Mary gave a huge grin. And then stuck her tongue out at me.

~~

Tasha opened the motel door and just about fell into the room, nearly tripping on a strap hanging low and loose. Rather than make two trips she carried everything at once, suitcase, purse, laptop, makeup bag, hair dryer, cooler, key card, and a sack of food from Burger King.

She closed the door with her behind, set the load on the table, and reached into the purse and cooler simultaneously with a deftness that came from practice. As the corkscrew pierced the foil and twisted, she mused.

The bottle of Kendell-Jackson came from a case Dax had given for their *anniversary*. 'To commend the beginning of our love and friendship,' he'd said.

It was corny for sure, even sappy, but damn if it wasn't also sweet. He was funny like that – tough outer shell with a soft, gooey center – and she honored his girly sentiment by drinking only one of the gifted bottles every month to commemorate his obvious adoration of her.

"Alright, girl. Let's dial it back a bit. He's still a killer. And you are . . ."

She filled a plastic Solo cup and took a long sip of wine that became a series of swallows. After a refill, she debated on whether to grab a quick shower or wait till the morning. The decision was deferred when a compelling aroma made her stomach growl. She hadn't eaten since last night at Dax's and the contents of the sack called out to her.

The fries went fast and furious, the Whopper slow and savored. The chicken tenders were saved for breakfast.

Tasha thought about watching TV but topped off her 'wine glass' instead. It'll help me sleep, she thought, needing both the rest and respite from thinking about Dax.

She wasn't any closer to knowing what to do, but, as Scarlett O'Hara once said, 'Tomorrow is another day.'

"Huh."

Jeri was right, Dax had infected her. She was butchering the English language for fun and quoting lines from movies just like he did. Like Mary was now doing, too. He was a contagious virus that affected the heart, tickled the funny bone, and inhabited the mind.

If loving you is siiick, I don't want to be well . . . she sang, not sure if the off-kilter, paraphrased lyric was the hoot her wine-addled brain thought it was.

Tasha took the path of least resistance by brushing and flossing her teeth, slipping out of her clothes, letting them drop to the floor, climbing into bed and turning off the light. As the top sheet slid across her breasts, Dax returned to her thoughts. Setting aside those that plagued her earlier, she imagined him lying next to her. A moan escaped her lips as his f*ingers caressed her in the way that always inflamed . . .*

"No, not yet," she said when the phone vibrated. It was a text from Jeri, with a yellow smiley face winking at her.

'Looks like you can't leave your kids alone for a minute.'

She clicked the YouTube video, and laughed out loud as Mary and Dax *Supered* the vehicle and its passengers. Even through the paint smeared on the news van's windshield, Tasha saw the smiles on their faces and wished she could have been there to join the fun.

When were those damned news people going to learn?

The next video was more sobering. As Tasha listened to Dax calmly and courteously threaten the camerawoman, her feelings were mixed.

His love for Mary was absolute, powerful and profound. It couldn't help but move her.

It also scared her.

~~

Alexi couldn't think of an organization that would allow a boy with no experience to take over the business affairs of a multi-billion-dollar company – unless it was a criminal enterprise formerly run by a ruthless man who'd raised an equally ruthless nephew. He considered killing the kid right off, regardless of the attention it would bring from the FBI. But patience was called for, and patience Alexi had.

For two years he'd bided his time, waiting for the right moment to *relieve* Dimitri of his responsibilities. It wasn't that he didn't like the man, but Anatovich was greedy and Alexi wasn't being paid nearly what he was worth.

And so, he'd been plotting to take him down.

Except, someone beat him to it. And that might be the kid looking at him with deadpan eyes, waiting for an answer to his question.

"Johnny said the guy was about your size, dressed in black and wearing a skeleton mask. The man spoke quietly, asked questions about Dimitri and Anthony, then left him tied to a tree. Other than that, he doesn't know anything."

"How can you be sure?" Miko said.

"I asked him nicely. With a blowtorch."

"Is Johnny still alive?"

"Barely. I figured you might want to talk to him."

Alexi hadn't given a single thought to keeping him alive for that reason and again contemplated killing the nephew. But he didn't know what he didn't know, and Miko might have already consolidated his power. Men could be waiting outside to relieve him of *his* life if anything happened to the boy. Such were the vagaries of the business they were in.

Besides, Miko might not be so easy to eliminate. There had been stories...

"I appreciate the courtesy, Alexi, but there's no need. If you're satisfied, so am I. You can dispose of him as you see fit. Now, what about my uncle's assistant, Marcus?"

"The Feds have him. He's probably spilling his guts."

"Just to be safe we'll shut down our operation, here and abroad. Tell the..."

"What are you talking about? We can't..." Alexi said, stopping when Miko's eyes darkened.

"Did you kill my uncle, Alexi?" he asked

The kid stared at him like he was looking at a dead man, and Alexi breathed deep the winds of change.

"Of course not. What the..."

"Good. Now," Miko said, "shut everything down. Stop taking them, stop selling them. Liquidate any we have in stock and tell our distributors to take an extended leave of absence from their lives. Tell them it is not a request. Non-compliance will have consequences."

Alexi nodded because he had to, not because he agreed. "It's going to cost us a ton of money."

"For now, yes. But we have tons and tons to hold us over. I want the Feds to think we're done, that the business died with Uncle Dimi. We'll resume sometime after their investigations are over. In the meantime, we'll restructure. Become more cost effective and thereby more lucrative. Is this something you'd be interested in?"

Alexi looked at him with a new set of eyes. His previous encounters with Miko had always been brief, mostly in the presence of the old man. But he had never heard him speak about the operation before. Perhaps the kid knew what he was talking about? It couldn't hurt to play along for a while. "Yes," he said.

"I'm glad to hear it. I loved my uncle, as much as I could, but damned if he wasn't a stingy son of a bitch. The man had more money than God and yet wouldn't share it with those who'd made him rich in the first place, so..."

Alexi took the paper he'd been handed with the many-zeroed number and looked up at Miko with wide eyes.

"I hope this adequately expresses my opinion of your value to this organization, Alexi."

"Yes sir," he exclaimed to the boy thirty years his junior. Thank you."

Miko nodded once and shook the offered hand. "Now, why were Anthony's men at that detective's house? And who killed Uncle Dimi?"

Alexi still thought Miko might be responsible but gave the answer he knew for sure.

"I don't know."

"Let's find out."

"Yes, sir."

chapter four

The words of a classic song by *Rush* echoed as I awoke. And yes, after I sighed and smiled, I lay a while in bed.

Of all the things to worry about, Tasha was uppermost on my mind. Not the yellow police tape that surrounded the space where the parked car had been, not the possibility of a retaliatory response if what happened up in Georgia was linked to me, or even the niggle in the back of my head that I might be leading Mary astray.

No, it was Tasha. And not because she might arrest me. Sure, I answered her questions, but I wasn't going to sign an affidavit to that effect. If she wanted me in jail, she'd have to build a case on her own without any more help from me. A *catch me if you can* kind of thing. It could be interesting. Then again, probably not.

Hell, I only said as much as I did for the very reason she occupied my thoughts this morning – I loved her.

Too damned much.

'Yes, I know,' I told myself, feeling more marshmallowy than manly. 'I sound like a schoolgirl.'

I heard Watson's nails clicking down the hallway with Mary in tow and decided to get up. I checked my phone for messages. No *Hi*, no *Hey*, no nothing.

When I walked into the living room, Mary was already in the kitchen making breakfast noises.

"Hey, Pumpkin."

"Pumpkin? What the heck is that?"

"A large, round fruit. Part of the Cucurbitaceae family that includes things like squash and watermelon. They're orange, grow in a patch? You make pies and Jack-o-lanterns out of them? Huh... I thought you were the smart one."

"Ha-ha. I meant where's your 'Whazzup, Buttercup?'"

"Thought I'd try something different. Why? Don't you like it?"

"No," Mary replied. "It makes me sound fat. And it's too cutesy. Better stick with the standards: Mare, hon, sweetie, smartass, little girl, little shit."

I grinned and looked around.

"Where's Waldo?"

"Get up on the whimsical side of the bed this morning?" she asked and nodded her head at the back door.

I picked up his ceramic bowl, rinsed and refilled it with fresh water, and set it down just as he walked in.

"Good morning, Watson." I reached inside the pantry for a large scoop of dry dog food from the plastic container. "How's my interspecies brother from another mother?"

When he growled, I just about laughed because there were barely any r's in his '*Grrr.*'

"What's that about?"

"He thinks he's mad at you." Mary turned on the faucet to collect some water on her fingertips, and then flicked the droplets on the griddle to watch them dance.

While not as fluent in *Retriever* as Mary, Watson and I talked all the time – although deciphering his words was purely speculation on my part. I knew one thing for certain though. He, like me, was never too upset to eat.

"What did *I* do? He's been gone for a week." I pulled a can of Pedigree, Choice Cuts in Gravy, from the pantry shelf, popped the lid and spooned the contents into another dish. "Want me to warm it up?"

He nodded, begrudgingly, and I slid it in the microwave.

"He really wants to be mad at me," Mary said, pouring the batter into circles that would start a stack of flapjacks. "As if it's my fault I have to defend myself from killers. But that's ridiculous, so he's trying to blame you."

The microwave beeped and I set the bowl next to the others. Watson said, "Thanks," I think, and walked by.

"Blame me for what?"

Mary seemed to hesitate but answered anyway.

"It's non-sensical, even paradoxical. If you weren't who you were or hadn't taught me what you had, I'd be dead instead of them. So one has nothing to do with the other. The truth is, he's angry at himself."

As I watched a pancake molehill become a soon to be buttered and syruped mountain, an unsettling thought gave me pause. Did Watson know what I'd been up to? You might think it wouldn't matter, but it did. I didn't want him to have a bad opinion of me.

"Why is he angry?"

"Because he's scared. He blames himself for not being around to protect me."

"Well, I can relate to that. I wasn't either. And I blame myself, too."

Mary shut off the burner and turned toward me.

"Dax, that's illogical."

"Still," I said and shrugged. "I can't help but feel it."

Watson and I shared a look and Mary shook her head.

"You're as bad as he is. Besides, and just so you know, y'all protect me plenty. In more ways than I can count," Mary said softly and then more firmly. "So knock off this blame game baloney or else."

She assumed an *En Garde* position, hand backward for balance with the spatula in the other like a fencer's foil, and advanced to attack. As I hadn't set the table there wasn't anything to counter her parry with, so I raised my hands in surrender. It didn't keep her from making the point, though, by pressing the hard-plastic edge into my neck.

"Are we clear?" she said with eyes that sparkled.

I chuckled and felt the *blade* tickle my Adam's apple. "Yes, Ma'am. I got it."

"Watson?"

Mary said she'd curtail his behind the ear scratching's if he didn't come round to her way of thinking, so he did. He had to. That itch was worth its weight in Snausages.

"Alright, then," she said. "Let's eat."

~~

Detective Brian Murphy massaged the smooth Navajo turquoise of his Bolo tie between thumb and fingers as he pondered last night's bloody murder. It was sloppy, messy. Not the work of the man he was looking for.

His killer was careful and deliberate, dispassionate – unlike the guy who stabbed the local woman twenty-seven times in an emotional outburst. That guy had no impulse control, which would make him much easier to catch.

"Did you see yesterday's news?"

"Are you referring to the St. Vincent girl?" Murphy said and set aside the murder book.

"Yes," Tim said. "That squirt-gun packing serial killer. Man, her and her guardian tore that news crew a new one. It looked like fun. Maybe we could put in for some Supers ourselves? Use them for crowd control, or just for the hell of it. They'd be great for morale. Ours, not the public's."

"We could call them Picasso pistols," Murphy offered, wondering if his partner would get the cubism reference. "And he's her new dad. Has been for about a month now."

"How do you know that?"

"Newspaper. They print weddings, births, adoptions, arrests, sentencings, estate sales . . . Don't you read, man?"

"Newspapers? No. Like too many twenty-first century Americans, I get my news from the twin pillars of truth – Fox and Facebook," Tim retorted with a grin.

"God help us."

After a chuckle, and flipping for the last Bearclaw, Tim asked Brian what he thought about Dax Palmer.

"He was firm but respectful, polite but resolute. And I believe him; he'll kill anyone who comes after his daughter."

"He seemed like a straight shooter. No pun intended. It's hard not to like a man like that."

Murphy agreed. "The minefield is a nice touch."

"Yeah. Oh, my friend at the St. Vincent PD said those guys the girl killed might belong to that mess up in Georgia."

"How so?"

"The detective who was held hostage is an old friend of an FBI Deputy-Director in Atlanta. Rumor is Jeri Ryan was being pressured and the detective was the *or else*. Then the Palmer girl pops the perps and all hell breaks loose."

"So, the FBI sends in a team and there's a shootout?"

"I don't know any of the facts, just the scuttlebutt. I'm surprised we haven't heard more about it on the news. They must be keeping a tight lid on the details."

"Must be," Murphy said and pushed back from the desk. "Let's go see if we can find Mr. Cole Parker."

"I doubt he'd stick around after stabbing the hell out of his girlfriend. Probably long gone by now." Tim stood and slipped on his jacket. "Don't you think?"

"Maybe not. Not yet anyway."

Brian Murphy had hunches. And he followed them no matter where they led him or how far-fetched they seemed. And, while they didn't always pan out, he had put too many people in prison to stop hunching now.

"Where are we going?" Tim asked.

"To see Parker's ex-wife."

~~

After the old wrestling mat was rolled out on the floor, Mary began to stretch muscles and ligaments in preparation for one of her favorite things – training.

Dax had a penchant for teaching, and she a proclivity to learn. She loved it, almost as much as making music. And as in playing the guitar, practice made perfect.

Just ask the men lying in the morgue.

"Before we get started," I said. "I've been thinking..."

"Uh-oh," Mary cracked wise.

"Funny girl. As I was saying, you made a valid point earlier. It is irrational for Watson and me to blame ourselves for things we can't control. It's also unrealistic to expect us not to worry about you, as I'm sure you do us. But as Forrest Gump sorta said, 'Shit happens.' So the best we can do to mitigate that concern is prepare for the possibilities in life: physically, emotionally, intellectually. Can I get an amen?"

Mary got into the spirit by giving me a hallelujah and a grin. Whereas Watson only gave a single wag of his tail. I smiled and sat with them on the mat.

"To that end, I'm wondering if it might not be helpful to talk about the other night so Watson can better understand. It won't eliminate his worry, but it might ease it some."

She'd already been debriefed by Dax, a review process that sought optimal solutions to confrontational problems – real or hypothetical. Their discussions were valuable not only because they added to her skill set, but how they built her confidence. Dax wasn't a 'do as I say' instructor, rather he encouraged her to think. Within, and outside of the box. And if she had a better idea, he was all for it.

With Watson, however, she'd only give as much info as needed, thinking she was protecting him.

"Well?" Mary asked, letting her fingers loose in his fur. "Want to know the gritty details?"

When he nodded, she began.

"Well, I drove over to Tasha's for our sleepover in my pajamas, thinking it would be fun, even though Dax tried to talk me out of it. But as soon as I got there, I regretted not listening because one of the bad guys looked me *all* over. Although, ironically, his pervy interest was their undoing."

The more he heard, the more Watson was intrigued. He thought Mary had accurately assessed the situation, looked for weakness to exploit, adapted to changing circumstances, formulated a viable plan, and acted when the time was right. All while remaining calm in the face of danger. He marveled at her courage and said so.

"I don't know about that."

"What did he say?" I asked.

"That I was courageous. But . . . I was pretty scared."

"That's why you were." I winked and patted her hand. "I'd like to give some praise, as well. First, you didn't just move your gun from the man in front of you to shoot the one behind you. If you had, and no matter how fast you were, he could've taken his gun off Tasha and shot you dead. But saying what you did before doing so was a clever ploy that gave you the time to put two in his buddy and return to your position during his confusion."

"Thanks," she said. "I thought so, too."

I smiled, loving how she lit up with the compliment.

"But I'm particularly pleased with the lessons you've learned from the movies. Like don't start running for your life after knocking out the bad guy until you make sure . . ."

"... he can't pop up later unexpectedly and try to kill you again," Mary said and laughed.

"You did good, kid. Thanks for not getting killed," I said on a more serious note.

"No problem. You, too."

Mary gave Watson a rub and I asked him if he felt any better. "Somewhat," she said he said.

"We can't run from the evil in the world or allow it to go unchecked. That's why we train. And part of the training is evaluation. So, can you pinpoint the key to your success?"

"I didn't panic," Mary said, fortified by the knowledge. She could've given in to her fear but didn't. And that made all the difference.

"*If you can keep your head when all about you are losing theirs?*" I said with a growing grin. "Yes."

"Where's that from?" she asked.

"My head."

"No, really."

"What, I can't define the moment with eloquence?"

"Oh, sure," she said. "You *can*. But often there's usually a made-up word or two sprinkled in with your articulacy. Am I right, Watson?"

"Articulacy? Sounds like you're calling the kettle black."

"Look it up. It's a real word. Unlike *grammerical* which can only be found in a Daxtionary."

I chuckled, enjoying the playful banter.

"It's from a poem by Kipling. After saying a bunch of 'if you can do this' and 'if you can do thats,' it ends with, 'yours is the Earth and everything in it.'"

"Ooh, I like the sound of that. Can you wrap a big yellow bow around it before you give it to me?"

Would that I could, little girl.

"Back to business, Buttercup. What would you say was the most significant mistake those men made?"

As she gave it some thought, Watson spoke up.

"That's exactly right, boy!" I said after Mary translated, sticking out my hand and asking for *five*. He gave me four. "They underestimated her. And who wouldn't?"

Watson looked at Mary who looked at me and smiled.

43

"No, seriously. I'm asking."

It didn't take more than a second before Mary nodded. "Anyone who knew what I was capable of," she said.

"Precisely. Given what happened at Tasha's and with your uncle, folks now know you can handle yourself, which has both up and down sides. It will keep the curious from messing with you, not wanting to get their butt kicked by a girl. But it's the ones who are serious that we'll have to be on extra guard against. I don't think those who sent the men to Tasha's will retaliate, but we have to plan as though they might and take precautions."

I stood and pulled Mary up by her raised hand.

"We need to raise our sense of awareness and discuss additional steps we can take in certain situations. Like what to do when you're being followed. But for now, let's add something new to the mix."

Mary's eyes sparkled as she took the Nerf-knife he gave her, looking forward to the knowledge he would impart.

~~

"So that's it?" Tim asked. "He pays his child support?"

"On time, without fail. And he never misses visitation."

"How do you know this? Another newspaper nugget?"

"I have a friend at the Friend of the Court, or what you call down here, Child Protective Services. And according to her, Cole Parker is a doting father to his ten-year old boy. Seems likely he'd try to see him before leaving town. Might even try to take him," Brian said, turning left on Leaf street.

"That's a tad thin, I'd say, as hunches go. Why... Shit!"

Tim reached to call it in, but Murphy shook his head.

"There's no time," he said and stopped the car, popped the trunk, and opened the door. "Be ready."

Cole Parker dragged his son from the front porch as his ex-wife pleaded for him to let go. He punched her face with the fist holding a knife and took two steps before he noticed a man with his palms raised standing fifteen feet away.

"Mr. Parker. I'm with the police. Please, let Robby go."

"Leave us alone!" Cole yelled out and took another step. "Get out of my way."

"I can't," Brian said, moving between him and the car. "Now, please. Drop the knife and let your son go. It's over."

"Cole," the ex-wife cried out. "Don't hurt him!"

When his eyes glazed over, Brian knew what it meant. As he lifted the knife, a red spot appeared near his shoulder. The thunder crack of a rifle sounded a second later. When he fell to the ground in a heap, Robby wrested his wrist from his father's grasp and ran into his mother's arms.

"Mr. Parker, you're under arrest," Brian said and cuffed his hands behind his back. "I would have bet money you wouldn't try to kill your kid. I thought you loved him."

"I do. But I wasn't gonna leave him with that bitch of a mother. That cunt, owww..."

Brian took his foot off the wounded shoulder and said, "Let's not have any more of that, Mr. Parker."

"EMS is on the way." Tim shook his head and grinned. "Don't you get tired of being right all the time? You said he'd be here, and here he is."

"I said he *might* be. And he was. Nice shot, by the way."

"Well, it was only ninety feet, so it better have been."

Tim left to talk to the mother and son while Brian took a crack at Cole after reading him his rights.

"So, Mr. Parker. Why did you kill your girlfriend?"

chapter five

After a restless, dream-filled night of Dax on the ground and bleeding out, Tasha was back in the truck and down the road. Hot coffee warmed the cold nugget breakfast as she tried to shake off the remnants of her nightmare. It had been too vivid, too painful, and the tears on her cheek when she woke were too real.

He could have died and part of her was angry with him. Of course, she and Mary could've too, but that was different. Dax had put himself in a position to get killed, whereas they ... hadn't? Was that the distinction? Did it matter whether death found you bound on a couch or out confronting evil? And by the way, wasn't that what she did as a detective? Protecting others from the wicked came with risk.

What made him wrong and her right?

'You are sanctioned,' the law said. 'He is not.'

With that opening statement, the jury of her mind was seated, and the courtroom called to order.

'By who?' the defense asked. Tasha winced, expecting the judge to have the grammar police haul off the objector. She had hoped for a Clarence Darrow to help argue her case, but now feared she'd gotten a Clarabell, instead. Only this Howdy Doody clown was neither mute nor articulate.

'It is the people from *whom* the authority derives,' the law said with a degree of derision.

'Which people? Who is this people?"

Tasha was about to ask for a continuance so she could find more competent counsel when the law contemptuously said, 'You must be joking.'

'Am I? So you're saying all of the people have come to an agreement about who can be killed and for what?'

'Of course not,' law scoffed. 'That's ridiculous.'

'Is it? Why?' the clown asked.

'You cannot expect a hundred percent of the people to agree on anything, let alone something as serious as this. But a majority...'

'Majorities are infallible, then? All knowing? Always?'

'Well, no. But...'

'A majority of Americans believe in capital punishment, yet twenty or so states don't have a death penalty. Why is that? There seems to be a difference of opinion about what is or isn't *right*. And in that discrepancy lies the flaw in your one-way fits all law. Wouldn't you agree?'

Mary had made the same argument the other night, and Tasha turned off the radio so she could listen.

'That is balderdash,' the law rebuffed, which surprised her because she'd never used the word. 'You can't possibly be advocating an abdication of lawfulness.'

'I could," Clarabell said, "but I'm not. Why don't we look at this more specifically? Take it out of the hands of the majority and consider a more singular perspective.'

'What are you proposing, counselor?' the judge asked.

'We the people decide what will or will not be, your Honor. And let's make no mistake, we've given ourselves the right to kill. We have, to parrot *the law*, sanctioned the use of death and bestowed upon some – soldiers, police – permission to dispense it with the consent of the majority. However, there is a fundamental truth about this authority.'

'And that is?'

'Who lives or dies under the law is often decided not 'by the many,' to paraphrase Mr. Spock, 'but by the one."

Clarabell might be a Clarence after all, Tasha thought, appreciating the reference of a Star Trek icon in her defense.

Police officers were allowed to use deadly force to save lives, similarly to what Mary did the other night. But the law didn't permit the preemptive use of that force.

Or did it? What about the military commander who orders an attack – to prevent an attack?

Isn't that essentially what Dax did?

'It doesn't matter,' the law interjected. 'He cannot be allowed to be judge, jury, and executioner.'

'And yet we allow some to do just that, like a President. He alone makes the call to kill a terrorist. Not a jury, not the majority. And as of right now, and as far as we know, Dax hasn't caused any collateral damage to civilians, has he? The same can't be said about an ordered drone strike.'

Tasha saw a convoluted logic in what Clarence said.

What if Dax were a commander-in-chief engaged in a war against evil? Would she feel differently?

When they went in to get Osama bin Laden, it wasn't to arrest him. They knew what he did, what he would continue to do, and knew bringing him to trial carried even more risk. He was put down to save lives. And to hold him accountable.

Technically it was legal, but was it the right thing to do? If yes, then Dax's actions shouldn't be any less valid.

But if everyone acted on their own, it would be anarchy. 'That's why we have laws,' she told herself. To curtail poor judgement. We took our chances on a select few, put them in charge for a while, and hoped for the best. The problem was she trusted Dax's judgement more than anyone sitting in an oval office.

'How can you think about absolving him?' the law said. 'You've sworn an oath. What about your integrity?'

"I'm not going to address that right now," she said out loud. "And my oath includes a responsibility to ensure the safety and quality of life in the community."

What messed with her head was visualizing Dax taking someone's life, regardless of the reason. It didn't square with the man she cared for, one who loved and listened and touched her with tender caresses. It was difficult to accept that the hands which gave so much pleasure were covered in so much blood.

How could she reconcile what he'd done with who she was? Or respect the path he had chosen?

'What if Dax were a Navy Seal, defending his country?' Clarence posed. 'Would it change the way you view him?'

"Well, crap," she said and turned the radio back on, not wanting to listen anymore.

~~

Two hours into our training, Mary's enthusiasm hadn't faded a wit. I wanted to stop forty minutes ago, but the joy on her face and glint in her eyes compelled me to continue. Of course, some of that shine was fueled by her attempt to wear me down and do me in.

What began as a Tai chi kind of ballet had evolved into a salsa of sorts, with moves and countermoves accentuated by colorful Nerf knives during the dance of a thousand cuts.

Mary amazed me by being both patient and aggressive, a combination not easily learned. She didn't rush to deliver a fatal blow but seemed to relish the wait, inflicting damage when the opportune time to strike presented itself. And as much as I'd like to take credit for it, I couldn't.

Sure, I'd shown her the correct way to hold a knife, but she had an intuitive sense of fighting that defied belief. It was remarkable! What had taken me weeks to learn took her all of a couple hours, which was why I wanted to quit earlier, before she Nerf-knife kicked my ass.

There it is! I lunged toward the mistake I'd waited for, hoped for. Except it wasn't one.

My little shit, little girl had suckered me into making a mistake of my own and she quickly, gleefully, cut my throat.

"You be dead, old man."

"Yes, I be," I said and fell to my knees for effect. "That was great, hon."

"Thanks. You were pretty good, too. Until you weren't."

"Thanks?"

She reached for a towel to wipe the sweat from her face, and I tried to catch my breath without seeming to, an effort that did not go unnoticed by Watson who smiled at me with too much delight. I shook a *Shh* at him, but we both knew he'd tattle on me later.

"Well, so much for lessons one through ten," I said after regaining my equilibrium. "Maybe eleven to twenty, too."

"Yeah," she said, grinning. "I don't know why, but I was in a zone. Like Neo with that Agent at the end of *The Matrix*."

"Well you seem to have a knack for it, that's for sure. Maybe we'll see how you do with Chinese throwing stars."

"It's funny you say that because while we were going at it, right before I killed you, I was singing a song in my head from a disco station – *Kung Fu Fighting*."

"You know, I heard those kids were fast as lightning."

We laughed and then I asked why she was listening to disco. "It's dead, you know."

"That's where ABBA lives. Besides, I have an affinity for things that are old. It's probably why I like you so much."

Watson snorted a canine guffaw.

"How about a bike ride to cool down?" she said.

"That's a great idea. I'd rather not have a ton of TV vans trailing us, though."

"I could deal with a newsie or two. We could take along our Super Duper, Red Ryders."

"You'll squirt your eye out, kid," I said and crooked my head at Watson.

"Would you mind taking a look? It'll give you a chance to practice some of what we were talking about earlier. Just stroll to the end of the driveway as if you didn't have a care in the world, take a look around like it's no big deal, and, if something looks disconcerting, act as if it isn't. We don't want them to know we know. You know?"

Watson barked an *okay* and headed for the door.

"Would you check the mail while you're there?"

He rolled his eyes before leaving, and I asked Mary if I could talk to her.

"Isn't that interesting?" she said as we stepped off the mat to roll it up against the wall. "Why is it when something serious needs to be said, people often ask permission first?"

"Apprehension about the outcome? To soften a blow, maybe, or give a heads up? An unconscious delaying tactic?"

"Why are *you* doing it?" She grinned and I reciprocated. "And what if I said no? Where would you be then, having asked and been answered?"

"Uh . . ."

"Exactly. So just say it."

"Okay. It's about our training," I said and got right to it. "How do you feel about killing those men?"

She shook her head and then answered the question I was really asking.

"No, I didn't like it. And I don't. Was there a satisfaction that came from being able to apply what I've learned? Yes. Most certainly. But I wish I hadn't had to. And if they hadn't tried to harm me or mine, I wouldn't have."

I wanted her to be safe, to protect herself and others. To be formidable in confrontations. What I didn't want was for her to follow in my footsteps.

A green light flashed and Booker T's song *Green Onions* started to play, indicating something or someone taller than Watson had triggered the alarm nearest to the road. As a precaution, Mary and I traded Nerfs for nine-millimeters on our way through the living room to the garage.

The clanging door opened slowly as the music changed to *Yellow Submarine*. And then *Red House*.

We watched Watson amble into the clearing from the driveway followed by Dominic.

"Thanks, boy." I took the saliva-soaked envelopes from his mouth and held up a hand to Dom in a saying *Hey* way.

"Dax," he said, winded by the nearly hundred-yard trek. "Miss Mary."

"Good morning, Detective Greer. How are you today?"

"More tired than I was a few minutes ago. That's a heck of a hike you have."

"Sorry," she said. "You'll have to blame Dax for that. It was there when I got here."

"I blame my wife's cooking. And her darn apple pies." Dominic patted his stomach and grinned. "How are you holding up?" he asked her after she'd tucked the gun away. "That was a mighty brave thing you did the other night."

"I'm alright. Just wish it hadn't been necessary."

"I'm with you there."

"What brings you up the long and winding road, Dom?" I asked. "Is this about what happened with the news folks? I saw you came by the house after we left for Tallahassee."

"Yesterday, it was. I wanted to let you know I talked to them and tried to warn them off for their own good. But it probably fell on deaf ears, judging from past experience."

"Are there any vans out front now?"

"Not yet. But..." Dominic shrugged. "I hear you have a minefield now?"

"Not really. I wanted to send a 'do not disturb' message with a little oomph, so I rigged a *one and done* event. With any luck, it will give them some incentive to stay away."

"Couldn't hurt," he agreed and asked Mary if she'd mind if he spoke with me alone. "It won't take long."

"No problem," she said. "I'll go tend to the Supers."

When she left, Dominic raised an eyebrow at me.

"Squirt guns. We're going for a bike ride in a bit."

"How is she really doing?" he asked.

"Good, actually. It's like she said, but she's not going to live in fear, either. She's tough, that one."

"Lucky for us she is," he said, knowing Tasha would be dead if not for her. "Hopefully, it'll make her stronger."

I acknowledged his 'what doesn't kill you' aphorism by nodding but wondered if Nietzsche meant that to be literal.

Dom reached into his pocket and pulled out a picture.

"Do you recognize this guy?"

"No," I said after a few seconds, lying through my teeth. "He looks dead."

"He is. Are you sure? Maybe you saw him somewhere."

I looked and lied again. "His face doesn't ring any bells. Who is he?"

"Don't know yet."

"You ran his prints, I assume?"

"He doesn't have any."

"Hmm," I said. "That's odd. Some kind of birth defect?"

"Something like that. Do you think... Would it be okay if I showed Mary the photo? I don't want to upset her, but she might have seen him around."

"Hey, Mare?" I yelled. "Can you come here for a sec?"

"What's up?" she asked as she drew near.

"Dominic is trying to identify a man who died. Would you see if he looks familiar?"

I handed her the picture, and she studied it, raised it to sunlight, brought it down, and then held a single finger over the photograph where his eyes were.

53

"He looks like the man I saw about a week ago on Indian Pass Road, the day before Watson went to stay with Isabel. He was parked on the other side of the street, talking on the phone, wearing sunglasses. He waved as we rode by on the mower. Did you see him?" She showed Watson the photo.

Dom smiled at her silliness, figured Mary was having a laugh at his expense, and asked if she remembered the color or make of the man's vehicle.

"I don't know the kind of car it was, but it was silver." Watson barked, and Mary corrected herself. "Sorry, I guess it was more a matted grey with silver flecks. And he says it was a Toyota Camry."

His smile retreated as he looked at Dax who shrugged. While not sure what was going on, Dominic didn't know how to feel about having his leg pulled. The color and make were a match, but why Mary pretended the dog knew things she didn't confused him.

"Do you happen to know the tag number?"

"No, sorry," she said, and Dom believed her. His many years as a detective honed his ability to detect the *bull*, and he knew she was sure as shit telling the truth.

"What about you?" he asked the dog for the heck of it.

When Mary told him what Watson had said, his mouth dropped open and I chuckled at his reaction.

"Welcome to our Dr. Doolittle world."

In the midst of his confusion, Mary asked Watson why he memorized it. When he told her, she said, "See? It's like I was saying at breakfast. You look out for me in more ways than you know."

"What did he say?" I asked.

"That he keeps track of the paparazzi, looky-loos, and weirdos that follow us around when we're out cutting grass. Just in case."

"You're still being pestered? I didn't know that."

"No?" Mary said with an air of innocence, knowing he didn't because she hadn't told him.

"No. Why didn't you... Wait," I said and looked at Dom. "Does this have to do with the car that was down the road?"

I did a good job of selling my surprise, especially since it was me who'd killed the guy we were talking about.

"Yes. The man was found in the trunk of the Camry. When was the first time y'all noticed that car sitting there?"

Mary hadn't seen it there at all, she said, and I told him about the second time I'd noticed it. But not the first.

"I saw it when I got home the night the girls were held hostage. You were guarding my driveway in a police cruiser. Remember?"

"Yes."

We didn't speak for a minute and I debated whether to try and direct the course of his investigation. It was tricky and fraught with risk, but I thought it would be okay if I just dipped my toe into the pond of what he knew or didn't.

"What was he doing there, I wonder?"

Before he answered, Mary put the bee in his bonnet I'd hoped to place myself.

"Could he have been involved with the guys at Tash's? Maybe they were out to get us too, but Dax had gone to play the gig in Georgia, and I'd already left for my sleepover."

"It's possible, I suppose. But why kill him? Because he let y'all get away?"

As they thought about it, so did I. This misdirection of motive would last only till the ballistics of this murder were tied to the other one, and then...

"Dax?" Mary said, looking at me with probing blue eyes. "What do you think?"

"I don't know. It's as good a theory as any without more to go on," I said and looked at Dominic, who shook his head. "Maybe he intended to use you as a bargaining chip to force Tasha's hand the way those guys were using her to force Jeri's. And killing him might have tied up a loose end, once their plans fell through."

"It sounds like you know what you're talking about," Dominic said with a raised brow.

I stopped his suspicion dead in its tracks by grinning and saying *thanks*. "We watch a lot of movies around here. Don't we, girl?"

"A lot," she said and smiled. "You'd be surprised how much you can learn from them. Like how to kill the walking dead in the event of a zombie apocalypse. Or what to do if suddenly thrust into the world of international intrigue."

Dominic found their sense of humor every bit the hoot Tasha said it was and added his grin to theirs.

"How *do* you kill a zombie?" he asked, just in case.

"It's all about the brain," Mary said, "and stopping its function. By bullet, knife, stick, rock, whatever gets it done. And don't let them bite you, or else you're a goner."

"Good to know," he told her and tucked the photo away. "I'm gonna let y'all get back to your day."

"Thanks for stopping by," I replied. "Maybe you'll keep us informed if something turns up we need to know?"

"Will do, Dax. Miss Mary, I appreciate your help. And your talking dog's," Dom said with curiosity and disbelief.

We shook hands like men do, with a firm grasp and two quick pumps. But before he turned to leave, I asked Mary to run in and get the extra gate remote from the junk jar.

"Here you go, Mr. Dominic," she said after grabbing it. "Next time, you won't have to blame your wife for her pies."

"Thanks a lot," he chuckled. "See y'all."

After he was out of sight and sound, I turned to face an arms-crossed cutie with a semi-scowl on her face.

"What?"

Mary didn't say anything, but I had a good idea why she glared at me that way and didn't really want to discuss it. However, as she seemed more curious than cross, I yielded.

"This one time, Mare," I said, a finger held for emphasis in an attempt to impersonate Al Pacino as Michael Corleone. "I'll let you ask me about my affairs."

She smiled in spite of herself, and the tension was gone. "What does the man in the trunk have to do with us?"

I took a deep breath then opened my hands into a scale. "In this hand is plausible deniability. The other, knowledge. Choose wisely, grasshopper."

It might seem inappropriate to joke around about such a serious subject, but we preferred it that way. Gallows humor made unpleasant realities easier to navigate.

She appeared to give consideration to my predicament, which I appreciated, but her response was as worrisome to me as it was funny.

"I'll take knowledge for six-hundred, Alex."

I nodded and said, "Hale Bedford."

Mary paused and then asked the pertinent question.

"Do we need to be concerned?"

"No," I told her. "Not anymore."

chapter six

Tasha turned right as instructed and received a *You've arrived at your destination* declaration even though she was still 1.3 miles from the house. She knew that because after she could reach the pedals of her father's one-ton truck, he'd let her take it up the driveway and get the mail – one of the many things she was taught as a kid that seemed as normal as calling cowboy clothes, *ranch dressing*.

She gazed out over the familiar sage-brushed, tumble-weeded, wind-swept plain, and saw four or five times more nodding donkeys than when she left some twenty years ago.

But the giant *penny horses* she used to ride were now eyesores. The crude oil machines' up and down motion still mesmerized her, though. How many hours had been whiled away watching them, happily thinking about her father and their life together?

"Too damned many," she said, shaking her head to clear cobwebs of memories she'd long ago taken a broom to.

Jeri's picture lit up her phone just as the sun set

"What's shakin,' Seven?" She'd called her that since the academy, after a favorite Star Trek character. *Seven of Nine* was self-sufficient, intelligent, and cool under pressure with a calm demeanor – qualities Tasha admired in her friend. And, though not as emotionally detached as her Borg alias, Jeri never let feelings interfere with her work. Which might be why what Tasha heard didn't register at first.

She shut off the pickup to listen. It sounded more like weeping than crying, and the anguish in it broke her heart.

"Seven?" she said softly as Jeri became quiet. But her voice grew firmer when she didn't respond. "Are you there? Seven?"

After a fumbling commotion, Jeri answered.

"Hey girlfriend. Sorry, I didn't hear your call. What's up? Did you make it to your dad's yet?"

"What's up? You called me."

"I did? Huh. Must have butt-dialed you. I forgot to take it out of my pocket before getting in the car. Everything alright with you?"

Tasha didn't hear a hint of the sorrow from before and wondered whether to ask Jeri about it or not..

"I'm okay. And yes. I'm heading up the driveway now."

"Sorry you have to go through this, Tash."

"Thanks. It is what it is. What about you?"

Tasha expected to hear a tremor, but Jeri spoke as if she hadn't just been crying all alone in her car.

"It's a mess. We're finding them stacked up two-three bodies to a grave. I say bodies, but they are only skeletal remains. Can you imagine the callousness it takes to pile dead children on top of each other like that?"

Her voice had a sharp edge Tasha hadn't heard before, and it made her uneasy.

"We're up to fifty-three so far, and we've only covered a sliver of the forest. Anatovich lived there more than forty years, so there's no telling how many he has buried. Could be hundreds."

"Seven..."

"Before you called me I was thinking about his gardens. They're scattered throughout the property, most of them wild, but many were maintained. Strawberries, blueberries, tomatoes, peppers, cucumbers... I bit into a Georgia peach that knocked my socks off. I'd never had one sweeter in all my life and ate it quickly so I could taste another. But then a cadaver dog came over with its handler and barked at the ground under my feet. Turns out, after those kids were stolen, raped and murdered, he found another use for them – as compost. Waste not, want not, I suppose."

The last was uttered with lifeless sarcasm. Tasha could only imagine the horror her friend had seen and tried to give comfort with the first words that popped into her head. In retrospect, she shouldn't have.

"It's going to be alright, Jeri."

"I don't think so. I'm afraid nothing will ever be *alright* again."

Before she could respond, Jeri said she had a long drive back to Atlanta and needed to go

"Thanks again for calling, Tash. Talk at ya later."

"Wait, Seven. I..."

But she was gone, leaving her worried about Jeri's state of mind – as well as her own because she wished more than anything that Dax had gotten to Anatovich earlier.

Much, much earlier.

'So, to hell with the law then?' a voice in her head said.

'I didn't say that. The law serves a purpose. But it's not the *be all, end all* it's made out to be. It's limited, constantly in flux and, too often, too late to address an injustice. In the meantime people suffer. They die. I'm not saying Dax was right, but...'

'Yes?'

'I can't say for certain he was wrong. Truth is, the law didn't save Mary from her father or us from Anatovich. And the three girls he would have surely thrown into the ground with the rest after he'd had his filthy fun. *Dax* did. Am I just supposed to ignore that?'

Her raised voice only became apparent in contrast to the calm question asked as an answer.

'What about the others? He getting a pass there, too?'

"I didn't... I don't know," she said and started the truck to drown out the buzzing in her brain.

Before shifting into gear, she sent Dax a text.

'I'm here. Let Mary know. Like you. Love her. Later.'

It was more succinct than usual, but she thought it best to be brief, not wanting to get into a discussion that might lead to a conversation. She'd like to share her concern for Jeri with him, knowing he'd care, but didn't think it wise. It could turn into talking, and she wasn't ready for that. Her heart, however, sent him a text of its own.

'Miss you.'

'Me too.'

61

His concise reply made her smile. He was as fretful as she was about where they were with each other after two days of being alone with her thoughts.

Shadows from the nodding donkeys galloped along as she drove down the drive to the ranch house. She imagined them a stampede of wild mustangs and longed to join them as they ran fast and free and far away.

The surprise of seeing her home after so much time turned to shock as she realized it didn't just look the same; it was *exactly* the same. And more than that, it appeared to be meticulously preserved and maintained.

A sadness welled despite her best efforts to squash it. Was this for her? He had no reason to expect she'd want to see him again. Ever.

But what if he'd been hoping all these years?

Tasha almost put the truck in reverse when long buried feelings threatened to resurface.

"Knock it off." She grabbed her purse and the cooler then walked to the front door, refusing to knock.

If it's locked, I'll leave, she thought, letting fate decide. When the knob turned, she stepped inside.

He sat in a lounge chair, his face gaunt and sallow, his body withered, shrunken. A tube attached to an oxygen tank connected to the nasal cannula affixed to his face, and a bag of morphine fed another tube imbedded in his arm.

But as pitiful as he looked, and in spite of her natural compassion, Tasha knew she would walk out if he so much as smiled or acted at all pleased to see her.

Just give me a reason, and I'll be on my way.

She returned his hello with a nod and walked past him, down the hall to her old room. After closing the door, she took a deep breath and fished the corkscrew from her purse. She was surprisingly calm, content with being able to keep her feelings in some semblance of check.

Her room was exactly how she had left it as a young girl. It wasn't a shrine but a snapshot in time. And when she sat on the bed, a waft of clean rose instead of the dusty, musty smell she expected.

He must have known her coming was a long shot, but her bed was made with freshly washed, Downey softened sheets and blankets on the million to one chance she would.

"Stop it," she uttered when the sadness welled up again. "He had no right to hope. And I've no business being here."

Tasha took a giant sip from the bottle rather than leave the room to find a glass. After another guzzle, she knew two things for sure. It was going to be a long and difficult night.

And she hadn't brought nearly enough wine.

~~

"Is this really necessary, Alexi?" Marcus asked.

"I'm sorry, yes. Miko is being overly cautious, but it's understandable considering what happened to his uncle."

"He can't possibly think I'd try to kill him."

"You've been in the hands of the FBI for days, Marcus. Frankly, he doesn't know what to think. Neither do I."

Marcus did his best to be at ease, but he wasn't.

"Look, he wants to talk to you but, if you'd rather not, feel free to go. It's up to you," Alexi said.

Yeah, right, Marcus thought, his situation untenable. How long could he expect to live if he refused?

"You just going to stand there?" he asked.

"Believe me, Marcus. I don't like it any more than you."

Alexi watched him undress and assessed his demeanor. When he stood buck naked, Alexi told him to hold his arms out to his side while he used a wand similar to one used in airport security, only his scanned for electronic devices.

"Open your mouth," he said, and, after a look inside told Marcus to turn and grab his ankles.

"Come on," was the reply, but he bent over all the same.

"Be glad I'm not putting on a rubber glove," Alexi said. When finished, he had Marcus set his glasses, wedding ring, and a nipple piercing on the table with his phone and wallet. "Kind of old for that, aren't you?"

Marcus blushed and said his wife preferred matching spikes instead of tattoos for their last anniversary.

"She sounds like fun. Maybe I'll meet her sometime."

"Maybe," Marcus said as if the notion weren't troubling. It was, however. Very much so.

"He's downstairs in the spa."

Alexi opened the hidden door and waited for Marcus to descend the spiral staircase before getting to work.

~

"It's good to see you, Marcus. Glad you could make it," Miko told him. "Please, join me."

Marcus climbed in the hot tub and tried to settle down. "Aahh, that hits the spot. Thanks for inviting me, Miko."

"Are you doing alright? In general, I mean."

"Yes. I'm fine."

"And the family? The twins must be what, twelve now? That's such a special age... On the cusp of womanhood and all the pleasures that await. I don't envy you the attention having such beautiful daughters will bring."

Miko sliced into a pomegranate and offered him a taste as he tried to mask his fear. The nephew just threatened to do to his little girls what Marcus would do with his uncle's.

"No thanks. They give me gas," Marcus said.

"That's too bad. So, you're working for the FBI now?"

Any thought he might have had of cooperating with the Feds vanished when he stared into the eyes looking into his. They were dark, cold, ominous, like a shark's must be, and Marcus began to worry about making it out of the tub alive.

"No," he said, struggling to keep his cool. "They offered, of course, practically promised me the moon if I gave them what they wanted. But I didn't."

"So you say. Why did they let you go then, I wonder?"

"Well, you're right. It looks suspicious, which is exactly what they intended, hoping it would coerce me to cooperate for fear of what the organization might do to keep me silent. But they know I'm an attorney and knew they couldn't hold me unless they charged me. The fact I'm here indicates they don't have anything, or they would have used it as leverage and kept me in custody."

"Then why are Juanita and the twins down in Miami? Just visiting her mother?"

It was alarming that he knew his family's whereabouts, but Marcus appreciated what Miko was doing. Or rather the way he was doing it. Dimitri had been a crude, blunt object. But the kid was subtle, and his threats more businesslike.

"Yes. I thought they'd be safe there, least until we find out who is involved with what happened to your uncle. Hell, if I hadn't left for home when I did that night, I would've been killed along with the rest of them."

The kid looked at him like he was already in the grave. But rather than climb in, Marcus took a stand.

"Look, you're going to do what you want, for whatever reason you have, but I had nothing to do with his death. Not one damned thing."

Miko found his denial believable. For the moment.

"Any thoughts on who it might have been?" he asked, using the knife to deftly peel the skin from the pomegranate. "A competitor, perhaps? Or someone on the inside?"

Marcus was under no delusion the threat of danger had passed, but he sat back and relaxed as if it had.

"It's always a possibility in business. Your uncle sat at the pinnacle of his profession and ruled with an iron fist, so, yes, he made a few enemies. I haven't heard anything from anyone who might know but then again, I've been a guest of the FBI up until an hour ago. As for it being an insider, your uncle said something once. At the time, I took it to mean one thing, but maybe I was wrong? I don't want to slur anyone's character, but given the circumstances . . ."

"What was it?"

Marcus looked around and leaned forward, noting the knife in the kid's hand had steadied and was pointed at him.

"He said, '*Keep an eye on Alexi. He's ambitious.*' But he never said anything more after that."

"Thanks for telling me, Marcus. Uncle Dimi told me the same thing – in addition to sharing insights into others who worked for him."

After another peel and slice, Miko got around to the girl. "Why were Anthony's men at that detective's house?"

Marcus sighed, unable to hide his exasperation.

"For some reason, Dimitri developed a livid hatred for the new Deputy-Director in Atlanta. Maybe it was because she wasn't Thompson, who had been as much a friend as a facilitator. Or her investigation, that could've put him in jail. Or just because she was a woman with power. I'm not sure, but he wanted her dead. I tried to counsel him, pointing out the catastrophic ramifications, but your uncle was adamant. It was Anthony, if you can believe it, who argued for a less destructive course of action – putting Ryan in Dimitri's pocket by threatening to kill her best friend in real time. He liked the idea of owning her more than killing her, so he gave his consent."

"And how did the girl factor into it?"

"Her involvement was accidental but pivotal. If she hadn't shown up, Ryan might have let herself and her friend die, both professionals familiar with the inherent risks. But the girl's arrival upped the ante and Ryan ended up folding. Then Anthony's men fucked up by failing to secure the girl, and she somehow managed to kill them both. Just like she did the former Deputy-Director. Did you know about that?"

"Yes," Miko said. "How do you know what Ryan did or didn't do? Or the girl? I haven't seen any news about it."

"Anthony has . . . had a mole in the Atlanta field office. He called just before the Feds pulled me in."

"Did you give this information to your FBI buddies?"

Rather than say they weren't his *fucking friends*, he just told him *no*. The kid then magically pulled pen and paper seemingly out of nowhere and told him to write the name of the contact down, which he did.

"How are you set for retirement, Marcus? Do you have sufficient funds to see your girls through college?"

He thought the question odd but answered honestly. "I'm alright."

Miko nodded.

"I'd rather you not become a witness for the FBI, but I guess you'll do what you think best. As will I. Regardless, there's twenty-five million in the Cayman account for you. Consider it a severance package. And if you end up arrested, we'll do what's needed to keep you from going to prison."

Marcus was stunned, and, when thanked for coming, he was afraid to take the offered hand.

"That's very generous, Miko, but you don't have to do that. I could just work for you as I did for your uncle."

"Your loyalty is appreciated, Marcus, but your services are no longer required. My uncle's way isn't mine, and I'd prefer to let his legacy die with him. I hope you understand."

Marcus shook his hand, expecting the knife to follow, but the kid just stood and smiled.

"Good luck, Marcus. Alexi will show you out."

"Thanks," was all he could say, worried if he'd ever see his wife and kids again.

Miko was taking laps in the pool when Alexi returned. "Well?" he asked.

"He was clean; so was his shit. But you were right. He has an FBI tail on his ass. Is he a dead man?"

"We'll see. Did you get the trackers installed?"

"Yes. Did he have anything on who hit your uncle?"

"Nothing definitive. What do you know about the girl in St. Vincent who killed Anthony's men?"

"Only what's been on the news. Did you see her old man threaten to kill that reporter the other day?"

"She was a cameraman," Miko corrected him. The teen was intriguing. And the man who must have trained her. "Let's give them a closer look. See who they really are."

"You think they're involved?"

"I doubt it. The dad wouldn't have left her alone after what happened, and Uncle Dimi was killed long before they could have driven there afterward. But they interest me. The girl in particular..."

chapter seven

Tasha got out of bed, exhausted and pissed. She threw on some clothes and walked quietly down the dark hallway to the front door. Once outside, she slipped on her shoes and took a deep breath of cool air, hoping to clear her head.

"Damned dreams. Fuck you."

The sun peeked over the horizon to brighten her mood but wasn't appreciated for the effort.

"Fuck you, too."

She tucked her shoulders against her neck to stave off the morning chill, thought about getting something to keep warm, but then stepped off the porch and said, "Fuck that."

When she rounded the corner of the house, as if to add insult to injury, a sunbeam lit the old swing hanging from a branch of the old tree, beckoning her to come hither.

"What the . . ."

The rope was new, and the wooden seat she'd swung on for years still intact. Like the clean bedding, his hope had paid off, and she eased herself down on the plank he called her throne because she sat so regally.

'You're a princess, sweetie,' he'd say. *'And my queen.'*

Tasha kicked the ground before she grabbed the rope and shoved her feet. Her eyes shut as she found her former rhythm and thoughts of her childhood reemerged.

Those were happy days, filled with fun and play, love and laughter. He told her there wasn't anything she couldn't do and taught her what she needed to know – like how to drive when she was eight.

'It's just us, darlin' he'd say. *'Only and always. We have to learn to do for ourselves. And each other.'*

Tasha was the love of his life little girl, and he, the sun her world revolved around. She'd never known a stern look, an irritated inflection, or a time he made her do anything she didn't want to. He'd been her light, her rock, her best friend, and they did everything daddies and daughters who love each other do...

She slammed on the brakes, fell to her knees, and threw up. Whether it was from dizziness, stress, or lack of sleep didn't matter so much as having something to heave. The nuggets she ate yesterday morning were long gone, and the wine from last night had found safe harbor in her bladder.

After a few dry attempts, and wiping a snot string from her nose, she pulled down her pants and peed.

"Don't look much like a princess now, do you?"

Tasha chuckled and gazed about, remembering how nice it had been to be by herself in the middle of nowhere. But that was then, and now... headlights were approaching.

She stood and zipped before taking a seat on the swing to wait. It was a long-ass driveway.

When the car pulled next to her truck, she walked over.

"Oh, hello," the large lady said as she lifted herself out. "You must be Tasha. I recognize you from the picture by his bed. I'm Tammy. Your father's hospice care provider."

Tasha gave a nod, not knowing what to say, ask, or feel. Fortunately, Tammy was talky.

"I'll bet he was glad to see you. It hasn't been easy for him, hanging on like he has."

"What do you mean?"

"He should be dead, if you don't mind my saying so. I think it was sheer will that he stayed alive till you got here."

"We've been estranged a long time."

"He mentioned it," Tammy said, reaching for her bag.

"Yeah? What else did he mention?"

"He hardly says anything, your father. But he loves you very much."

"Did he tell you that?" Tasha asked, irritated he might have cast himself in a light much brighter than deserved.

"No, however... I don't want to cause you any pain, Miss, but your father's been in agony because of the cancer. The morphine won't eliminate it, and he doesn't use enough to get even marginal relief. Said he wanted to be..." Tammy paused to remember and then said, "Functionally coherent. For you."

Tasha took a breath and counted to five. Six. Seven...

"What do you do here? With him?" she asked.

"Nurse stuff - clean him up, change the sheets, check his vitals, and spend time with him so he doesn't suffer alone."

She didn't hear a judgement in her voice but felt a tug of recrimination anyway, which was straight-up bullshit!

"Tammy, how long do you usually stay?"

"Until four or five, depending. But you'll probably want me to leave early now you're here, so you two can be alone."

Tash's feelings about spending time with him were not ambivalent, and her nod was a lie, plain and simple.

"I need to go to town this morning and get a few things, but I should be back before long."

Tammy saw something in the daughter's eyes, but she wasn't her concern. He was.

"As you wish, Miss. Now, if you'll excuse me."

Tasha followed but went to her bedroom. With purse and cooler in hand, she glanced into his room on her way to the door, caught his eye and left.

~~

It wasn't until early evening that the mower drove onto the trailer for the last time. We'd cut, whacked, blown, and sprayed twenty-nine lawns and I, for one, was feeling every bit of it. "I can't believe we got 'em all done in a day, Mare."

"We kicked butt, for sure. But that's not all of them. There's another thirty-one to do next week."

"What?" I said, rolling the windows down to let the hot air out as the cold streamed in through the vents. "I didn't realize you had so many now. How's that working for you?"

"Well, Dr. Phil," she said with a grin and a back-country twang, "I don't usually do like we just done did, but instead round ten a day, three times a week, till I's all done."

Watson winced in the rearview as she mauled the lingo, but I wasn't going to rebuke an impertinence I encouraged.

"So tell me, Mary, Mary. How does your garden grow?"

I'd given her a three-hundred sixty degree, zero turn radius riding mower for her last birthday, and she used it to form the *Quite Contrary Lawncare Service* company.

"Good. I had to limit customers to sixty to comply with your all work and no play policy, but it's working out fine."

"I appreciate your compliance," I told her. "And your play. How much money are you making, by the way?"

"Why? Do you want me to start paying rent?"

Her eyes shined as she playfully poked my funny bone.

"Not unless you're still living there when you're thirty. I was just curious about what's in your piggy bank."

"I only have a little over forty-eight thousand right now. But my projected yearly earnings should exceed sixty-five."

I glanced over and got a nonchalant look of satisfaction. She'd gotten me, one way or the other, by hook or by crook.

"Really?"

"Really."

"Holy cow! What are you charging, an arm and a leg?"

"More legs than arms. And an occasional foot."

"Huh," I said and turned my attention back to the road in front of me after a car honked its horn. "Huh?"

"I get fifty to a hundred bucks per yard, That averages to seventy-five times sixty times four for the slow months, and double that for the busiest. Then there are the odd jobs. And, of course, the tips."

"Tips?"

"They call it paying the *cutie tax*. I try to give it back, but ..." Mary shrugged as if saying, *What are you gonna do?*

"They?" I asked, knowing she was goading me but irked all the same.

"Sorry," she said, sensing my consternation. "I'm just kidding about the tips. But I'll do an occasional odd job."

"Like what?"

"Trim and haul away dead palm fronds, mow a patch of grass not part of the yard, clean their pool in a skimpy bikini. That there is the money maker."

Mary punched my arm when I gave her 'the look.'

"You're getting to be too easy to get; you know that?"

"I knew you were kidding right off."

"Oh, yeah? How?" she asked with doubting smugness.

"Because you didn't blush after you said *cutie tax.* Cutie pie."

And there it was, a bright red glow where her smile had been, followed by another harder punch to the arm.

"So, rent, huh?" I said. "Where did we leave that?"

"Fourteen years down the road," she said and smirked. "Maybe by then, you'll be living with *me.*"

"And why would I . . . . Oh, because I'll be an old man. Ha-ha."

"You're already old. I was thinking rickety and feeble."

"Sounds like a geriatric country duo. That reminds me, we've been asked to play a couple two-hour sets over the Labor Day weekend from a wooden deck with a shaded roof overlooking the sand and water along Cape San Blas. Are you interested? Might be fun."

"Is it just you and me, or can all of us play?"

"I don't see why not. It's a little more than a week away, so maybe Tasha will be back by then."

"Isabel is already planning to come down, so that just leaves Aunt Jeri," Mary said, excited by the idea. "It would be great to have the whole family rocking and rolling again. Do you think she could make it?"

"Give her a call and find out."

I loved to watch her eyes dance when she got animated. It made me wonder what she was like as a little girl, and sad because I'd never know.

"I'll shoot Tasha a text and ask her to ask," she said.

"Have you heard anything from her today?"

"No. You?"

"No," I said, not wanting to wonder about *that.*

Watson barked something that made Mary say, *Aww.* "Of course I meant you, too. You silly dog." She ruffled and scratched his head as it settled into place on the console.

We rode to town without saying much and pulled into St. Vincent RentAll minutes before they closed. In addition to renting equipment and hand tools, they sharpened saws, chains, and blades, and sold plants, fertilizer, and propane. They were a versatile mercantile.

After dropping off the lawnmower for maintenance, I suggested we get some chicken from the Pig. Watson's ears perked and Mary grinned like I knew she would.

Colonel Sanders had nothing on Piggly Wiggly, or so we believed. And until a Kentucky-fried franchise came to town and proved us wrong, we were *dancin' with the one that brung us*, so to speak – albeit poorly.

We left a window rolled down for Watson and moseyed across the Piggly parking lot like we were heading to an old-time western saloon. Mary brandished a mini- super squirt gun on her hip, and me, a concealed weapon in the crook of my back. I whistled *The Good, the Bad, and the Ugly,* and she finished the refrain by singing, *Mwow, mwow, mwoww.*

Once inside, we split up to save time.

"I'll get the chicken and some fixings while you grab the eggs and what not."

"What if they're all out of whatnot?" she asked. "What then?"

"That'll work. I haven't had a bowl of *whatthen* in ages."

After commemorating our clever repartee with a grin, I went to the far side of the store and stood in line at the deli counter. Three places in front of me, two from being served, was a man with a young girl I assumed to be his daughter. They stood side by side, his hand on the crook of her back.

She looked about Mary's age, maybe younger, although my deduction was based solely on viewing her from behind. Her long hair was curly red, arms covered in freckles, and I thought it sweet that she let him display his affection for her – in public no less!

The girl said something to her father I couldn't hear and left to sit on a nearby bench. I recognized her immediately but pretended I didn't and turned my face away. Instead of leaving like I should have, I stepped forward when the lined moved and hoped she hadn't noticed me.

Damned chicken. Why did it have to taste so good?

As I moved in accordance with others who wanted to get their food and go, I could feel her eyes on me and, in my periphery, saw her shift on the bench to get a better look. Unable to avoid the inevitable, I looked at her and smiled.

Leigha started to stand, but I shook my head and placed a finger to my lips. She nodded, mouthed *Thank you,* and smiled back. It looked good on her.

Much better than the fear I'd seen the other night.

But she was safe now, back in the arms of her family. And the men who used her were dead and done.

When her father returned with styrofoam containers, she stood, slipped her hand inside his arm, and glanced back as they walked away. Her expression conveyed hope, and my nod was an assurance that everything would be okay.

I stepped to the front of the line just as Mary rolled her buggy beside me.

"Hey, do you think Watson would rather have meatloaf with gravy instead of chicken?" I asked.

"Instead of, no. In addition to? Yes."

After getting a little of this and a lot of that, I put it all in Mary's buggy and led us to the salad stuff – Romain lettuce, tomatoes, cucumber, mushrooms, and a fat purple onion.

"So who was the girl?" she asked.

"What girl?" I said, grabbing the bacon bits and tossing them in the cart. "We got everything?"

"Yes. Except an answer to my question."

"What was that again?" I tugged on the buggy, and she pushed toward the check-out lanes.

"Who was the girl?"

"What girl?"

One of the things I like about Mary is she doesn't get too frustrated with me. If I square dance around an issue, she's happy to Dosey Doe.

"That pretty little redhead."

"What makes you think I know her?"

"You smiled and nodded."

"I'm sure I was just being friendly, to pass the time."

Another thing I like is her tenacity.

"Were you now? Because it looked like you were trying to hustle up another daughter," she said, a grin in her eyes.

"Well, it doesn't hurt to keep one's eye out. Just in case you leave me someday. "

"One might get one's eye plucked, if he's not careful."

75

"That's a good one, hon. Very nice turnabout wordplay. I'm going to take credit for that if it's alright with you."

I raised my brows and she gave her consent, both of us aware that our little dance was nearing the end. I did take a last twirl, however, when she asked if it was the girl from Wewahitchka.

"I think the song you mean is *The Girl from Ipanema*," I said as we approached a lane full of people.

Her confusion was compounded after I finished singing a verse ending with a robust, *Aahhh*. I received a smattering of applause from those of a certain age, and a *Not bad* from a lady working the cash register.

From Mary, I got a snicker, a headshake, and a look.

"Yes, she is," I told her when we were outside.

"Is that going to be a problem?" she asked, keeping her eyes peeled for anyone up to no good.

"I don't think so. Tasha said Leigha was adamant about not giving them a description. The others, too."

"It doesn't seem..."

"What?" I said when she quit talking.

She dawdled and looked at me in a curious way.

"It wasn't very smart to let those girls see your face, and then show it on television like you did."

"No, you're right. And now that you've brought it up, you might as well know the truth. I'm... I'm not perfect. I know it's hard to comprehend such a thing, but sometimes, I... make mistakes."

She cracked up in the middle of the parking lot, causing people who passed by to smile at her amusement.

"That was quite a performance, Dax. All that's missing is an *Oh, woe is me* hand to the brow," Mary said, shaking her head. "*I make mistakes.*"

"Glad you liked it. I'm going for the Oscar this year."

"But seriously, I think we should have a full debriefing, like you do with me, to replace errors with sound solutions. What do you think?"

What I thought was I didn't want her to know what she knew, but it was too late for that. And as we approached the truck, another thought occurred.

"How much does Watson know, about me?"

Mary stopped in her tracks and cocked her head.

"He asked me about a time you two were in Lynn Haven playing a spur of the moment gig with a band that was a man short. Said his leash smelled funny after you let him run loose in a nearby neighborhood, one where a guy who raped and killed a grandmother was later found strangled."

"What did you say?"

"According to him, the same thing you did. *Ask me no questions and I'll tell you no lies.*"

"And he accepted that?"

"Watson knows what's up, but we don't talk about it," she said, lifting an eyebrow. "Sound familiar?"

I nodded and patted her hand. "I just don't want him to think badly of me, is all."

"Watson is his own dog, so he's going to think what he will about what you've done – and what *I've* done, for that matter. But I don't believe he'll ever take the witness stand against you if it comes to that."

"Because he loves me so much?" I asked her with a grin. But Mary shook her head.

"Because he loves *me* so much. And I, you."

~~

She began to squirm as he touched her.

"Do you like that?"

"Yes."

"You sure? We can quit if you want."

"No, please," she said, undulating. "Don't stop . . ."

Tasha woke covered in sweat, and her face burned with anger and shame. She threw back the sheets and marched down the hall to his room.

How could he have done that?

She lifted the fallen pillow from the floor by his bed and squeezed it in frustration.

Why? WHY!!

He opened his eyes and saw her standing over him.

"How could you?" she asked, furious and foreboding.

When he smiled, she squashed his face with the pillow and held on tight, pushing down harder and harder.

Tasha woke again and peered through the darkness. "Damned dreams."

She reached for the cell phone, her eyes squinting from its light as the time made her groan. Too groggy to stand, she rolled to the floor and used the bed to shove herself up and toward the bathroom.

When her bottom hit the seat, she put elbows on knees and plopped her face in her hands.

What the hell am I doing here?

Despite her intention to leave, she'd spent most of the day aimlessly putzing around town and all night drinking at a local bar. Sometime after midnight, she decided she was too drunk to drive back to Florida and walked through his front door and fell into her old bed.

She didn't flush, as was their custom to keep the other from waking up too early for work or school.

What do you care if he wakes up now or not?

Similar questions had plagued her day, and no amount of alcohol had helped answer or drown them.

Why'd you come here? Yeah, she thought, like that one.

Tasha stood still in the hallway, listening to the rasp of his breathing. Without meaning to, she moved toward it. A pillow lay on the floor like her dream, and she picked it up, held it against her chest, and then sat in the chair by the bed.

You damned well didn't come for closure.

She'd created most of that by herself over time, and the rest had come from loving and being loved by Dax and Mary.

What was she looking for, then?

Any apology would be meaningless and far too late, any explanation an attempt to excuse himself. And if he tried to pull that crap, there was no telling what she might do.

You'd be dead if Dax knew what you did to me.

Whether it was said out loud or not, she didn't know. But a deep satisfaction came from knowing it was true. Dax loved her the way she should be. Not the way she'd been.

Tasha laid her head against the pillow, closed her eyes, and began to rock back and forth, trying to reconcile her *all over the place* feelings.

She'd loved her father as much as any child ever had, and it made her sad to think of that little girl's daddy dying. Would it be so wrong to shed a few tears for the man who stayed by her bed all night, wiped her fevered face with a cool washcloth when she was sick, or read a bedtime story again and again with as much enthusiasm as the first time?

Had his affection and devotion been a lie, or a truth she could believe in and hold on to? And if true, could she honor the good while condemning the bad – tuck the happiness of her youth in a safe place to keep from being tarnished by the vile things he'd done?

Wouldn't it be wonderful if she could separate a father she loved from the one she despised.

Perhaps it was as simple as that?

The possibility inspired hopefulness and offered her a chance to change how she felt about the past. They could spend the day together, maybe laugh and reminisce about good things, the happy times.

She might tell him about Dax and Mary.

Tasha was neither forgiving nor forgetting. But while he was still here, she could make his leaving less lonely and show compassion to a dad who gave her the gift of music and made ice cream from scratch.

Cause where he was going there'd be no such kindness.

~

The Hospice worker was surprised but pleased to see his daughter's truck when she pulled up, and teary-eyed when she found her asleep in the chair holding her father's lifeless hand.

chapter eight

Tasha listened to the morning noises and smelled the freshly turned dirt mixed with the scent of a cedar elm tree under which her father rested.

He died without having remarried, making friends, or caring about his neighbors enough for them to bear witness to his burial. Even Tammy could not attend because a lady the next town over needed her, like he had.

"What a waste of a life," she said and wiped at her face as another tear rolled down her cheek.

Loving father, he'd inscribed on his tombstone.

How would she have reacted seeing that, if not for her resolution to glean the good wheat from his chaff?

"Badly," Tasha muttered. "Very, very badly."

Crying jags were an unexpected result of that decision, but she'd rather bawl than continue to live with the hate.

"Of course, your being dead makes it so much easier. Now, doesn't it?" she told him.

To his credit, he didn't speak or try to climb out of the grave, so she agreed to accept his contention that he'd been a loving father in the context of her new construct.

"Context of construct? Holy cow, I sound just like Dax," she mumbled and then addressed the hushed mound of dirt. "You don't know who that is, do you?"

She told him how they'd met and everything since then, including the murders he had committed and why she'd left. By the time it was all said, the sun had moved from one end of the sky to the other.

Her stomach growled at her, just as it had yesterday, a reminder it had yet to be fed. Tasha grunted in recognition, but she didn't have much of an appetite and what did make it down didn't stay long before coming back up.

Her body must be more stressed than her mind was coping with her dad dying and worrying about Dax and Jeri. But she could handle it.

Tasha bent over suddenly and began to heave, thinking, *The joke's on you, because there's nothing in the cupboard.*

While waiting on hands and knees for the episode to be over, a ray of thought brightened her gloomy morning. Why couldn't she do the same *gleaning* with Dax? After all, her father's crimes were far worse. Right?

When the law failed to respond, she said it out loud.

"Right?"

Although given reluctantly, Tasha heard the nod in her head. "Well, at least we finally agree on something."

~~

"Let me see that."

"Now, sweetie," I said.

"Give it."

Mary held out her hand, and I gave it up.

After hefting, turning, tossing, rubbing and staring at it, she stuck it in her pocket.

"You're just going to keep my quarter?"

"Yup," she said and began to fill the sink with hot water.

For the third straight time, I'd gotten out of washing the dinner dishes by winning the coin toss. Not that I minded doing them, but I'd been having a good time at her expense and twenty-five cents was a small price to pay for it.

I left her in the kitchen, picked up a guitar and sat in my favorite chair; a rocking, rolling, sometimes squeaky and always swivelly, reclinable Barcalounger with a mold of my behind in the seat.

Watson joined me in the big room and jumped on the couch before the television spoke up. As he tried to find the most comfortable position, the channels started to change.

"I think you're lying on the remote." I asked him to turn it off but said, "Wait," when CNN came on.

"That sounds like Aunt Jeri," Mary called out.

"It is."

"She looks tired," she said, walking into the room. "Oh my God . . ."

Pictures of mass graves and skeletal remains assaulted us from the big screen TV as her hand fell to my shoulder.

"Did you know about this?"

I shook my head, listening to Jeri lay out the facts with a deadpan delivery. When a reporter asked if there were any leads on the man who'd killed Dimitri Anatovich, she told him an investigation was underway. And when asked if his murder had anything to do with the bodies of children being discovered, she said it was too early to know.

"Assigning any motive at this time would be premature and speculative."

"Did what happened to him and his men have anything to do with the St. Vincent detective who was held hostage?" another reporter asked.

"I don't see how," Jeri said. "Detective Williams was used to compel me to drop a criminal case, but I didn't know *what* case until the men who held her were killed. By the time we got a warrant for his arrest, Mr. Anatovich and his associates were already dead."

"So you say," a voice from the back said.

"Excuse me?"

"They threatened your friend... You could've had your FBI stormtroopers kill them like y'all did at Ruby Ridge and Waco as part of George Soros' master plan."

Jeri looked long and hard at the *so-called* journalist, and I imagined her frustrated and fed up with the stupidity of conspiracy-theorists.

"I suppose I could have, but someone else beat me to it. Thank you, ladies and gentlemen," she said and then left the podium as questions continued to be shouted out at her.

"Geez, Dax. Do you see that?" Mary said.

The information beneath the ubiquitous and annoying 'BREAKING NEWS' banner read - 107 found dead so far.

I didn't know my jaw was clenched until she put a hand on my fist, and I looked up and shook my head.

"It's not the number, because one is too many, but what it says. No one seems to be doing anything to stop this kind of thing from happening."

"You are," she said, her eyes filled with conviction.

"It's a drop in the bucket, Mare."

"Maybe, but that bucket doesn't get filled without them. And every single one matters, Dax."

The way she said it left no doubt that one of those *drops* was her. And she was right.

"So, you're saying Rome wasn't built in a day?"

Her face softened and she kissed my cheek. "A journey of a thousand miles begins with a single step."

"A two-steps forward, one-step back kind of deal?"

"Well, you can't make an omelet without breaking some eggs."

"Or leave till the fat lady sings," I said.

Mary looked at me funny and made me laugh.

"Okay, that one might be a bust, but I hear what you're saying. Thanks, sweetie."

"If you really want to thank me, let's double or nothing," she said and pulled my quarter from her pocket.

"How about an even or else instead?"

"A what?"

I recovered the coin and began to toss it up and down. "If you win, you're back where you started with me helping with the dishes. If you lose, you make me a rootbeer float. Agreed?"

The quarter missed my hand and fell to the floor, so I bent over and deftly traded it for another.

"Dax, I'll make you a float if you want."

"I know; it'll just taste a tad sweeter if I win it from you. Here, you flip this time."

When I gave it to her, my grin was understated.

"Alright then. Call it."

I smiled when the two-sided counterfeit left her thumb, looking forward to the taste of my ill-gotten A&W treat.

~~

Miko turned off the television and tried to recall how many of the bodies buried on the property belonged to him. Forty? Fifty? More? It was like asking how many pairs of sox he'd worn over the last ten years. Who knows?

Who cares?

Besides, his contribution paled compared to his uncle's. The number of carcasses reported by the *take me-fuck me* brunette on cable news was a small percentage of the total scattered around Dimitri's one-hundred-twenty acres and the state's twelve-thousand next door.

He leaned back in the leather chair and closed his eyes. It had been a long time since he'd thought about the past. His mom needed an operation and Uncle Dimi was his only living relative, his dad having left them alone long ago. He'd never spent much time with him before and was not eager to stay at his house while his mother recovered.

After dinner, Uncle Dimi asked if he still liked to play with toys, and Miko nodded.

" As long as they're fun."

"Good, good. I have a couple you might like."

When Miko followed him to his room, two nearly naked girls not much older than himself were on Uncle Dimi's bed.

"Say hello to your new playthings."

As a young boy, he had no interest in playing with girls. They were stupid, yucky, and always giggling. But when his mom came to get him a week later, he didn't want to leave.

She was touched by the strong bond he formed with his uncle and nurtured the connection by letting him stay every other weekend as long as his grades didn't suffer.

Miko began to get straight A's, something he continued to do in high school and college, so that he could spend more time playing with his 'toys.' But as can happen when you play with them too hard, sometimes they break.

The first time was an accident, and he was distraught. Not because he killed her but because she was his favorite.

'Never get attached, son,' his uncle told him. 'There are more where she came from, many new toys to play with.'

At some point, he began to break them on purpose for the added pleasure of watching them die. But that teenage fantasy phase only lasted for a summer and a half.

Now, he was more disciplined, his killing less frequent. No longer interested in low hanging fruit, he preferred a girl who was particularly ripe for the taking, one he could spend days, maybe weeks with.

"Come in, Alexi," Miko said when the door knocked.

Alexi pulled a folder from his briefcase and set it down. "It's light right now, mostly internet searches. I have a man in St. Vincent poking around, but it's going to take time if we don't want to raise alarms."

Miko held up some artwork of the father-daughter duo. "I want you to show the *I'll shoot you dead* video to Johnny. I know he said Uncle Dimi's killer wore a mask, but he might be able to identify his voice. Don't tell him what it's about, though. I don't want him lying to save his ass."

"I can't do that," Alexi told him.

"Why not?"

"He's dead."

Alexi's skin grew damp as one moment turned into the next. Even though Miko said he didn't care what happened to Johnny a week ago, it wouldn't matter if he had a temper like his uncle.

"I see," Miko said, pulling a sticky from a desk drawer. "We have a mole in the FBI, according to Marcus. Arrange a meeting. If he's legit, ask about Uncle Dimi's murder."

Alexi took the note and stood to leave.

"And give him Palmer's name to run on their database. So we can cross him off the list."

"Yes, sir."

~~

To sleep or not to sleep was one of many quotes from literature, film, or television I'd co-opted since going to bed four hours ago. But it was an iconic line from a Brady Bunch episode that most accurately expressed my feeling about all my thoughts being about her.

Tasha, Tasha, Tasha.

I resisted the urge to look at my phone knowing no call, text, or message would be there. And while that in itself was unusual behavior for her, mine was even more so – because there hadn't been a single day since we'd said our *I love yous* that I hadn't talked, texted, or touched her.

Giving her space was cramping my style, because as the song said, *'I'm just a love machine.'*

Hey, I thought is was funny . . .

After repositioning the pillow once more in a string of many times, I gave some thought to the other lady in my life.

Mary again asked for a debriefing, and I had put her off with a joke hoping to make her smile. And she did. But there was disappointment in her eyes I'd never seen before, and it hurt like the dickens – if *dickens* were an old English word meaning 'to reach inside and squeeze one's heart.'

When I tried to explain my reluctance, she said it wasn't necessary, and she understood. But thinking about it now, I wonder if I'd hurt her feelings?

Yes, she was young. A kid, though not really. She was also a friend, a joy, and a partner - in crime and out. Was I doing her a disservice by refusing to discuss details of things she never asked about but already knew?

How could I do that, though?

It felt irresponsible to say, *'After leaving that night to play the gig in Georgia, I noticed a suspicious looking car not far from the house. So I pulled into the trees, confronted the driver, and what do you know? He was there to kill you, me, Tasha, and Watson. He'd been sent by the man who blamed me for killing his sister and thinks I killed his best friend. too.*

Well, I stuck him in his car trunk and put one in his head because I couldn't take him with me in case I got pulled over. And then I decided to pay Hale Bedford a visit before he found out his hitman was no longer the hitter, but the hittee.

I called the club on the way, said I had car trouble, raced to Bedford's house, and killed him with the assassin's gun.

Then you and Tasha were taken hostage. So, as long as I was in the area, I rushed further up the state to deal with the scumbag responsible for that.'

Actually, and contrary to how simple I made it sound, a debriefing might be beneficial. If only to discuss the danger in seat of the pants operations versus those well planned. While the men who had tried to kill us were themselves now dead, I made mistakes that could come back to bite my ass.

Our ass, I amended, because those missteps could harm us all. So maybe talking to Mary was worth thinking about.

Okay. Now, can I get some damn sleep?

Apparently not till I checked my phone one more time.

87

chapter nine

Murphy set his coffee on the end table and stretched before taking the chair beside it. After a few sips from the cup, he reached past the murder book for the newspaper, pushed back in the recliner to lift the leg support, and slid the News-Herald from its plastic sleeve.

Brian loved the smell and feel of the paper in his hands, savored the small but significant pleasure it gave him. It also brought with it a sadness as the printed page would soon become a thing of the past, replaced by digital media.

He was surprised to see the St. Vincent girl and her new dad on the front page below the fold; although, given recent events, he shouldn't have been.

The picture was copied from a poster promoting their appearance at an upcoming Labor Day *BLOWOUT*, as advertised in big block letters. It was difficult to believe the smiling little girl he saw singing and playing a guitar killed two men by shooting them dead in the head. After seeing her dad on the television, however, it was clear the apple didn't fall far from the tree. That man was capable.

When finished reading everything on every page - want ads, job listings, births, deaths, weddings, arrests, what have you - Murphy set the paper aside and got up to get a refill before going over his murder book. Again.

Not that he didn't already have it memorized.

As coffee poured from the pot, he mentally reviewed. Of the twenty-two cases, eight were clearly tit-for-tat. Like the drunk who ran down the elementary kids at a school bus stop getting run over himself, or the low-life who raped and strangled a grandma in her home, strangled in his own.

The rest, though not slain as poetically, shared a similar *had it coming* characteristic. They were known or suspected offenders who killed or caused suffering.

And while he wasn't sure six of the twenty-two were murdered by the same person, two things were undeniable – *this* serial killer didn't prey on the innocent or vulnerable. No, he took out the garbage.

And it was a *he*.

In addition to having hunches that consistently paid off, Murphy had profiling skills that led him to believe the killer was a white male, thirty-five to fifty, intelligent, disciplined, capable... *Hmm*.

What about that?

He returned to the living room with his coffee and gave some thought to what popped into his head. Fortunately, he no longer questioned whether something was too crazy to consider, not after all he'd seen over the years. So, after the caffeine kicked in he picked up his phone and asked Siri.

Besides what he knew from the news, the internet said Dax Palmer won the Bayou Bash tournament in St. Vincent three years running five years ago. In a kayak. And while it spoke to his fishing acumen, Murphy saw something else – patience and planning skills. Palmer was a man confident in his ability, in this case, to out-fish those who used boats.

What Siri showed him next made him tingle.

Link after link to this bar or that club featured his 'rad riffs' or 'soulful sounds.' Apparently, Palmer not only played a mean guitar, but he also got around. Mostly in the Florida panhandle and occasionally in Alabama and Georgia.

The word *opportunity* lept to mind, and he reached for the murder book to satisfy his curiosity.

Of those the serial killer shot, four had two in the head, nine had one, and one had three. He checked the dates, and three of the four with two had Palmer playing a bar nearby. Brian felt the excitement and looked for another match, the strangled guy in Lynn Haven.

Nothing, but...

He took the murder book to the kitchen table, grabbed the laptop, poured another cup, and began a search for bars, clubs, dives, and honky-tonks near an unsolved murder.

It was all speculation and could easily fall apart, but it was the best lead he'd had in over a year.

~~

For Dominic, it was a glass half-full kind of morning. After waiting over a week for the FBI to process his request, which for them was lickety-split, he now knew the identity of the man in the trunk. But not why he was parked there.

And as thankful as Dom was that they ran the guy's face through their database, he wished the ATF were as quick in getting back to him about the bullet casing evidence he'd entered into their Ballistic Identification System.

He supposed the easiest way to find out if Terry Lamb worked for Anatovich would be to call the feds, but he didn't have any contacts there. So he decided to wait for Tasha to return and have her ask her Deputy-Director friend.

Dominic looked over Lamb's rap sheet and saw he was really a wolf in sheep's clothing with a history of violence, stints in jail, prison, and two murder convictions he only served six and nine years for.

Why even bother arresting these scumbags if we're just going to slap them on the wrist and let them go?

It was disheartening to see men like that released for good behavior as if what they'd done no longer mattered. What about the families of those they murdered?

He shook his head, tried to let it go, and stuffed half a breakfast burrito in his mouth. It might not be good for him, but it wasn't as bad as the bearclaw in the bag would be.

~~

Jeri closed the door to her office so she could sit at her desk and take a few needed minutes. Even though the judge had issued a temporary freeze on Dimitri Anatovich's bank accounts prior to a forfeiture hearing, it did not lighten her mood, which had taken a dark turn of late.

Angry, troubled, and depressed, she read the succinct results from the facial technician – *unable to identify suspect.*

Not that she cared right now. Catching the man who'd killed a mass murdering pedophile wasn't her top priority.

Identifying the dead would be a nearly impossible task that would take years and money, and the reason for trying to seize as much of that monster's assets as they could find. But attempting to do right by those kids didn't bring her any relief or satisfaction. Instead, Jeri felt a deep emptiness.

So many children. So many skeletons...

The phone made her jump, and she picked it up with a sense of dread, afraid it was Donald with a fatality update.

"Oh, hi Tash."

"Sounds like you're not too glad to hear from me. Sorry I haven't kept in touch."

"You don't have to apologize. I haven't either. And I am glad. How are you holding up?"

"Better now that he's dead," Tasha said and left it there. "How about you?"

Jeri thought it an odd response but didn't press for an explanation, hoping she would return the favor.

"I just got back from court," she said and told her why. When it came to telling about the bodies, she kept it short.

"We need a break, girlfriend," Tasha said.

"I hear ya, sister."

"Dax and Mary have invited us to play music with them over Labor Day, and I think it would do us some good."

"I don't know, Tash. I don't feel much like a party."

"Me either... And we don't have to. We'll just sit in a chair on the beach with our toes in the sand and drink wine. What do you say?"

Tasha could hear her vacillate, which, though similar to wavering, had a slightly lower pitch in frequency.

"Seven, Mary told me to 'ask Aunt Jeri to come so the whole family can be together.' She also said to say *please*. Now, how can you say no to that cute little girl?"

Jeri smiled for the first time in a week, and it hurt.

"She's cute alright, but not all that little."

"Which makes the love she has for her *Aunt Jeri* all the more adorable," Tasha said, grinning as she continued to pile it on. "Why, it's so precious, it makes me want to cry."

"Alright, alright. I'll come," Jeri said with a laugh. "Geez, woman. Is that how it's going to be?"

"Yes, ma'am. What's the use of having a daughter card if you're not gonna play it?"

"Do you think she really loves me?" Jeri asked.

"How could she not, Seven. I sure as hell do."

The moment's respite from the recent turmoil in their lives was interrupted by the very life they lived.

"Sorry, Tash," Jeri said, "I have to take this. It's Donald."

"Okay, then. Later, gator."

"See ya, croc."

Tasha left the worry for her friend behind and began to think about what lay ahead. She was on her way home.

But to whose?

Que sera, sera . . .

Whatever will be, will be.

~~

Despite trying to change her mind, Mary was adamant with me. We were done for the day.

"Come on. We can knock off a few more, easy peasy," I said, giving her grief because it was fun.

"Instead of trying to run my business," she said with a grin, "maybe you should start your own? I'm thinking a tree stump removal service. You can call it Dax's Picks and Axes."

"Why wouldn't I use a backhoe, instead?"

"Where's the challenge in that?"

"I could start a car detailing shop called *Dax on, Dax off.* Get it?"

"Very clever, Daniel-son," she said in Mr. Miyagi's voice. "Now show me *sand the floor.*"

We played out the scene from *Karate Kid* in the middle of a stranger's driveway and fell out laughing when Watson joined in by nipping at our ankles. Anyone who saw us must have thought we were nuts. We bowed to each other with respect at the end, as was required.

"Ahhh," Mary said and smacked me on top of the head. "Look eye. Always look eye."

"I was looking eye," I said.

"I know. Just wanted to get in one last whack."

"And did you find it gratifying, oh soon to be grounded grasshopper?"

"Hai," she said in Japanese with a twinkle.

We loaded up mower and equipment and left for home. On the way, I thought now was as good a time as any.

"Hey, Mare?"

"Yes?"

"I think I hurt your feelings the other night, and I'd like to talk about it."

"You don't have to. You're the dad; I'm the kid. I'll get over it."

"You know you're more than that to me, girl."

She didn't say anything but nodded.

"What do you know about lying?" I asked her. "Did you know there's been quite a bit of scientific research done?"

"No, but I never really gave it much thought."

"That's good. Because it means you're basically honest. It's also bad for the same reason. Do you understand?"

"Uh, not as much as I will in the next few minutes?"

I grinned.

"Guilty people act differently than those who aren't. Same with lying – defensiveness slips into the conversation, hesitation in responses, the body reacts reflexively. You can prepare to defend a lie, but the efforts to undermine your attempt by those trying to ascertain the truth are not always straightforward. Some are subtle and will try to trip you up. And once suspected, difficulties beget huge complications."

"Beget?" she asked with a lift of an eyebrow. "Couldn't you have just said *cause*?"

"Silly girl," I replied. "When pontificating, one must use the proper verbiage. Don't you know nothing?"

"I know a pain in the butt when I see one."

Her expression made me like her all over again.

"Anyway, lying is a tricky business and best left alone. However, that's not always possible. Let's take you, for example. There is a difference between what you *know* and what you *think* you do. And that distinction is significant. One is a fact, the other conjecture. And a guess, even one that's educated, is still not an actuality. And that matters, because when you're asked about something you're not a hundred-percent sure of, the answer will be truthful. And that eliminates the need for deception. Understand?"

She nodded and scratched the furry head propped in between the seats to listen.

"The only fact you know for certain has to do with your father, because you were there. The guy in the car and those up in Georgia are only *inferred* – although, you could still use them against me in court, I suppose."

"Dax, I'd never do that! How could you even think..."

"Sorry, I didn't mean you, you. No, I'm afraid *you* would lie to protect me, come hell or highwater. Am I wrong?"

"Nope."

"What about you?" I asked Watson who shook his head, belatedly.

"Thanks, boy. Listen, I don't want us to be a family of liars, but, should the need arise, the less you know, the less lying you have to do. So, unless you have an absolute need to know, Mare, I'd prefer we didn't discuss my... affairs. At least till you're old enough to date, in twenty-thirty years."

She took a long minute, and then a shorter one.

"You seem to know a lot about lying. How come?"

"From reading about it?"

"Uh-huh. Have you ever lied to *me*?"

"No," I said. "Not once in all the time I've known you. And I never would. I told you that in the beginning."

"What about him?" she asked, turning Watson's puppy-eyed face my way.

"Only a few white ones, almost all of them food related. But he knows that all is fair in love, war, and spaghetti."

My phone sang from the console, and I glanced at Mary.

"Well, the only way to know what Tasha wants rather than *infer* is to answer it."

"Funny," I said and picked it up. "Well, hello stranger. What's up? What's happening? What it is?"

Mary lowered her window to give me privacy, and then raised it when I hung up.

"Well, *what it is*?" she said, mocking me.

"She's a few hours away and wants to do a sleepover on Bird Island. We'll have to fill her boat with supplies and haul it to our place so we can all leave as soon as she gets here."

"Cool! Won't that be fun, Watson?" She ruffled his fur and asked how Tasha sounded.

"Tired."

chapter ten

The first thing I noticed was she not only sounded tired, she looked it. And that kind of fatigue came from more than just being on the road all day. I was responsible, at least in part, though I was fairly sure her father's death didn't have as much of an impact on her as I did.

And before you start thinking *what an ego on that guy,* let me explain. After I told her how sorry I was for her loss, Tasha gave me a perfunctory *thanks* and didn't say another word about him. So it had to be about me. Right?

She was quiet on our way to the boat launch at Indian Pass, preferring, by my inferring, to listen to what Mary and I'd been up to instead of talk about herself. And when we reached the sandbar she still remained subdued, until Mary pulled her into the water, with Watson's help.

I setup camp while they played like ten-year old girls and talked about silly things of little consequence. Perhaps everything was going to be okay?

Did I mention she'd lost weight?

Not so much I'd have to trade her in, (that's a joke, btw) but more than seemed possible in the time she'd been gone.

While Mary, Watson, and I fed on hotdogs, buns, beans, and salad, Tasha only ate two leaves of lettuce and a quarter wedge of chilled watermelon for dessert.

"I haven't been hungry, lately," she said. "Must be a bug or something."

Yeah. Or something, I thought, feeling guilty as sin.

"Do you have a fever?" I asked, hoping she did, which was pitiful, but then it wouldn't be all my fault.

"No," she said and looked at me like it was.

When the sun began to set, we listened to the wind and water as the sky changed color. I reached for Tasha's hand,

and she opened it so I could caress her palm. It's hard to say who enjoyed the tender moment most, but as I am a manly man, I'm sure it was her.

When the flames from the fire lit the darkness, Mary invited Watson to join her for a walk.

"Before you go, want to do a *what if* scenario?" I said.

"Out here?' she said with a dubious inflection. But the firelight revealed the interest in her eyes. "Okay. Sure."

"Let's assume someone is out to get us, just your garden variety baddie up to no good. How would you proceed using what you're learning about situational awareness? What is there to consider?"

"Does this bad guy have money?" Mary asked.

"Yes," I said, liking the way her mind worked.

"Well, right off the bat, we'd be screwed if they were in a boat nearby with a parabolic microphone, wouldn't we?"

"Yes. And don't say screwed. It's not very ladylike."

Mary and Tasha chuckled at me, but I didn't know why.

"Assuming their rocket propelled grenade launcher is at the shop for repair," Mary said, "I suppose someone could be sitting out on the water or the island next to us with a night-scoped, high-powered rifle. If that were the case, we wouldn't know unless they were noisy. Or smelly. They could also try to sneak up on us by kayak, innertube, paddle boards, floaties... Even scuba divers."

"Can you think of any other way they could get to us?"

Tasha had seen this kind of interaction between them before, and it never failed to fascinate her. He was teaching her to navigate the violence of the world by encouraging her to accept its existence without the fear that would cripple most people. And Mary had learned to think with a clarity that enabled her to save not only her own life, but her dad and new mom's. How could that be a bad thing?

"How about a skydiver?" Tasha offered.

"Nice," I said. "And that's in keeping with what we were talking about the other day, Mare. What would you do If you heard an airplane overhead, or a drone for that matter?"

Watson barked and Mary said, "I was going to say that. *Not look up at it.*"

"And if y'all hear a sneeze coming from the darkness?"

I grinned when they both answered at once.

"Pretend we didn't," Mary told me. To Watson she said, "No, I did."

"What did he say to you?" I asked.

"That he said it first," Tasha said.

I looked at her with surprise. "How do you know what he said?"

"Deduction, Dax. I am a detective, you know."

Mary laughed and said, "She's right. But *he's* wrong. *I* said it first. By a split second."

Apparently Watson disagreed, so Mary offered to call it a tie. When he accepted, she said, "Alrighty, then. We're gonna skedaddle and let y'all have some smooching time."

"Take your gun, sweetie. Just in case someone shows up riding a jet ski," I said.

She smiled and went to her tent with Watson in tow.

"It's cute how you do that with her," Tasha said as her fingers meshed with mine.

"She thinks overcoming adversity is fun."

Mary came out wearing a wrap around her bathing suit that hid a Kimber Micro nine-millimeter in the small of her back. As she walked away, we heard her singing, '*Dax and Tasha sitting in a tree. K-I-S-S-I-N-G...*'

"Does she wear that out in public?" Tasha asked. "She's not old enough for a concealed weapons permit."

"No, ma'am. That would be against the law."

What I thought to be funny might not have been, given our situation. But to my relief she didn't remove her hand, so I ran my thumb over the engagement ring on her finger.

"Dax, we need to talk."

I suddenly had a lot more empathy for Mary because I'd had a few conversations with her that started the same way. And what followed wasn't always pleasant or well received, at least in the short term.

"Can we smooch first and talk later? And if we talk first, will there be a later?"

Tasha looked at me with sad eyes and kissed me long and slow. When it was over, she leaned back in her chair.

"I've missed that," she whispered, seemingly to herself. "I want to thank you for giving me space while I was gone. That couldn't have been easy. I know it wasn't for me."

I nodded and started to feel anxious.

"It comes down to this, Dax. I'm not sure our views on right and wrong are compatible, but I've come to believe you are trying to do good as you see it. It's hard to argue that Mary's life would be better if you hadn't intervened. Or that those girls wouldn't have eventually ended up buried along with the others. And anyone else you've *helped* would probably agree. But your way isn't my way."

She lifted my fingers to her face, and I could see the end of who we were around the corner.

"Where does that leave us, then?"

"I've been thinking about old boyfriends," she said.

"What?"

"I could never understand why a grown-ass man would let himself get jealous of an old boyfriend. I mean, really, where is the logic in that? If I wanted to be with the old one, I wouldn't have gone out and got a new one. And if I'm okay with it, why shouldn't you be?"

"Me be?" I asked.

"Sorry. Other men."

"Oh. Well, for the record, I don't get jealous. And I don't know what the heck you're talking about."

"Are you saying you don't love me enough to be jealous, Dax?"

I couldn't tell if she was kidding or not, but this wasn't my first rodeo. Okay, I'd never been to an actual rodeo, but ... "Tash, I love you enough NOT to be jealous."

She cracked a smile that seemed incongruous with the ending of our relationship and asked me another question.

"So, it wouldn't bother you if I had fifteen boyfriends?"

"Well, it would explain why you're so good at that thing you do, but no. I might be curious about where I stood in the rankings, though."

We'd taken a detour from driving ourselves over a cliff, but it worked for me. For her too, I think, because she looked at me with bedroom eyes.

"There's never been anyone like you, Dax."

She was joking around, I thought, but the texture of her sultry voice moved me, nevertheless.

"That sounds like a stock response, girl."

"Well, if I said someone was the best I'd ever had, they'd rest on their laurels and stop trying so hard to please me,. Like the guy stuck at number three. Or four, in your case."

Her smile lit the night and I resolved never to forget it. "So, you've only been using me for sex?"

Tasha moved her body to the beat in her head and said, "I like the way you work it."

"Are you sure you want to break up? We seem to like each other an awful lot."

Her smile faded, and I feared we were back to driving Thelma and Louise's Thunderbird into the Grand Canyon.

"I could look at your past as an old girlfriend I have no reason to be jealous of and no right to judge. It wouldn't be easy, but I'd like to try. However, what you do from this point forward I can and will judge. So I need to know if what you're doing is more important to you than us. If it is, tell me now and we can go our separate ways."

Tasha had gotten down to the nitty. And I, the gritty.

"Mary told Dominic the other day that she wished she hadn't had to kill the men who'd threatened the two of you. That's how I feel, as well. I wish I hadn't had to. But I could. So, I did. And I believe it's necessary because the world isn't getting any better on its own. That's why Mary is out there preparing for the worst with the best of intentions. When she's confronted by evil, I want her to win. To live. And Tash, it *is* important. But nothing means more to me than you, Mary, and Watson. Period. And you can believe it cause if I were going to lie to you, I'd have done it last week."

I expected a smile, kiss, nod, or tear, but her eyes were circumspect and solemn.

"Are you saying you want us, you and me?" Tasha said.
"Yes."

"Will you stop doing what you're doing?"

"Yes. With one stipulation. Anyone who threatens my family will die. Without exception. That is non-negotiable."

I looked at her as seriously as she did me, afraid it was a deal breaker but willing to lose her because of it. After minutes that felt like hours, she responded.

"If I accepted your caveat, would you accept mine?"

"Which is?"

"We can put what's happened behind us and go on from here. But I'm telling you Dax, if you cheat on me we're done. Because if I ever suspect you of being involved in an incident not related to family, I'll catch you if I can and put you away. Regardless of how much I love you. Do you understand?"

Her tone and countenance left no room for doubt.

"I do," I said. "And you?"

"I do."

Our fingers tightened in each other's grasp before the tension let loose and slipped away into the night.

"Does this mean we're married now?" I asked.

"I think so."

~

Tasha listened to the steady rhythm of his breathing. She thought about waking him, but it was too late and too quiet to keep even the slightest sound from being heard.

They'd be all over each other if by themselves, but with Mary so close, the house rules were in force – no groans, no moans, no sex.

Well, not in the conventional sense.

Since the rule's inception, Dax had taken his sensual caress on the road, so to speak, and he'd touch and tease her to the brink and beyond – as long as she didn't make a sound Mary could hear. It became an erotic game she loved to play, and the pleasures he gave were some of the most intense she'd ever known.

But what he giveth he also took away the moment a too loud *Mmmm* escaped her lips. And regardless of how much she would plead, he'd just grin and shake his head. While damned frustrating in the moment, it made her work harder so she could come better. And Dax, for his part, learned to play her more like a Stradivarius than a fiddle, so the music of their passion could go on and on well into the night.

Tasha laughed at herself for waxing poetic, but it felt good to think of them that way.

She left the air-mattress, said she had to pee when Dax called out, zip-a-dee-doo-dahed the screen door of the tent, walked a ways downwind, and fell to her knees to throw up.

Expecting to vomit but glad she didn't, Tasha squatted and felt the worry about Dax dissipate.

On a side note, she didn't think there was anything sexy about a woman peeing outside and would rather he saw her writhing in ecstasy than in the position she now assumed. Although, the breeze did feel pleasant on her behind.

Maybe that's why guys did so much peeing outdoors?

She saw fiery embers leap into the night and assumed Dax was responsible. She would love to sit and watch the darkness swallow up the remnants of the dying fire, leaving them alone and together in the middle of the night.

Keeping with the *bad guys are out to get us* theme of the evening, Tasha snuck up behind him like a Ninja assassin.

"Gotchu," she whispered in his ear.

"Why Tasha, I didn't know you liked me like that?"

"Oh, my. I... I..." she stuttered, stunned and flustered. "I thought you were your dad."

"I figured that," Mary said with a smile as wide as Texas. "But if you don't move your hand from my boob, I'll have to figure something else."

"Oh, sorry. Yeah, that should have been my first clue."

Tasha took a seat, and Mary asked if she'd like water, juice, or wine. "I'm buying."

"Wine. Thanks, honey. What are you doing up?"

"Same as you. But I didn't go further than two feet from the tent. Not very ladylike, I suppose, but practical."

"Wasn't it funny when Dax said that about your saying *screwed*? I mean he's been encouraging your smartassitude, as he calls it, since I've known you."

"Yup it was, and yeah he has. It's a little late to turn me into a debutante, and I'm too old for a Cotillion." After some wine and some silence, Mary asked Tasha about her father. "How did it go?"

"We didn't talk for two days, and then he died."

Mary was the only one she'd told about the relationship she had with her father growing up. "Why didn't you tell Dax about him?" Tasha said. "It would have been okay with me."

"It's not mine to tell."

Tasha nodded, and, after more wine and more silence, Mary asked if she was going to be alright.

"I think so." She explained the *good-bad* epiphany and how it altered her perspective. "Hopefully, it'll stick."

"Here's to sticking," Mary said and raised her glass.

"To sticking."

They clinked quietly and emptied their glasses.

"More?"

"None for me."

"Me, too," Mary said and asked her another question. "So, are you taking Dax to jail?"

"No."

"Why not?"

Tasha watched an ember burn out and die. The extent of what Mary knew about Dax was an assumption, and she was apprehensive about asking or saying anything.

"We've reached an understanding," was all she said.

"What kind of understanding?"

Saying it was none of her business would not only be a lie, because it certainly was, it would also be stupid.

"What he's done is *done*. Now we can move forward."

Tasha knew the answer was vague and likely to prompt another question, but to her surprise it did not. She glanced at Mary who sat silent and seemed to bristle.

"Mare, what's wrong?"

"I love you, Tash, as a friend and a mom. But I'm not at all happy about this."

"Why?" Tasha was confused and alarmed by her tone. "I thought you would be."

Mary shook her head before looking at her.

"While you were gone, a woman in the Middle East was stoned to death for infidelity. Not the man, mind you, just the *whore*. And a young girl accused of *flirting* was raped over and over by her brothers, then killed and thrown into the sea with the father's blessing. And it was all legal."

"Those are terrible, awful things, honey, but why..."

"The law is worthless if it's not doing what's *right*. And until the world gets its shit together, we will continue to be thrown into the sea. Dax was doing something about that."

As Tasha pondered her words, one thing became clear – Mary didn't just love Dax, she admired him.

"I understand. I do. But he said he'd rather have *us*."

"You mean *you*, because he already has me." Mary had never spoken so contemptuously before, and she regretted it even before the tears welled up in Tasha's eyes.

"Tash, I'm sorry. Really. I'm just upset. The truth is you matter a great deal to Dax. To me, too. And his decisions are his to make."

They stared at the fire and retreated to their thoughts.

As Tasha watched the last ember burn, she went ahead and asked. "How much do you know, Mare?"

"About what he's been up to?"

"Yes."

"Well, we don't talk about it so most of what I know is based on speculation that began a year ago cause of the way his rocking chair squeaked. I *do* know about my rotten, no good, son of a bitch, bastard of a father, though."

"Honey, you're swearing an awful lot tonight. It's not very ladylike, you know."

"Oh, ha-ha."

chapter eleven

Tasha woke up to the sound of line peeling off the reel. "You're gonna have to toss that little guy back after you land it. It sounds like a puppy-red to me."

"My ass," Mary said. "It's a monster, and you know it."

"Sweetie, I don't think your butt's *that* big."

"Dax," she said, trying not to laugh but failing, "it is *not* big. My boobs are, but not my butt."

"First off, I didn't say it was big. I said it wasn't *that* big, after you called it a monster. And second, *but not my butt* has a Shakespearial ring to it, don't you think? Sort of like, *To be or not my butt.*"

"It's Shakespearian, not Shakespearial . . ."

Tasha stretched long and hard, thinking their banter was a hilarious introduction to the day.

She rolled off the still firm mattress and pulled the plug, unzipped the screen, rolled it back so the tent could air-out before being packed up, and then watched Mary bring in a redfish that was three-feet if it was an inch.

"See? Told you it was a puppy," I said, a little jealous. "Are you going to throw it back?"

"Yup," she said and removed the circle hook, careful to cradle *the monster* horizontally. If lifted vertically, it might cause trauma or internal damage to a fish so heavy.

" It's a beauty, Mare. And a beast. So, we're even then?"

"Nice try, old man. I'm up by two."

"Morning." Tasha yawned and then smelled the coffee. "Nice catch, hon. Did you use that scent I told you about?"

"Thanks. Morning. Yes."

"Scent, what scent? Are you two conspiring to keep the bigun's for yourselves?" I said and called out to Tasha as she walked away. "Is that why Mare's butt is getting so big? You know, because it's seeping through her skin?"

I thought I might need to duck to avoid getting hit, but Mary had already thrown her line back in the water.

"Did you bring creamer by any chance?" Tasha asked.

"Blue cooler. There's some pre-cooked breakfast fixin's too, if you're hungry."

"Bigun's and fixin's? Are you hillbilly sweet talkin' me?"

"Well, like the song says, "I'm bringin' sexy back," I said and winked. "And how are you this morning? If you're half as good as you were last night . . ."

"I'm fine as wine, thanks. As for last night . . ."

"Woohoo," Mary yelled.

I looked up and damn if she didn't have another fish on. "That darn kid is up three, now," I grumbled.

"Well, we can't have that. Go get her, Dax."

No sooner than said, he had a rod in hand ready to cast.

When Tasha pulled out the breakfast *fixin's*, the aroma grabbed ahold and didn't let her go until the food was gone. Happy to have an appetite, she asked about the watermelon.

"Green cooler," he said, reeling in a huge speckled trout.

She forked a piece, then another and another until only the rind was left. Not that there'd been a lot to begin with, but it was a whole lot for her. More than she'd usually eat. And it tasted better than any she ever had.

Tasha watched her big, beautiful *kids* try to out-fish one another and sipped at the coffee in her cup.

"It doesn't get any better than this. Does it, Watson?" she said, scratching and petting and enjoying the view.

"Congratulations, kiddo," I said and took a break from the ass-whupping Mary was giving by sitting next to Tasha.

"Thanks. If you'd like, I could give you a lesson."

"I think you just gave me one. In humility."

"Ha, you humble?" Mary scoffed. "I don't think so. And don't even try those puppy eyes. I'm not buying it."

"You two looked good out there," Tasha said.

"Why thank you, Miss," I told her. "You look pretty darn good yourself."

She smiled and said she wished they could stay all day. "Why can't we?"

"I have to get home and rip out the carpet, take out the couch, wash blood from the wall and floor..."

"It's already done." Mary reached into the red beverage cooler for a soda and asked if anyone wanted anything.

"Wait, what? When?" Tasha said.

"We started the day you left. I'll take a Coke, sweetie." I popped the top and finished half the can right off. "Ahh. Thanks. Did you know you had oak under the carpet, Tash?"

"Yes. But it has to be sanded and stained."

"Not anymore," Mary said. "We also repaired the bullet holes, replaced your couch, and repainted the walls with a bright, airy color. Oh, and added a nice throw rug to the mix. Everything looks brandy new."

"Aw, guys. Thank you. That was very, very thoughtful. What do I owe you two?"

"I don't know? Mare, what could she give us in return? A lifetime of happiness? A promise to laugh at our jokes be they funny or not? Maybe have her wait on us dressed as a serving wench?"

"*I'd* like a pass anytime I come home smelling of booze with my blouse misbuttoned and askew," Mary said.

Before I could say anything to her, Tasha beat me to it.

"You got it, Mare," she said.

"What the hell? You're supposed to be on my side?"

"Well, Dax, you shouldn't have made me a wench."

They laughed at me, and so did I.

"You don't owe us anything, Tash. It's like throwing a rock through someone's window – if you break it, you fix it. Mary's a good kid with a big heart, and a big butt. She is also a rambunctious little girl who needs to learn that you can't just go around shooting bad guys in other people's houses. So I'm keeping her allowance until it's paid off."

"Since when do I get an allowance?" Mary asked. "And don't think that *big butt* went by unnoticed."

"How could it? It's a monster."

After another round of laughter, a faraway disturbance in the water caught our eye.

"My god," Tasha said. "Are those Tarpon?"

"Dax and I saw them early this morning. He thinks they might shoot the pass between us and Little George Island."

"Wow, even from here that school looks *huge*. Did you happen to bring any heavy rods with you?" she asked.

"Oh yes. We heard they were running."

As I estimated their number, Mary said something new.

"Mom?"

"Yes, dear?"

"Huh. I've never been a dear before. I like it. How come you never call me that, Dax?"

"A *dear* wouldn't tease me about a blouse being askew. A little shit would, though."

"I see," she said and grinned. "Uh, Mom?"

"Yes, dear?"

Mary glanced my way and stuck out her tongue.

"Are you still gonna marry this guy?"

"That's a good question," Tasha said and looked at me. "Am I?"

"It depends. Will you at least try on the wench outfit?"

"I will if you will."

"Great!" Mary said and jumped from her chair. "Let's do it before the big *Blowout* while Aunt Jeri and Belle are here."

"Honey, that's in two days. There's not enough time."

"What's there to get ready? It's casual, catered, and you already have the license."

Tasha raised her eyebrows, and I shrugged.

"She's right. It's bada bing, bada boom. The only thing that needs doing is your signing a prenup."

I couldn't have asked for a better wedding gift than the expression she gave me.

"A prenup? What, are you afraid I'll get your twenty-year old truck and soccer-mom van in the divorce?"

"Hey, that van carts many manly things. Including me."

She shook her head and then jerked it toward Mary.

"That there's the most valuable thing you have and the only thing I'd want. And as Watson goes wherever she goes, I guess I'll be taking your little dog too, Dorothy."

I couldn't help laughing when Watson took issue with being called *little*.

"It's alright, boy. You are also a manly man. Or a doggly dog? Anyway, I'd be happy to lend Mary to you, Tash, but I could never let you take her. Nobody makes spaghetti sauce like she does."

"Okay, you two. Let's not have a custody battle before y'all get married. There will be plenty of time for that later."

"You're right, hon. But maybe a prenup isn't a bad idea. Seeing as how I've recently become a very wealthy woman."

"Oh, have you now?" I said to the shine in her eyes.

"As it turns out, I'm the sole beneficiary of my father's estate. In addition to a house on four-hundred acres, there are two-hundred and forty-six pumpjacks drawing crude oil from the ground, the annual income of which is substantial."

It wasn't like her to be so elaborate in our running gags, not to mention using her dead father to help sell the joke. But I played along.

"So what are we talking, a few hundred thousand?"

"Millions."

'Was that million*s*, with an s?"

Tasha nodded, and her sparkle deepened.

"I guess the next night out is on you, then," I joshed.

"I'm not kidding, Dax. That doesn't even include stocks, bonds, and cash."

If this was a *get* it was the mother of, because she didn't crack or flinch.

"Really?" I said, swallowing the bait like a guppy.

"Really."

I waited for her to yank the hook, but she didn't. And no one said a word for the longest time, until . . .

"You were always my favorite, Mom," Mary said.

I called her a fair-weather daughter. "Don't let the old truck and mom van fool you as I am also a man of means."

She raised her hand like a second-grader and waved it all around until called upon.

"Yes?" I said.

"Did you mean to imply your fiancée is also a man?"

Mary giggled, Tasha snickered, and I grinned.

"As I was going to say, I have a couple of bucks myself. So you may have traded me in prematurely, little girl."

"Oh, really?" Tasha asked, still sporting a grin. "Are you like one of those old, eccentric millionaires you hear about?"

"I can vouch for the old and eccentric part," Mary said, having the kind of fun that always deepened my love for her.

"It just so happens; I started a business from scratch a few years back that became very profitable. I also took over a failing business, increasing its customer base five hundred fold. I eventually sold them, retired early, and then..."

"Yeah, right," Tasha said.

"Tash, please," Mary quipped. "Dad's talking."

"Tash? I was Mom a minute ago."

"Children can be fickle, sometimes," I said, watching the silver-kings start to track toward us. "We should get ready."

"Well, are you?" Mary asked as we ambled to the boat for the stouter rods and colorful lures.

"Am I what?" I said.

"A millionaire?" Tasha said, curious but not convinced.

"Where did you get that idea?"

"You said you were a man of means. A rich man?"

"I *am* rich, in the love and respect of my family."

"Uh-huh. And the couple bucks?" Tasha mocked.

"Well, I have about sixteen in my wallet."

"What about your businesses? Did you make them up?" Mary asked. She didn't look exactly crestfallen, but she was sure as heck cute in her disappointment.

"No. And they were quite successful. That lemonade stand made me enough money to buy the paper route when I was nine, which in turn allowed me to get a sweet, cherry apple-red Schwinn ten-speed bicycle."

Mary tried to knock me down by jumping on my back, and Tasha jumped on hers to help.

~~

Murphy hung up the phone and yawned for a good ten seconds before leaving his desk for more coffee.

"Was it Rita down in personnel?" Tim asked him. "You two finally hook up, bump some uglies? She looks like she knows how to keep a man up all night. Know what I mean?"

"Yes, I do. And she does. But no, we didn't. I told you, I was up late with the murder book."

"Have you even asked her out? I heard she likes you," Tim said, dialing the next number on the list. "That book is never going to sit on your lap naked and... Hello. Detective Burel? This is Tim Hanlon from the Panama City PD. Yes, it's that time again. Yes. I know."

Brian filled the cup for the third time since he arrived, his fifth of the day. He'd pay for it later but needed the boost because it had, indeed, been a long night.

There were a ton of bars, clubs, and other venues in his search area, and most of them didn't have a Facebook page or website showing who had performed and when.

Even when he called directly, it was frustrating. Some places weren't open until evening, and evening could mean six PM to midnight. And then there was the effort to get information. Many didn't keep records after a few months, some not at all, and trying to speak to people who could find them was a nightmare all its own.

He also discovered that if he said he was a detective, folks generally said they had to *get back to work* and did. He had to get creative, pretend to be a fan, or claim he'd lost something the night that 'Dax guy' was there.

It wasn't a complete bust, however. Palmer had played in places near enough to have killed at least twelve, maybe fourteen. But it was circumstantial at best. And the reason they were calling area detectives this morning was to see if they'd added anything new to their case files – something he did every couple of months so he could update his own.

None of the crime scenes had any evidence that pointed to anyone. No prints, fluids, shell casings, shoe impressions. And, while most autopsies put time of death sometime after Palmer was in town, a few were a day or more earlier.

Then there was the anomaly.

Whether subconsciously or purposefully, serial killers didn't deviate much in how they murdered. It was their signature, that which distinguished them from others. But unlike the Gainesville Ripper, this guy was all over the map when it came to method and weapon. Where your ordinary, run of the mill serial killer used the same *modus operandi* in committing their crimes, Palmer never did.

But was he really the guy?

Brian didn't know and hadn't said anything to Tim yet. He'd been hunching, though.

The murders began shortly after Palmer found the girl who later became his daughter. She'd escaped a father who repeatedly raped her over Christmas vacation from school and hadn't been heard from since. Sometime later, Palmer put three guys in the hospital with multiple injuries, men he thought were raping a woman at a local raw bar.

Now that Brian suspected him, it seemed reasonable to assume Palmer killed the father. And given the nature of the beatings, an extrapolated *motive* now existed to go with the *opportunity*. But while his hunch was strong, the evidence was thin, inconclusive, and not enough to take to his captain or the district attorney.

Maybe something would shake out over the weekend.

chapter twelve

"Marcus called. He said he hasn't heard anything new," Alexi told him. "That, by itself, says something."

"I agree. In fact, I'm beginning to think our competition had nothing to do with Uncle Dimi's death," Miko said. "And his crotch being shot all to hell . . . No, this feels personal. Those girls were rescued."

"By who? A father? Brother? And how would they know where they were? Dimitri barely let them out of their room, let alone the house."

"Could be. As for the how, someone has a big mouth. What else has Marcus been up to?"

"He's still in Miami with his family, still being watched by the Feds. He doesn't leave the house except for groceries, and he hasn't met or talked to anyone that we know of. So far, his nose is clean," Alexi said.

"Maybe. How did your meeting go with the FBI snitch?"

"He wants a raise."

"Don't they all," Miko snorted.

"He told me where they were in the investigation and agreed to run Palmer, or anyone else, if his terms were met."

"So, where are they?"

"They don't have a clue who the killer is, and the only camera that saw him didn't see enough to tell us anything. But they're thinking he's probably a pro, because everyone he came across had at least one or two in the head, including Dimitri. Sorry, I . . ."

As Miko stared, Alexi thought about what it must have felt like to be a gladiator in the Roman Colosseum, waiting for the Emperor to lift his thumb up or down.

"Give him what he wants but be sure he understands. When we ask, he delivers," Miko said.

~~

"Morning, Dax. Where's Mary today?" she asked after I loaded the lawnmower onto the trailer.

"Good morning, Miss Barbara," I said. "She's gone with some friends to the airport to pick up another friend."

"She's a sweetheart of a girl, isn't she?"

"Yes, Ma'am."

She bent over to give Watson a pat. "You doing okay?" He said he was and wagged his tail.

Mrs. Radcliff owns and operates the *No Name Café*, a book store on Reid Avenue where one can peruse a passel of pages as disco music plays in the background. You can even sit and relax, have some coffee, a doughnut, and spend some time reading what you find.

I wouldn't take advantage of her generosity, however. Word is that behind the sweet exterior and those dazzling baby blues is a lady who doesn't take too kindly to sampling the wares for over an hour and then not buying the goods. Rumor is Miss Barbara has a .357 Magnum handgun under the counter, but I don't think she has shot anyone.

"Say hello to Mary, and you two take care," she said.

"Will do. Thanks, You, too."

Watson jumped into the truck after I opened the door and made himself comfortable in the passenger seat.

"Well, Indian Pass is done. Let's head over to the Cape and see if we can knock out the rest of the yards."

On the way, I thought about tomorrow's big event.

"Hey, boy? How'd you like to be my best man?"

He cocked his head and raised a furry eyebrow.

"To tell the truth, you're the closest male friend I have."

He squinted.

"No, you don't have to wear a penguin suit. I'm not." It's funny how much I understood if I just imagined I could. "Thanks, Watson. It would be an honor for me, as well."

I began to look beyond tomorrow and envision what it would be like to turn a blind eye to the suffering of others. How was that going to work, exactly? A big part of me was struggling with not just *if* I could do it, but if I *should*. I'm sure Tasha was every bit as conflicted about what *she* was giving up, and, like her, I'd have to find a way to live with it. I wanted us together. Hell, I might even need us to be.

I drove to the far end of Cape San Blas Road and worked my way back to the mainland, hoping to finish in time to shave and shower before the girls got home. I'd asked Mary to give a heads up when they were an hour away, and she texted as I pulled into the Scallop Cove parking lot to fill the five-gallon gas cans and top off the truck.

"I think we can get the last two done if we hurry," I said and asked Watson if he'd like anything from the store.

'I wouldn't kick a beef jerky outta bed for eating crackers,' he answered, or so I thought, but probably not.

The store was packed with people down for Labor Day, and, as I stood in a crowded line, a couple cut in front of me – or rather a man pulled a young woman along.

When she tried to say something about it, he squeezed her arm, and she looked at me and said *sorry*.

"It's alright. I'm not in a hurry."

The man yanked at her to turn around, and once more as the line moved. I almost said something and then noticed the bruises on her arms, legs, and the back of her neck.

This wasn't the first time she'd been manhandled.

I felt a calm come over me which, in turn, kept the anger at bay and my emotions in check. After they left the store, I paid for the gas and jerky and followed them next door to the bait shop.

"Hey, Dax. How 'bout it?"

"Ferd," I said. "I'm good. You?"

"Ain't nothing to it."

Alford, or Ferd as he was known, observed the couple without appearing to as they moved about the shop.

"How's Mary?" he asked.

"She's good too."

"Heard she handled herself alright the other night."

"Yep. Hope she doesn't keep having to."

"I hear ya," he said, ringing up the MirrOlures the man laid on the counter. "Is that gonna be it?"

"Yeah."

After they left, Ferd walked by me to the glass door and watched them get into their car and drive off.

Alford was intelligent and intuitive with many innate abilities. He could tell what scent you were wearing as soon as you walked in, and if a shelf was unlevel by a sixteenth of an inch just by looking at it. He also had a good sense of humor, a great singing voice, and knew everybody in town.

"Are they tourists?" I asked, knowing he'd seen what I had and hoping they weren't locals so I could leave it be.

"That's Marvin's youngest boy. He lives down the road from Melissa next to the golf course."

Serendipity was like that sometimes, telling you things like *who* and *where* when you'd rather not know.

"What can I do you for, Dax?"

"I need a couple packs of Poopah's white worms."

Poopah was a man named Steve, and the worms were a plastic bait he hoarded and hated for anyone else to use. It had become a hoot and a half for Ferd to sell them to the rest of us just to get a rise out of him.

"Got some coming in on Thursday. I'll set them aside."

"Thanks. Hey, it's short notice but I'm getting married tomorrow, and, if you and Laura don't have any plans..."

"Is this the same girl you were gonna marry last week?"

"Yes."

"Still having it on Bird Island?"

"Yes. Wedding's at noon, reception starts right after. You don't have to bring anything except bait, rods, and your appetite. There'll be a pontoon ferry leaving the Indian Pass boat launch at eleven if you don't have a way out there. And it's still Hawaiian shirt optional."

"I'll talk to the missus and see ya if I see ya."

"Alright, then. Have a good'n."

"Is there any other *'n* to have?" he said and grinned.

I walked outside, waved an apology to the car waiting behind me at the pump, and drove away peeling the plastic from Watson's beef jerky.

"Sorry, boy. I got distracted."

And I was, because instead of turning down the street where the remaining lawns needed to be cut, I kept going, driving off the Cape and heading toward the golf course.

"A little drive-by isn't going to hurt anything. Right?"

Watson was busy chewing and may not have heard me.

The speed limit on County Club Road was thirty, and I slowed to a fifteen mile-an-hour crawl as we got closer. His car was in the driveway and the house sat back from the road surrounded by trees on three sides. The ninth hole tee was adjacent to the fourth, providing an unobstructed view of the left side of the home.

As we drove past, a tentative plan began to emerge.

I glanced at my watch and stepped on the gas, believing I could still get those yards done in time.

~

We decided to stay in and eat Mexican. Not *a* Mexican mind you, but your tacos, burritos, enchiladas, etceterados. Then we sang and played for hours, laughing, joking, liking and loving – until I apparently hugged and kissed Tasha one too many times.

"Okay," Jeri announced. "It's time to go. No more seeing, tasting, or touching the bride until after the wedding."

"I think he's already had the milk, Aunt Jeri," Mary said.

"Mary Jane," I said as everyone stared with wide eyes. "It's not nice to imply your mother to-be is a proverbial cow. Although, she is a fine heifer, at that. And if the hoof fits . . ."

I thought she'd take a swing at me, but Tasha grinned and jumped into my arms, doing her best to hold on as Jeri, Mary, and Isabel tried to drag her away. When they finally succeeded, we were out of breath and laughing our asses off.

As they piled out the door, I gave her a parting shot.

"Noon-sharp, girl. I'm in a marrying mood, and if you're late, I'll grab the first woman that'll have me."

"So," Tasha said, "you'll still be available if I show up at three, then? Or four? Five, even?"

"I'm only going to wait for the rest of my life."

I heard Isabel and Jeri say, "Aww," and saw Tasha get teary-eyed, but my little shit-little girl wasn't so enthused.

"Sounds like something you'd hear on *The Bachelorette*. Geez, Dax, you don't watch that show, do you? Perhaps you should just go ahead and turn in your Man Card."

They laughed and left Watson and me to ourselves. I opened the garage door and unlocked the cabinet that held the drone, a full three-footed circle outfitted with multiple cameras for an up, down, three-hundred sixty degree field of vision. It was waterproof, whisper quiet, and could stay aloft for close to forty minutes.

I stuck in a new battery, took it outside, put it through some preliminary paces, and checked the ten-inch monitor. The wind was light, the moon was low, and I was ready.

"Are you coming?"

Watson sat there and said nothing.

"It's only a reconnaissance mission."

He cocked his head.

"Look, I'm not going to do anything; I've given my word. But I need to verify my suspicion. If I don't, it'll eat at me like an earwig tunneling through my brain."

He raised a brow.

"Yes, I know they don't really do that."

"And if he's hitting her? What then?" he said.

"I'll tell Tash about the bruises and let her handle it."

"You could have told her before she left."

Watson was right, and I didn't have a good explanation. So, I asked him again. "Are you coming?"

I removed the dome bulb from inside the vehicle before we left, so light wouldn't shine when the door opened later. And then I turned my phone off so we couldn't be tracked.

~

As we backed into the foliage I'd seen earlier in the day, lightning flashed across the sky followed by a loud crack. I hurried to get the drone out of the van and on its way before someone drove by, and then jumped back inside.

"Would you please keep an eye out for people or cars? I don't want anyone to see the glow from the monitor."

Watson said *sure,* and I flew to the tee box and hovered. After visually clearing the area, I moved closer to the house looking for outdoor cameras, telephone and cable wires, or anything else that might impede my efforts to look inside. Another flash of lightning revealed a stack of lumber, and a boom of thunder shook the van.

A smattering of windows dotted the side of the home, both upper and lower, but I wanted to peek into the kitchen first. I hadn't done the research, but in my experience most domestic abuse occurred there. I don't know why, it just did.

And tonight was no different.

They were in the middle of an argument, or rather he was yelling at her while she said nothing and tried to cook a meal he probably wouldn't appreciate. When she didn't respond to his verbal abuse, he grabbed her like he had in the store and yanked.

And still she said nothing, even when he got in her face. She was in a damned if you do or don't situation and must have found *don't* the option that worked best. It appeared to be effective, even as he pushed her, but I knew it was only a matter of time before she got hit.

And she did, though not like I'd expected.

He grabbed her by the hair, bent her over the back of a kitchen chair, and spanked her with his hand like she was a willful child who'd disobeyed.

I squeezed my fist as she seemed to whimper, clenched my jaw as the wind rose, and cursed when it began to rain.

Serendipity must have been surprised at my reaction, as she had given me a golden opportunity to stop this abuse. I could use the storm to throw things at the house until he came out to investigate, and then beat him to death with a two by four when he did.

But, of course, I wouldn't.

I'd need more time to prepare, for one thing.

And killing so close to home was like defecating where you ate. It had been a necessity with the man in the truck, but that kind of stink drew flies, like Dom asking questions he might find answers to.

There was also my promise to Tasha to stop doing what I'd been doing, an oath I had no intention of breaking.

But what exactly had I pledged? I assumed she meant murder . . . Did it include not breaking his arms and legs so the woman could leave safely while he took time to mend?

How would I go about getting such a clarification? Ask? Would she allow it?

She's a cop, dumbass. What do you think?

And if I didn't ask and went ahead, could I then claim a *misunderstanding of our understanding* if she found out?

He stopped hitting her when she started sobbing, and I breathed a sigh of relief. Then he pulled down her pants and took off his belt.

"Fuck that," I said and rammed the drone into the glass. I saw him turn when it shattered but he didn't see me cause I'd flown straight up to break the big bay bedroom window.

"That'll keep him busy for a while."

I flew back in the howling wind and pouring rain and was drenched after I got out and put the drone into the van. As we drove away, Watson asked if I felt any better.

"No. Worse."

"Why?" he said.

"Because I can't do anything to stop it."

"But you can. You'll tell Tasha about the bruises, and maybe Dominic, as well. They'll go see him, talk to him. Talk to her, too. He'll be warned. Maybe that will be enough."

"I doubt it. He'll forget his fear one day and be right back at it. And then what?"

"I noticed you held your hand up as an umbrella of sorts when you stepped outside, presumably to keep from getting wet. Yet here you sit, soaked to the skin."

"Your point being?" I asked.

"You can't stop the rain, Dax. No matter how hard you try. But you *can* soak up the sun, as much as you can for as long as you can. While you still can. It's your choice."

In the midst of my turmoil, he presented a perspective worth considering.

"That's very profound, Watson. And something to think about. Thanks. We should talk like this more often."

"We're not talking," he said with his usual half-grin. "You only think we are."

chapter thirteen

"Oh, hey girl," Dax yawned as he answered his phone. "What's up?"

"See, that's the difference between men and women in a nutshell. Y'all can roll out of bed and be ready to go in five minutes, but we have to primp for an hour to look good."

"Tash, I've seen you roll out prettier than you crawled in. And where are you going that requires primping?"

"Someone said something about getting married."

"Oh, is that today? Hmm. Guess I better get a move on, then. Can you tell me again what time it starts?"

He made her laugh, and she asked if he were going to do that every day.

"That's the plan."

"Shoot, I have to go, Dax. Jeri's giving me the evil eye. See you out there," she whispered and hung up.

"Where are the girls?" Jeri asked, pouring some wine.

"They're out in the driveway fixing up the boat."

"That's nice of them. And cute. Would you like a glass?"

"I'm going to wait, thanks," Tasha said.

"Are you nervous at all?"

"You know, maybe I should be, but I'm not. He's going to make me happy, Seven."

"I think so too, girlfriend."

They hugged the way friends who love each other do.

"We better get cracking if we're going to get you to the church on time," Jeri said.

After two hours of havoc and horseplay, they stood in front of the mirror before heading out the door.

Mary and Isabel wore matching sundresses, as did Jeri but in a different color and print. Tasha wore a white, wrap-dress that was loose but form fitting.

"We look gooood," Isabel exclaimed.

"We sure do," Jeri said with a little bit of country twang. "Ain't nobody got nothing on us."

When they arrived at the boat launch, the railings were decorated with bows and streamers, the posts wrapped in candy-cane stripes with bouquets of flowers sitting on top.

"That's so cool," Isabel said.

"Yes, it is," Tasha replied and pulled up alongside a man in a golf cart so she could back the boat into the water.

"Miss Tasha?" he said.

"Yes?"

"Dax asked me to save this spot for you, so you didn't have to walk so far after you parked your truck."

"That was nice of him. And you. Thank you."

"You're welcome, Miss."

She backed down to the launch, waited for Jeri and the girls to unhook and drive the boat off the trailer, then pulled forward into the place reserved for her.

"Thanks again." Tasha walked down and onto the boat, but not before she stopped and literally smelled the roses.

"Let's get movin,' Ma," Mary said. "We're gonna be late."

She powered back and then headed to the sandbar by driving along the twelve mile length of St. Vincent Island.

About a half-mile from the launch, they passed a candy-caned pole sticking out of the water. A half-mile from that, another pole. And then another, and...

"Those have to be artificial, right? They can't be real," Tasha said to Mary who shrugged. She stopped at the next one and saw the long stems of a colorful floral arrangement stuffed inside the red striped PVC pipe driven into the mud.

"Wow," Jeri said, fondling the flowers and inhaling their fragrance. "This is above and beyond."

"Yep," Tasha replied and pushed the throttle forward, needing the wind to dry tears that might let loose.

As they skirted the oyster bed end of St. Vincent, the tip of Bird Island came into view.

Fishing rods stood in sand spikes spread out along the eastern and most of the southern shoreline of the sandbar, with ten to fifteen boats beached on the west, two party-

murder in the light of day

barges next to those, and a pontoon moored offshore. The north was vacant, save for a sign that read *Insert Bride Here* in front of a path that led up and through the waiting folks.

"Holy moly," Tasha said as she throttled down. "I didn't think there would be so many people."

"And I thought we were going to use beach umbrellas?" Mary uttered.

A wide area of shade had been created using anchored pillars and triangular sun sails. There were also twice as many chairs as they'd talked about.

"That's your dad contingency planning, I'll bet."

Tasha drove the boat onto the sand, and, after a quick brush of their hair with their hands, they all disembarked.

The crowd hushed as Mary and Isabel walked up the marked path followed by Jeri, then the bride. When they reached the aisle, Tasha stole a glance at the handsome man in a white shirt and Dockers standing with the minister. Dax's smile washed away the remaining doubts and fears, and she looked forward to the rest of their lives.

Her body tingled when the *Bridal March* began. Then someone said, "Let's drop a beat," and a syncopated rhythm got the toes a tapping.

Mary started singing *Going To The Chapel*, with Isabel coming in at *ma-a-a-rried* and Jeri joining soon after.

Tasha smiled as their sweet harmony filled her heart. They began to swing and shuffle toward the alter while the people clapped in time, adding *whoa-oh-ohs* when needed. She saw Dax nod his head and snap his fingers like the old-time beatniks used to do, looking all kinds of cool.

When the song wound down, Mary, Isabel, and Jeri took their places and the folks all listened quietly as they vocally climbed the choral ladder of, *love, love, love, love, wooooffff.*

"Nice job hitting that high note," I said to Watson as the people cheered and clapped their appreciation. He smiled and then resumed his role as best man.

"You look beautiful, Tash."

"You, too," she said, brushing my hair with her fingers.

"Dearly Beloved. We are gathered here today..."

125

~~

The reception offered something for everyone: fishing, drinking, sitting, dancing, singing, kayaking, sunning, eating, swimming, and sand-castling for the few kids who came.

Tasha and Dax spent much of the afternoon kissing due to the *clinking protocol*, be it a wine glass, beer bottle, or soda can. Some tapped their plastic forks on red solo cups.

At day's end, the people left fat and sassy before the sun got too low to safely navigate the oyster beds on their way back to the boat launch. The shady structure was loaded on one of the barges along with tables and chairs, and then left soon after with the catering crew close behind.

"Anyone have a deck of cards?' Mary asked. "We could get a game of hearts or gin rummy going."

"That sounds like some fun," Isabel said, playing along. "Maybe we could all sit around a fire and make smores, too. Oooh, and tell ghost stories that'll keep us awake all night."

When they giggled, I hoisted them over my shoulders like sacks of potatoes and carried them to Tasha's boat as the girls squealed and Watson yapped.

"It's sweet how much he likes those girls," Jeri said.

"I think so, too."

"Now listen up, girlfriend. I should've had this talk with you earlier, but, when a bird and a bee get married, they're gonna want to do things to each other. And you need to know what goes where and why."

"What kinds of things?" Tasha asked as if afraid.

"He's going to stick his . . ."

She laughed and then hugged Jeri tight.

"I love you, Seven."

"Back at you, Sis."

"Can I get in on that?" I asked as I drew near.

They opened their arms and welcomed me inside.

"Dax, you treat her right, now."

"I will. And thanks for not saying *or else*."

"Oh, that's implied." Jeri gave me a last squeeze and let us go. "I better take off. I'm not familiar with the lagoon."

"I used glow tape to stripe the poles, so you should find your way back alright," I told her.

"The bouquets on a stick were a nice touch, by the way," she said and smiled. "Very redneck chic."

"Come on, Aunt Jeri," Mary called. "We're going to miss Dax's favorite show. I think Jared is going to ask Brittany to marry him tonight. Or make-out with her in the hot tub, one of the two."

"Will you tell your daughter to stop being a smartass?" I said to Tasha, who grinned. We watched them leave until they were out of site and then walked hand in hand along the shore. I poured some wine when we reached the cooler and asked if she'd like a fire with that.

"Please."

The sun seemed to take its time, giving us a chance to sit and enjoy its fading glow. Tasha opened her palm on the arm of the beach chair, and I slid my fingers into hers.

"Dom said you told him about a man abusing his wife?"

"Yes. I saw bruising that looked like it."

"He also said someone was found dead in a car down the road from you."

"Yeah, I think he thinks the man might have been a part of what happened to you and Mary."

"He asked Jeri about him," she said.

"Did the guy work for Anatovich?"

"She didn't know offhand, but she'll look into it."

"Good," I said and left it at that, hoping Tash would too. I felt tension in her fingers and saw her mouth open out of the corner of my eye, but she didn't say anything.

The sun bid us farewell with an array of vivid colors before passing the baton to the darkness. Solar lights on the pontoon boat became brighter, and the subtle fire warmed and fascinated with multihued flames. We listened to the crackling wood, watched stars move in their celestial orbits, and didn't say a word until the fire turned into coals.

"Take me to bed, Dax."

We let loose our clothes, leapt into the water and swam the hundred and fifty feet to our 'honeymoon suite.'

~~

Jeri glanced at the clock when the girls finally settled down, wishing she had half the energy of either one of them.

She smiled and thought about her day on the sandbar. It had been fun, full of laughter she hadn't had in a long time. And it was forever ago since she'd danced. Dax had been surprisingly light on his feet, twirling her about with ease.

She envied what Tasha had but in a good way, wanting to be in a loving relationship with a decent man who cared for his family the way Dax did. It was endearing how he'd cordially asked Mary if she'd like to dance, and then held her hand as he led her to the sandy floor.

Jeri felt a sudden sensation that made her dizzy, as if someone spun her around as quickly as they could.

When Dax escorted Mary, he rubbed his thumb on the back of her hand just like the man who saved those girls.

In exactly the same way!

Don't be so silly, she thought. There were only so many ways to move a thumb, so of course it looked similar.

But she picked up her phone anyway and watched the Anatovich crime scene video over and over again.

chapter fourteen

At the risk of sounding like the chauvinist my friend in Michigan accuses me of being, there is nothing like waking up and seeing your woman make breakfast for you.

Or in this case, root around in a cooler.

"Good morning, Mrs. Palmer."

"Why, good morning, Mr. Palmer. How did you sleep?"

"Sleep? What's that?"

I stand corrected. There's nothing better than hearing your woman's sensual chuckle *as* she makes you breakfast.

After slipping on some shorts, I asked for my shirt back.

"Yeah, no. Our clothes are still on the beach chairs, and you packed yourself something to wear but nothing for me."

'Would you believe I forgot?"

"I don't think so. You like to see me naked too much."

"I do, but I really did. Sorry."

We ate cold sandwiches and had wine instead of coffee because I also forgot to put the generator on the pontoon.

"How does it feel being married?" I asked.

"It's wonderful. You?"

"I was alright until you started taking my stuff."

She grinned and said *get used to it*.

"When do we need to be back?"

"George will be at the launch to pick up the boat in less than an hour, so we'll have to go soon. Maybe we could do this again, sometime?"

"I'd like that," Tasha said and emptied her glass before shoving the last half of her second sandwich into the cooler. "Are you still hungry?"

"Yes," I said and reached for her.

~~

The folder Alexi left on the desk contained information about Palmer and his kid that Miko found interesting, but not as much as the St. Vincent Star did with its banner:

*** Don't tread on me or mine Dad gets married! ***

There was something too cozy about Palmer's new wife being the detective Anthony used as a pawn to get her maid of honor, Deputy-Director friend to play ball – the same Jeri Ryan who ran Palmer's name more than a year ago after the girl and her father went missing.

Why did she do that? he wondered.

The only thing that made sense was the FBI suspected him in their disappearance and then changed their mind.

Not that Miko cared. And so long as it didn't turn out that Palmer killed his uncle, he'd leave him be.

As for the girl... She was an impressive piece of pussy.

While older than he preferred, her talents were many – valedictorian, analytical mind, musically gifted, and deadly. His interest in her was more carnal than cerebral, however. Though she'd make an excellent courtesan for some middle-aged millionaire with daughter issues.

What intrigued him was the spark in her eyes, a latent flame he'd seen countless times in much younger girls. She liked to be taken, even against her will. Her father must have given her a taste for it, and she probably asked Palmer to feed her as well. It was what damaged girls did to feel loved and would explain why he kept her a secret for so long after finding her in the woods .

Because no man can resist the allure of a little girl, Miko thought. Especially if she called him *Daddy*.

~~

George gave us a ride to my place, and, after unloading chairs, coolers, bags, and twenty-seven PVC pipes, I thanked him again for the pontoon and the lift home.

"Y'all take care now," he said and drove off.

"He's one heck of a nice guy," I told Tasha. "You know, he wouldn't let me pay for the boat? Not even for the gas."

"He must be a good friend."

"That's just it. We don't spend a lot of time together, but he has always been friendly to me. Maybe it's cause we are simpatico when it comes to things like racial injustice or how people could be if they just stopped being assholes."

I grabbed two coolers by the handles and started down the long driveway. "I'll come fetch the rest with the truck."

"What are you going to do with all those candy-canes?"

"I think I'll save them for the next time I get married. They seemed to be a big hit."

"I can give you a big hit now, if you'd like," she razzed.

As we trekked toward the house, I asked her something I should have earlier.

"Do you have a preference on where we live?"

"Here is fine. It's more private and right on the bay. I was thinking we could build a dock out back," she said, and then added, "If that's alright with you."

"Look at us being respectful and giving. We've got this marriage thing in the bag."

"Yep. If the next twenty-four years are anything like the last twenty-four hours, we'll be singing songs and sonnets."

Tasha slipped her hand through my arm and then took one of the coolers. I started to say something, but the way she looked let me know we were in this *thing* together.

"I should put my house on the market then," she said.

"Hang on, let's think about that. I mean, now that you have a couple of extra bucks there's no rush, right? Perhaps we could hold on to it for a while."

"We could, but why?"

"Interludes and trysts."

The sparkle in her eyes burned bright. I think she saw wisdom in my solution to having relations with a teenager underfoot. At least the kind we had last night.

"I'm glad you said that, Dax. I was worried how I'd be able to keep fooling around with my other men and woman. Thanks. You're like the best husband ever!"

"Woman?"

"So the guys you're fine with, but not poor Annabelle? Geez Louise, that's pretty sexist," she teased.

We set the coolers on the porch, and I opened the door.

"Would you like to know how the tradition of carrying the bride across the threshold got its start?"

"As long as you have to hold me while you tell it," she said and jumped into my arms. "We'll see how strong you are based on which version I get: long, short, or in between."

I pretended she had some heft and took a deep breath.

"When Roman soldiers would capture a city, they'd pillage and rape. Of course, the ladies were not as agreeable, so the men had to take them, kicking and screaming. Years later, citizens in Rome thought it fun to recreate the exploits of the men they wished they were, and they symbolically *took* a girl from her parents and carried her into their house so they could . . . You know."

My intention was to grunt and struggle and give a *whew* when I set her down, but then she said, "Is that what you're going to do to me when we get inside, Dax? *You know?*"

It would be easy to lose oneself in the lust and luster of her eyes, and I think I did for a bit as I stood still holding her.

"Damn, Tash. You look good enough to eat."

"Well, then . . ."

But like a sweet dream that ends too early, the moment gave way to a honk.

"Wait, wait," Mary shouted out from Isabel's hatchback. "Don't take her in yet. I want to get it on video."

"You can put me down, Dax."

"Never," I said. "Me strong like bull."

We waited as they parked and climbed out of the SUV, and Mary took her phone from a back pocket to record us. "Look her in the eyes and say how much you love her, Dax."

"I just told her she looked good enough to eat. Does that count?"

Jeri grinned, Isabel giggled, Watson yawned, and Mary blushed before saying, "Ha-ha. Very funny. Now tell her."

I did as I was told and, again, looked into her eyes.

"Shall I compare thee to a summer's day?"

"Not with Shakespeare," Mary said.

"You're my sweet little thing, Tash. My pride and . . .."

"No Stevie Ray, either."

"Uh, here's looking at you, kid?"

"Dax..."

"What if I sang, *If ever I would leave you?* But it wouldn't be at breakfast. And surely not at dinner. I might take off after lunch, though."

Everyone laughed but Mary, and when she asked again, I couldn't refuse.

"Dad, come on. Please?"

It was the first time she said *Dad* for real. And between that and holding a wife in my arms, I was genuinely happy. So I spoke from the heart and left everyone teary-eyed.

"Now, was that so hard? Geez, you're such a big baby," Mary said, giving me shit and wiping my face with a sleeve.

"Hey, those aren't tears," I told her. "It's sweat. Tasha is a lot heavier than she looks.."

"I hope somebody loves me that way someday," Isabel said as we crossed the threshold one after the other.

"I don't see why they wouldn't," Tasha said and pinched me after I set her down. "You are worthy."

"Worthy is exactly the right word for you, Fluffy," I said. "You're a peach of a girl. A plum. A strawberry shortcake with whipped-cream and a cherry on top."

"You think so?" Isabel asked.

"I do. Ain't nobody got nothing on you."

"That's funny. Miss Jeri said the same thing yesterday."

"Did she now? Well, she may have said it first, but I'm sure I said it best."

I winked, and Jeri rolled her eyes.

"Maybe I'll see if there's an earlier flight out," Jeri said. "Before your over-inflated ego blows up and makes a mess."

"How can I not big up myself? I have a wife, a daughter, a backup daughter, and a new sister-in-law – all beautiful, all intelligent, and all completely enamored with me. You have to admit, I got it goin' on."

While hard to hear in print, my 'on' sounded like *owune*.

"God help us," she said.

"I wish you didn't have to go so soon, Aunt Jeri," Mary said. "I like it when we're all together."

"Me too, Mare."

"When do you need to be at the airport?" Tasha asked.

"Around five-ish. Plane takes off at six-fifteen."

"That doesn't give us much time to sit on the beach and do nothing before we have to get ready for the blowout."

"Tell you what, why don't you ladies go on? I'll load the van and get us setup onstage. All y'all have to do is be there five minutes before we start playing at two," I said, prepared to overcome an insistence on their part to help.

But Tasha left to take a quick shower, Mary and Isabel went to make some snacks, Jeri said she'd do the drinks, and Watson grabbed his treats.

Twelve minutes later, they were out the door and gone.

~~

When asked to get more bags of ice, Dominic jumped at the chance to leave a house that held one too many relatives attending his annual holiday cookout. Namely a sister in-law who talked incessantly and criticized relentlessly about his grilling, his drinking, his breathing.

He loved her, of course. Mostly because he had to.

To maximize his efforts to continue feeling that way, he created a timeout for himself by stopping at the precinct to run the tag number Dax had given him.

Daniel Turley was the registered owner of the vehicle. He lived out by Joseph's Bay Country Club, and, according to the reports, the police had been called to the Turley home four times in as many years without an arrest being made. This struck him as odd because five years ago in New York he was arrested, charged, and sentenced to six months in a county jail for assaulting a former girlfriend.

Dominic thought his not being charged in St. Vincent probably had to do with who Turley's father was. That, and the good ole boy mindset of a woman's role in the scheme of southern things – to obey and do as she was told.

Thank goodness, he had been taught better. His father would have tanned his hide if he ever treated a girl like that. Not to mention his older sisters, who would have kicked his butt and then some back in the day.

Hell, they'd do it now if I ever got out of line.

Not ready to return to the constraints of his castle, Dom drove out to see how Mrs. Turley was doing.

He trusted Dax had seen what he said, but there were reasons other than abuse that might account for the bruises. She might be hyperactive, or athletic. An injury on the job. Heck, it could be from having rough but consensual sex. He wouldn't know until he spoke to her alone or spent some time with the two of them.

Of course, she may say nothing's wrong or refuse to say anything at all out of fear. Or resignation.

Dominic called his wife and said he needed to tend to a work related issue before coming back. Carmen never gave him grief and was always understanding and supportive, She just added a few things to his *get from the store* list.

When he pulled in the Turley's driveway, Dom heard a man barking on the far side of the house.

"Goddammit, Lisa, lift it up higher."

"I'm trying. It's heavy."

"Don't give me that shit. Just do it."

"I can't."

"Jesus, you're worthless. You know that?"

As he came around the corner, Dominic saw a big man at the top of a long ladder trying to take a four by eight sheet of plywood from a small woman at the bottom straining to give it to him with arms stretched as high as they could go. He also saw marks on her legs and back as the blouse lifted.

"Let me help you with that, Miss. It looks heavy," he said taking it from her and handing it to him. "Is that from the storm last night? I heard the winds broke a few windows."

"Who the hell are you?"

"Detective Greer. Are you Daniel Turley?"

"What do you want?"

"For you to answer my question. Are you?"

"Yes," Daniel said. "Why are you here?"

"Are you Lisa Turley, Miss?"

"Yes," she said, barely.

"Can we go somewhere and talk? It won't take but a minute. It's about a friend of yours."

"Who?" Daniel said. "What friend?"

"If your wife wants to tell you later, that's up to her," he said, "but I would really rather talk to you first, Mrs. Turley. Would that be okay?"

She nodded and turned to walk to the front yard.

"Stop," Daniel said and scrambled down the ladder. "Whatever you have to say, Mister, you can say right here. She's going to tell me anyway."

"You're probably right, Mr. Turley, but I think it's best if we talk privately first. It won't take long."

"No. You can tell it now or be on your way. Right, Lisa?"

Dom saw the struggle in her eyes and decided to make it easier as there was no need to drag this out any further.

"Is that what you'd like, Mrs. Turley?"

She started to answer and then nodded.

"Someone noticed bruises on your neck, arms, and legs and thought you might be in trouble."

"That's bullshit..." Daniel said, but Dominic continued.

"And while you were trying to lift the plywood to cover up the broken window, I saw more marks on your back. So I'm asking, has he been hurting you?"

The silence broke when she looked at him.

"Don't answer that," he warned. "I mean it."

"That sounds like a *yes* to me, Mr. Turley. You're under arrest. Turn around and put your hands behind your back."

"You can't do that," Daniel said. "She didn't say I did."

"She doesn't need to, at least not at the moment. Now, turn around and do as I said."

"And if I don't?" he sneered.

"Then I'll make you."

Daniel's bluster couldn't overcome the quiet resolve of the detective. One way or the other, he'd be taken to jail, so he let himself be handcuffed and played his trump card.

"You wait till my daddy hears about this. You'll be fired, sure as shit."

"I'll worry about that when the time comes," Dom said. "Miss Lisa, would you walk up front with us, please?"

He lowered Daniel to the grass near the car and kept an eye on him as he spoke to his wife out of earshot.

"I'm sorry if I embarrassed you."

"You didn't," she said.

"Has he been hurting you?"

She looked away but wouldn't confirm what he knew. Dominic thought she might be too afraid to say anything or too scared to believe the abuse could finally be over.

"Do you have someplace safe you could go? A friend or family member you could stay with for a while?"

"Yes."

"May I make a suggestion?"

When she nodded, he told her to pack her bags and go. Now, before the sun sets.

"Take some time to think about what you want to do. And don't be alone with him or his family until you're ready. Okay?"

"Okay," she said and nodded. "Thank you."

"You're welcome."

When he turned to leave, she stopped him.

"Who was the friend you wanted to talk to me about?"

"It was a stranger who wanted to help if you needed it."

She looked away again and asked him to thank them.

"I will. Good luck, Miss."

Dominic walked over and lifted him to his feet, opened the door, and put Daniel in the back seat.

"Mr. Turley, this is my wife's car, so I'd appreciate your respecting her property."

"Fuck your wife. She'll probably leave you anyway after my dad gets rid of your ass. You fucked up big time."

In fairness, he asked him to respect his wife's property, not her personally, so Dom let it roll off his back. And the young man might be right. Arresting the mayor's son might be a major *fuck up* as far as his career was concerned.

chapter fifteen

I sat to take a short break and listened, humbled by the accumulated talent of the girls. Not only could they sing like songbirds, individually they played multiple instruments. Me too, if starting and stopping a drum machine by stepping on a button constitutes *playing*.

Isabel was classically trained on the violin, with a bent for playing bluegrass when the mood struck – as it did now. Jeri picked the mandolin like she'd been born to it, and Mare and Tash played twelve-string and folk guitars as the crowd whooped and hollered.

I might have accompanied them if I'd had a proper jug, but, as the soda can in my hand wouldn't quite cut it, I didn't. Besides, playing a jug might not be as easy as it looked.

Best to stay in my guitar and foot-pedal lane.

After they finished, I thought to rejoin them until a long lonesome plea from Isabel's fiddle stopped me cold. I stared at her and shook my head, but she grinned and began to sing *You Will Be My Ain True Love.*

A good song can evoke a powerful emotional response. For some, it's the lyrics that move them; for others, it is the imagery. For me it was a beautiful harmony, sweet chordal tone, or a haunting refrain.

This one had all three, and it always pierced my soul.

What's worse, Isabel caught me in the kitchen a while back with a tear in my eye after she played it in the big room. I told her it was the chopped onions, but she didn't buy it.

As the song neared the end, I figuratively patted myself for hanging tough – until Isabel sang a verse she must have made up. Mary then played a poignant guitar solo followed by another new verse sung in exquisite four-part harmony.

Of course, Isabel had done it all on purpose. And I knew this because she winked at me, even as the mournful moan of her violin reached into my chest and tore out my heart.

Apparently, she had some *little shit* in her, too.

~~

Mary volunteered to stay with the equipment as Dax walked Tash and Jeri to the car, and Watson followed Isabel to the porta-potties. She sat under an umbrella and watched boys in swim trunks toss around a football in the sand.

Their aesthetic qualities were pleasing to the eye, but Mary didn't *feel* anything. It hadn't always been that way... Before her father, she'd felt plenty.

The boys began to act like kids and tackle each other, but another strolled barefoot in front of them. Instead of parading around half-naked like the others, he wore khakis, a nice summer shirt, and carried himself in a quiet confident manner that felt familiar. So she gave him a discerning eye.

Mary looked him over and checked off criteria he met, which was all physical because she couldn't know anymore unless she talked to him. And that was when things would break down because boys will be boys and always would be.

Then, he looked at her.

Everything got quiet, or rather she didn't hear a thing. Not the wind, the birds, the ocean, or the people. Even her breathing seemed to stop. And then everyone disappeared, leaving only the two of them.

When he smiled, she wasn't sure if she'd reciprocated. And when he nodded, she didn't because she couldn't. Only after he left did her heart begin to beat again and a measure of thought return, along with the birds, beach, and people.

"What the heck was that?"

Mary was stunned, confused, thrilled, annoyed, excited. Words like *thunderbolt*, *thunderstruck*, and *at first sight* raced through her mind and she rejected them all.

"Don't be ridiculous. That's just..."

"Just what, sweetie?" I asked.

"What?"

"What's just what? You just said it."

"I did?" she said. "Huh, I must have been daytalking."

"Daytalking?"

"Daydreaming's chatty nephew."

"Well, what were you *That's justing?*"

"I can't remember. Must have been in a daytrance."

When I asked for a clarification she said it was a second cousin once removed.

"Uh-huh. Are you ready to get back at it?"

"Yup, as soon as Isabel and Watson get here. Are Tasha and Aunt Jeri on their way to the airport?"

"Yes. They'll stop and collect her stuff first."

"I'll miss her," Mary said.

"I know, but I got her to commit to having Thanksgiving with us, so Happy Birthday and Merry Christmas."

"Nice try. You can give her for one or the other but not both. You'll still have to break into your couple-bucks bank, I'm afraid." She grinned and gave me a kiss on the cheek. "That's just for being you."

"Thanks. You know, I'm me all the time, with plenty of room on both cheeks, so . . ."

"Yeah, well, a little of you goes a long way, so . . ."

"So," Isabel asked. "What did I miss?"

"Your sister wants to keep my cheeks all to herself, but I said she'd have to leave some space for the rest of y'all."

Mary rolled her eyes and Isabel smiled.

"How about here?" she said and kissed me there.

"Why, thank you, Miss Belle. About a thousand more of those, and I might forget what you did."

"What did she do?" Mary asked.

"I can't tell you, hon. Sorry. But she knows darn well."

"Why, whatever do you mean, Mr. Dax?" she said and winked, not subtly but right out in the open.

"Ha. Funny," I said. "Mare, do you want to start us off?"

"Sure," she said, stepping on the stage intending to sing one song before inexplicably singing another after spotting him in the middle of a crowd that vanished in plain sight.

Isabel later said her version of *Vision of Love* had given Mariah a run for her money.

~~

"Are you sure, Dax?" Mary asked.

"Yes. Y'all go mingle amongst your fans and bask in the glow of their praise."

"I don't want to bask, just get my feet wet."

"Either way, enjoy. I've got this."

"Alrighty, then," she said and took off with Watson and Isabel, feeling guilty about leaving him alone to break down and load the gear but eager to be going.

Mary heard but didn't listen while Isabel prattled on, instead employing Dax's *someone watching but act like they aren't* method of moving through a crowd. Only she used it to search without seeming to, a thing much harder than she would have thought.

Scanning one's surroundings, even casually, looked like looking, so she glanced briefly and then carefully, naturally, glimpsed again. It was arduous, and unsatisfactory because blind spots formed that could be a problem in real life and death situations.

"He needs to go," Isabel said, and Mary watched them walk away. Her eyes moved toward the coastline and, after receiving many compliments along the way, she eventually stepped into the warm water.

"It's you again."

She turned, and there he was.

"I've never been serenaded before. It was nice, thanks. I assume you were singing that song to me?"

She'd sung over two dozen but knew the one he meant.

"No. Sorry. It was just the next tune on the playlist."

He seemed to see right through her, but his smile didn't reproach or judge. She thought it warm and kind, a *with her* instead of *at her* kind of grin.

It also made her tingle.

"You were great, by the way. Remarkable, really."

"Thanks," she said, too riveted to think about blushing.

"So was the rest of your... Family?"

"Yes. They are. Thanks."

"Your dad is like Jimi, Stevie, and Carlos all rolled into one. Seems like I've seen him somewhere before."

"Maybe the news," Mary said, not wanting to go there.

"I hardly watch it, so probably not. Does he play up in Georgia? I'll go to a blues bar now and then when I need a break from studying."

"Sure. He was just up there, actually. So, what are you studying? Which blues King do you prefer – B.B. or Albert? Can you play?"

She was on the verge of becoming a jabbering idiot, but after a minute they fell into a funny, friendly conversation. He was nice, quick-witted, quick to laugh, easy to like, and, when her hand slipped into his as he introduced himself, Mary definitely felt something.

~~

Six, seven, eight...

No, I wasn't a helicopter dad. Nor was I spying, because I didn't consider keeping an eye on her snooping so much as prudent, given what happened at Tasha's.

Thirteen, fourteen, fifteen...

Where the heck had Isabel and Watson run off to, and what was taking them so long to get back?

Twenty-two, twenty-three...

No sooner had my concern of men coming to hurt Mary begun to fade than another threat materialized – young men who'd come after her for different reasons.

Twenty-nine, thirty, thirty-one, thirty-two!

His holding her hand for so long wasn't as troubling as her letting him – and smiling so generously while he did. I swear, I'd almost rather she killed bad guys than like boys.

Damned kids. Why can't they just stay little?

Watson and Isabel joined her in the water and I relaxed. A temporary respite, because they weren't always going to be there to help run interference.

~

"Mr. Palmer?" Brian Murphy said.

"Yes?"

"I just wanted to say how much I enjoyed y'all. You in particular. For once, the internet didn't lie."

"Oh yeah? What did it say?"

"Among other things, you were a 'blues playin' bad ass.' And you are. I liked your Robin Trower tribute. He's one of my favorites."

"Mine, too. I don't think he got the credit he deserved back in the day, but his new stuff is as good as the old."

"Perhaps, but I loved hearing *Too Rolling Stoned* again. And your *Daydream* is every bit as good as his."

Brian didn't say that only for effect; the man could play. But a little flattery sometimes greased the wheels, steering a suspect somewhere he might not go otherwise.

"That's kind of you to say, Detective, but we both know better. Thanks, though."

"How..." Murphy said, miffed that he'd been detected.

"It could be the haircut, and how you comport yourself. Or the way you give everyone a once over as they walk by," Palmer said before grinning. "There's a silhouette of a badge and ID wallet in your favorite blue jeans. Ergo..."

"What makes you think they're my favorite?"

"You've worn them often enough to create a flat square outline, unlike regular wallets that are fat and rounded. My wife is a detective and has one just like it."

Brian was impressed with both his observational and deductive abilities but didn't feel the need to comment on skills Palmer already knew he possessed.

"That's right, the paper said you got married yesterday. Congratulations."

"Damned newsies," Palmer said with a blatant disgust. "What paper was that?"

"The News-Herald. There was a wedding picture, too."

"Vultures," he muttered under his breath. "Sorry, uh?"

"Brian," Murphy said, and then, "Murphy," after Palmer raised an eyebrow.

"Call me, Dax. And thank you for the congrats," he said, removing a microphone from its stand.

Murphy waited to be asked some variety of *what do you want* like most people he unexpectantly dropped in on, but Palmer appeared to have already dismissed him as he set about packing up his gear.

murder in the light of day

At the junction of fish or cut bait, Brian threw a line in. "Would you like some help?" He expected a *no thanks* but got a *sure* instead.

"You can start by handing me the loose cords, and then put the guitars in their cases."

As Dax zip-tied the cables, Brian began to engage him. "I agree with you about the press. They can be a nuisance, especially when they're getting into your business. But you have to admit, threatening to shoot one of their own on live TV might not be the best way to keep them out of your hair."

Palmer chuckled.

"Yeah, that may have been a mistake. I was trying to deter the local creeps and curious from coming around like they did the last time Mary was in the news. But now there are more people to worry about. She told me that clip got over a million views on YouTube. Can you believe it?"

Brian saw an opening and took it.

"That's how I found out you were a blues bad ass, after an internet search. By the way, I think it's great how you're training up your daughter, Dax. It's unfortunate it has to be that way but, damned if it isn't necessary given the times we live in. It's part of the reason I came, to say so."

Palmer looked him over a second or two before saying, "I appreciate that, Brian. And you're right. Because without it she'd be dead. Twice, now. Will you bring those cases? And the other part?"

"What other part?" Brian asked.

"Of the reason you came."

"Oh, to hear you play. And enjoy the day." He smiled, as Palmer did, and trailed behind him trudging guitars and amps through the sand to a van and then back to the stage.

"I came across something interesting during my search that might help with a case I'm working on. Care to hear it?"

"Sure," Dax said.

After they grabbed another load, Brian went to work.

"I'm trying to catch a serial killer, and after seeing the places you ..."

Palmer stopped and looked him dead in the eye.

145

"We have a serial killer in the area? Why hasn't it been reported on the news? Who's at risk? Women? Children?"

The concern for the safety of his new wife and daughter was palpable, and Brian found it compelling and sincere. In fact, it created doubt and made him reevaluate his tactics.

"I'm sorry. Let me explain. This is just a theory of mine based on specific unsolved murders here in the Panhandle."

Palmer's stare penetrated at first, and then withdrew.

"I see. So my family isn't in any *known* danger, then?"

"Not from my guy. He only goes after criminal types."

Dax nodded, and then walked toward his van.

"How do you know it's a he, instead of a she?" he asked. "You aren't one of those chauvinists who thinks a woman's place is in the home and should leave the serial killin' to the menfolk, are you?"

Brian couldn't see it but imagined Palmer was grinning, because he was, too.

"No. I've learned that a woman's place is wherever she says it is, and I'm fine with that. But these kinds of killings are usually done by men, statistically speaking. And in this case, he's white, smart, and around our age."

"Is that *your* assessment or an FBI profiler's?" Dax said, opening the sliding side door.

"Mine. But I've taken a couple of classes at Quantico."

"Nice. So you were saying you were searching and saw places I'd . . ."

It was the first time he'd asked about the investigation, which could be telling. Then again, maybe Palmer was only being courteous by helping him remember where he'd left off? It was hard to know which was what.

"I noticed you play all over the Panhandle, and it got me to thinking. Maybe the killer does the kind of work that puts him where he needs to be? Like you."

It was as close to an accusation as he'd come, and Brian watched for any sign or reaction that might give Dax away.

"Hmm, you might be on to something," he said. "But I wouldn't limit myself to musicians. There's a host of other occupations that might fit the bill; service industry jobs, construction crews, landscapers, UPS or FedEx drivers . . .

Like that delivery guy who killed the grandmother in your neck of the woods but was let go cause of a legal technicality. What ever happened to him?"

"He was strangled to death. Same as she was."

"Huh, well, that seems fair. Anyway, another plausible person of interest, given the criminal aspect you mentioned, could be a cop who has had his fill of felons. Or better yet, a detective. Working active crime scenes and having access to autopsy reports would be helpful in learning to cover one's tracks, I imagine."

"I hadn't considered that," Murphy said. And he hadn't.

"Ahh, Brian, these are my girls," I said as they walked up on us. "Mary, Isabel and my good friend, Watson. Ladies, this is Detective Murphy. He came to hear us play."

As he praised their performance, I took stock. Based on his artful interrogation, he had a suspicion that was as yet unsubstantiated – else he'd have come with a warrant. And while disconcerting, it wasn't unanticipated as I'd prepared for the possibility of being questioned by the police from the very beginning. Starting with Mary's father.

That's how Tasha and I met, actually.

"It was a pleasure, Dax," Brian said, extending a hand.

"For me, too," I replied and shook it. "Thanks for your help. And for coming out. Good luck and take care."

"Will do. You, too."

After he left, I asked the girls to follow me home before heading to Tasha's for their *just the two of us* sleepover.

"Don't worry, I'll let y'all unload the van by yourselves. I know how much you love it."

"Be still my heart," Mary said, and Isabel laughed.

~~

I handed Tasha a chilled glass of wine and took a seat at the other end of the couch, patting my lap.

"Really? You've never rubbed them before. What's up? What did you do?" she asked.

"Now that is a perfect example of looking a gift horse in the mouth. Not to mention kicking the poor thing in the teeth as well, with an accusation of unfounded wrongdoing.

Fortunately, I'm a forgiving man," I said and patted my lap. This time her feet found their way lickety-split.

"It's partly your fault, by the way."

"How's that?" she said, shifting for maximum comfort. "They don't stink, do they?"

"No. Well, not enough to push you out of bed."

"What *would* be enough?" she asked with a tilted grin.

"Anyway, my rubs usually begin at your neck and then move downward. But I never make it to your feet because, for some reason, you always stop me in between."

I'd said it as innocently as I could manage.

"Yep, it's a mystery why that keeps happening, for sure. "Ooh, Dax . . ." she said as I kneaded the balls of her feet. "That feels so good."

"That's exactly what you say when I'm in the middle, which could explain how we get stuck there so often."

"Mmm, don't stop."

"Yeah, that too." I began to massage her heal and asked if Jeri got off alright.

"She hardly said a word along the way, claiming fatigue. And I'm sure she's tired, because I am, too. But something was bothering her. Those dead kids, no doubt. I'm worried about the effect they are having on her psyche."

"It can't be easy dealing with that."

"No. I know. Oh, I got a call from Dom. It turns out the couple you saw in the store lives here in St. Vincent."

"Really? Where?" I said, even though I knew.

"Out by the golf course. He ended up arresting the guy."

"That's good news. The man was hitting her then?"

"According to him, she didn't confirm or deny it, but he saw and heard enough to believe so and took the man to jail. Whether he stays there or not depends on the D.A."

"That's a load off my mind," I said, perhaps with more relief in my voice than I should have shared. But she didn't seem to notice and settled further into the pillow. "I forgot to ask, what did your captain say about getting the time off?"

"He said don't bother coming back to work till I'd been properly honeymooned. So we're good to go."

Tasha yawned and stretched until she cracked. "You okay having Mary stay with Isabel at FSU while we're gone?"

"I think so," I said and moved from her toes to her calf.

My apprehension about leaving Mary was mitigated in thinking she'd be safer on Florida State University's campus surrounded by faculty and students rather than home alone where peep-creep-bad guys could show up at any time.

Or detective Murphy.

I wasn't as worried about him talking to Mary. First, he didn't strike me as a man who'd question a teenager without a parent's consent. Second, he wouldn't know where to find her, and, if he did, it was a long way out of his jurisdiction – something that wouldn't go over well with his superiors. And third, but most importantly, she wouldn't give him the time of day where it concerned me. And, because of that, I didn't need to give her a heads up.

Tasha on the other hand...

I didn't doubt her willingness to protect me, and from that point of view, a warning could help her prepare in the event she was asked about things I was suspected of doing.

However, I had no right to make her an accomplice to something she would have arrested me for if she'd known. And even if she'd want to be told, it wasn't fair to put her in such an untenable position.

It was, of course, a mess of my own making that could only get worse once the man in the trunk *shoe* dropped.

How to resolve it was a dilemma all its own, but rather than try at the moment, I slid my hands up Tasha's leg to the promise land – only to be rebuffed by a snore.

Instead of questioning my manly appeal, I chalked it up to a case of *snooze you lose*, with her snoozing and me losing. I should have kept my eye on the prize, my shoulder to the wheel, nose to the grindstone, hand on the...

As I'm sure y'all are aware of by now, I have a penchant for platitudes. Also an affinity for alliteration.

Sorry about that.

~~

Mary felt the old pleasure of cool fingers on warm skin, except they didn't belong to her.

He explored her body, from the burgeoning peak of her breast to the silken valley below, slowly schussing through her pristine snow toward the opening that lay ahead. She didn't understand the skiing motif of her thoughts because she'd never been, but, as he drew near the slippery mound, Mary writhed in anticipation.

Her eyes opened and her ears listened, worried that the moan in her dream had been uttered out loud. Except for the slow and steady breathing, Watson and Isabel were still. She sighed in relief, wondering what the hell just happened. And why.

You know why.

'Stop it,' she said to herself. There was no way she was head over heels with a boy she'd just met. No effing way!

But smitten?

Yup, she was surely that.

chapter sixteen

After a big breakfast and playful banter, we loaded the vehicles with bags, coolers, suitcases and guitars as Watson ambled down the drive to see what was what.

"Did you pack your gun?" I asked while Tasha followed Isabel to her SUV.

"Yes. Plus three extra clips," Mary said. "I also grabbed a Nerf-knife, just in case."

"That's my girl."

Her incandescent smile only highlighted the fact this would be the longest we had been apart since I'd found her, and a sudden sense of loss washed over me.

What if something happened to her while I was gone? How could I ever live with that? Maybe I should just ...

She gave me a hug and said, "I'll be fine."

I squeezed her tight and asked if she'd ever tell me the truth about listening in on my thoughts.

"Probably not."

"Can I get one of those hugs for the road?" Isabel asked when we walked over.

"Of course. You can even have one for the heck of it."

I opened my arms and she snuggled in. "Y'all be safe and have fun," I said and kissed the top of her head.

"We will. Y'all too."

"We will," Tasha said, slipping an arm around my waist. "Oh, Dax. Did you turn off the alarms? We don't want Dom to get spray-painted for doing us a good deed."

"I did. It's nice of him to keep an eye on our houses. And for letting me take his work-wife on my honeymoon. Remind me to bring him back something."

"Oooh, us too," Isabel said.

"Sure thing, Fluffy."

When Watson returned, he said there was a news truck parked on the shoulder, according to Mary.

"That's unfortunate," I said. "When you two get to the gate, stop and I'll go have a word."

"Dax, I don't think that's a good idea," Tasha said.

"I'm just going to reason with them. It'll be fine."

Tasha frowned and shook her head, but Mary grinned. "Let's go, Belle," she said and piled into the car with Watson.

At the end of the driveway, Tasha put a hand on my arm when I opened the door.

"Don't threaten them, Dax. I mean it."

"I won't," I told her and reached beneath my seat for the pair of red handles. As I approached the van, a cameraman jumped out and started to shoot.

"Morning," I said. "Beautiful day, don't you think?"

I made my way to the passenger side and spoke to the driver/reporter through the open window.

"Listen, I know you're doing what you think is your job, but for safety reasons, I'm asking you not to follow us today. And if you'll give me your word you won't, we can all be on our merry way. What do you say? I'll even throw in a *pretty please* to offset the excessive rhyming."

When she didn't say a word, I asked her to nod if she'd heard me.

"So, it's a no then?" When she nodded again, I said, "That's too bad. Oh well, y'all have a good day," and then bent down, placed the sharp edges of the wire cutters on the valve stem of the front tire and squeezed.

As the air howled in its effort to escape, I walked to the rear and snipped off another stem, all of it *caught on tape* as the cameraman smiled behind the lens.

I gave him a grin and left them to their troubles.

"What did you do?" Tasha asked as we drove away.

I was about to ask if this was to be a standard question from here on out, then stopped and thought it reasonable given how far she had to come to find a way to be with me. My past might be overlooked, maybe someday forgiven, but I doubt if it would ever be forgotten.

"Nothing nefarious., my sweet. A little *snippy* maybe. I'm sure you'll find it funny when you see it on the news."

"Uh- huh ... What am I going to do with you? Really, I'm asking."

"Anything you want, Tash," I said with bawdy inuendo. "Well, almost."

Tasha smiled and put a hand on my leg.

"Why do you always qualify, Dax?"

"If I didn't, you might try to get me into a French maid's uniform or something."

"And what worries you most?" she asked as her fingers began to wander. "That you'll do it, or that you'd like it?"

"That you'd make me clean the house."

We rolled down the windows and let the cool morning air fill us with a sense of adventure as mile after scenic mile rolled by in blissful silence.

When we reached the fork in the road east of Lanark Village, I beeped the horn and flashed my lights at the girls who continued on through Sopchoppy to Tallahassee, while we turned toward an eight hour drive and the Florida Keys.

~~

Jeri set the report down and looked out the window of her office. It was only a niggle, as Tasha would call it. Not a serious consideration or suspicion but more of an irritation, like a breeze that tickled the hairs at the back of your neck.

So the hair and height were similar, so what? It wasn't definitive. Or proof. Neither was the familiarity of his gait, nor the affection he'd shown the girl when he took her hand and led them away from that monster's lair.

But it was curious. Circumstantially coincidental, even. Could Dax be *the man*?

She'd thought about it for the better part of a day now and, again, considered it to be an utterly ridiculous notion.

Then why the persistent niggle?

"I'm just tired," she said and turned her thoughts to the reason for it.

The excavation on Anatovich's property was on hold due to lack of storage space, personnel, and resources. The sheer number of skeletal remains had overwhelmed their capacity to . . . *To what?* she wanted to scream. Identify them? Give their parents closure? How? It could take years to discover who those children were, if at all. And if not, then what? Put them all back into the cold ground, alone and unknown?

She loosened her fist and tried to stretch the ache from her fingers as she grabbed a tissue from the desk drawer to wipe the blood on her hand. Although she'd cut her nails to the nub the last time, they'd grown enough over the three days since to break the skin . . . A guttural, macabre sound left her lips thinking how much it would lift her spirits if just one of the skeletons had even a little left on the bones.

Jeri tried to clear her head and climb out of the deep hole she was in by reaching for the phone.

"This is Detective Greer. How can I help you?"

"Good morning, Detective," she said. "This is Jeri Ryan, Tasha's friend? We met at the wedding."

"Deputy-Director, it's nice of you to call so quickly."

"Jeri, please. And may I call you Dominic?"

"Yes, Ma'am."

"Just Jeri. Ma'am makes me feel old."

"Alright, Just Jeri. I'm just Dom."

"I can see why Tasha likes working with you, Dom."

"Thanks. Can I assume you have something for me?"

"I do in that I don't. It doesn't look like your man in the trunk worked for Anatovich or his underlings or associates. You know from his file he was a killer, but we have nothing linking him to sex trafficking. My guess is he wasn't part of what went down at Tasha's. But I don't know everything."

"Are you allowed to share that info with outsiders, Jeri? Because I've never heard an FBI agent admit to not knowing something. Ever."

She heard the humor in his voice and liked him for it. "Well, seeing as how we're sort of family now . . ."

"That we are," Dominic said and nodded to the captain waving him into his office. "Thank you for looking into that for me. I owe you."

"You're welcome, Dom. Please, don't hesitate to call if you have a need."

"Yes Ma'am... Sorry,," he said before she chuckled and hung up.

The captain asked him to close the door and take a seat after Dominic knocked.

"I got a call from the mayor this morning. And one last night from the acting chief."

"I thought you might."

"Tell me what happened."

When he finished, his boss said he made the right call.

"I appreciate that. And his Honor? Does he agree with you or want my head on a pike?" Dominic asked wryly.

"I wouldn't give him a worry. His son is a problem that should have been dealt with years ago. Now, he can explain his poor parenting to a hostile press in an election year."

"I should stop by the jail, see how Daniel's holding up."

"He's already been O-R'd. Daddy got him in front of his fishing buddy Judge first thing this morning."

Dominic wasn't surprised he was released on his own recognizance instead of having to post bail like anyone else, but the indifferent message it sent to battered women stuck in his craw. That, and the overall nepotism of it.

"Do you know if the County Attorney's office will follow through and press charges?"

"I guess that depends on what Mrs. Turley has to say – once they find her. The mayor said she packed her bags, emptied their bank accounts, and left town."

"Good for her," Dom said. "Hopefully, she'll get squared away somewhere safe."

"Agreed. Give me your report when it's written up."

"Yes sir," he said and left for his desk feeling upbeat knowing that wife-beating sack of shit wouldn't have her to bounce around anymore.

"You've got mail," the computer told him, and his eyes lit upon discovering the long awaited email from the ATF. But as he read their ballistics report, the first thought that popped into his head was the last thing he wanted to think.

~~

"Alright. Let me know what you find out," Alexi said and hung up as Miko came into the office.

"Good morning, Alexi."

"Morning, sir. I just spoke to our man down in Florida. Something interesting with Palmer. He may have been here instead of there like we thought."

Miko took a seat and gestured for Alexi to sit.

"Why do we think this?" he said.

"Our guy had to get a broken fan belt replaced at a local auto shop and saw a poster of Palmer hanging on the wall. The mechanic mentioned him bringing in his vehicle. Said he'd been on the way to a gig in Thomasville, but a flat tire and intermittent engine problems kept him from it."

"When was that?"

"The day after your uncle was killed."

Miko gave it some thought and said the obvious.

"It's intriguing, Alexi, but inconclusive. Was it even the same night? Do we know where he was supposed to play?"

"Not yet. But I'm taking the tail off Palmer to find out. He needs to leave St. Vincent anyway, before someone gets suspicious about his hanging around asking questions."

"What is it, eighty miles north from there?" Miko said.

"About that. And you're right, if he couldn't make a gig because of a broken-down van, how'd he get to Dimitri's?"

~~

After his partner left for a court appearance, Murphy decided to do a drive-by in nearby Lynn Haven before lunch. On the way, he replayed the exchange he'd had with Palmer.

Everything about his demeanor suggested he was an innocent man making casual conversation with a stranger. Even the indignation displayed when he thought the police withheld information about a local killer was believable and seemed genuine. He was intelligent, direct, and likable, with a good sense of humor and a willingness to engage.

So why was he still looking at him?

There'd been no hesitation in his response or inflection in his voice that said either *uh-oh* or *catch me if you can*.

However, his asking about profiling was not typical of your everyday citizen. Neither was his suggestion the killer might have access to autopsy reports. Maybe it was because of his law enforcement wife, or perhaps he watched crime shows on television. Even Brian had his favorites – *Monk, Columbo, Law and Order: Criminal Intent.*

But what interested him most was the grandmother. Why had Palmer mentioned her?

He conceded it was part of a discussion he'd initiated, and Dax may have only been making a point – the police screwed up and let her killer go free. Yet he couldn't help thinking it was more than that, much more, even though he had nothing to go on but his gut.

The only way to resolve a problem was to work it, so he turned down Eddie's street and stopped at his house.

Dax was right about one thing; Eddie being strangled like his victim was fair. The coroner said the mark on his neck was an inch wide and dug into his skin almost twice as deep, concluding some sort of strap was used.

Eddie Johnson reaped what he'd sown. Tit for tat...

Brian drove back to the main road and then pulled into the Blue Moon parking lot some fifty yards away. The smell of food on the way to the door made him hungrier than he thought he was. Once inside, he ordered the 'burger special' and took a look around.

When the waitress returned, he said, "I notice you have a stage. Is there live entertainment?"

"Only on Saturday nights," she replied, setting the plate on the table with a tall glass of Coke. "If you need me, wave."

"Before you go, can I ask a quick question?"

"Sure."

"Do y'all keep records of who plays on any given night?"

"I don't know. You'd have to ask the manager."

"Is he or she here today?"

"No, but Jocelyn is. She's the assistant manager."

"Could I speak to her, please?"

"I'll ask," she said and walked away.

Brian took a bite and, *oh my god*, it was the best burger EVER. He'd heard it said about this place but took it with a grain of salt and hadn't bothered to believe it could be true.

"Speaking of salt," he said, lifting the lid of his sandwich and sprinkling some before taking another bite.

"They're pretty good, aren't they," a young woman with a wide grin said. "Hi. I'm Jocelyn."

"Mmff," was all he could manage with a mouthful, so he nodded and said *sorry* when he could.

"That's alright. Sandy said you asked about bookings?"

"Yes. I'm trying to find out who played here about three months ago and wondered if y'all had a list."

"No. Well, yes, but it's not a priority so we don't always keep it up to date. Why do you want to know?"

"Just tying up a loose end on a case I'm working."

"Are you a cop?"

"A detective. My name is Brian Murphy."

"Is who you're looking for in some kind of trouble?"

"No," Brian said disingenuously. "I'm trying to verify a person's whereabouts. She said a man named Dax Palmer was playing the night she was here."

"The name sounds familiar. When are we talking?"

Brian gave the date and she left to look. In her absence, he slipped a couple of fries in his mouth, and damn if they weren't also delicious – even without ketchup.

"Sorry, detective. There's no information for that night. But I remember why Mr. Palmer seemed familiar."

"From his being on the news?"

"Well, I saw him on TV looking out for his little girl," she said, "but that's not why. He was here, with the cutest dog you've ever seen. They had burgers and fries, just like you. Later, he filled in for a band member who was a no show."

"Can you tell me when that was?"

"I don't know the exact Saturday, but a man was found dead down the street later that week. It stuck in my brain."

Brian tried to contain his excitement and asked her to start from the beginning and tell all that she remembered. When finished, he thanked her and asked one last thing.

"Did you happen to notice if the dog had a leash?"

chapter seventeen

For the fourth day in a row, Watson gave her a stink eye after Isabel left for classes, but before Mary went to hers.

He knows, she thought, though she hadn't said and he hadn't asked. "See ya later, alligator."

He watched her close the door without a *crocodile* back, and she felt like crap as it clicked shut. But the moment her feet hit the stairs there was a pep in her step.

She'd been pretending to audit a few classes, 'as long as I'm here,' and had purposely deceived them for days.

You mean lying, don't you?

Okay, yes, if you want to get technical, she admitted. But there were reasons for it, one being she was still in the process of collating and analyzing the data. Also, she wasn't ready to share him or their time alone together.

Not yet anyway.

A grin formed as she gave an old melody new lyrics – O*n the first day of Michael, my true love gave to me, a warm smile near a pine tree.*

He'd mentioned his intention to visit the FSU campus in his search for a graduate school when they met and she'd kept an eye out, if only to test the validity of fate.

Only?

When she saw him standing in the copse that first day, the rational part of her tried to hold him up to scrutiny, to see the *why* of how she felt. But after his eyes found hers, he smiled, and her need to understand no longer mattered.

They'd taken to taking long walks, gravitating toward the solitude of out of the way places on paths less traveled. Their conversations were effortless and wide ranging over a myriad of topics, similar interests, hopes and dreams.

On the second day, Michael told her about a man who'd raised him being brutally murdered months earlier. Mary's heart went out, and she put her hand on his. He held it for a long time and then began to trace his thumb across its back, causing gooses to bump and tingle.

She received similar displays of affection from Dax and saw him give Tasha the same many times, but, as Michael caressed her skin, she came to know something else. What Dax and Tasha did was intimate, sensual, exciting. When Mary gave Michael access to her naked palm, he took her offering with humility and slipped his fingers into hers.

They hugged at the beginning and end of the third day, with another somewhere in between, just because.

And then yesterday, she told him about her father and what he'd done, something she couldn't conceive of doing only days earlier. But Michael wasn't just anybody, and she began to believe he felt the same toward her. He was a patient, caring listener, and when tears fell, he wiped them away with kisses, three on the cheek and one on her lips that lingered...

Though sad Michael left for home, Mary skipped up the steps to Isabel's dorm as she thought of her day in the nook by the understated stream. She'd twice caught him gazing at her longingly, at least that's how she read it based on how Dax or Tasha would look when the other was unaware.

It made her feel wonderful. And womanly.

By the time she reached the door, the number of gazes was amended to conform to the *Days of Michael* jingle she sang to herself.

Five longing looooooks. Four-r kisses sweet, three nice hugs, two touching hands, and a warm smile near a pine tree.

They hushed when she stepped inside, and their heads seemed to squeak like rusty hinges as they swiveled.

"Well, my ears aren't burning, but I'm guessing you two have been talking about me?"

"Is that the guy from the beach I saw you with today?" Isabel said.

Determined to ride the euphoric horse she'd ridden in on, Mary was lighthearted. "What guy are we talking about? There were so many of them."

She ruffled Watson's fur and gave a scratch behind his ear, hoping to win him over to her side if things went south. He tried to rebuff her, but his back leg moved in rhythm to her fingers.

"You know what guy," Isabel said. "And why were you two holding hands? You just met him a few days ago."

"Are you my mother or my sister?"

"I'm your sister. And your friend. But..."

"Hang on," Mary said and walked to the refrigerator to grab a soda – to defer, delay, and deter.

"Y'all need anything? No? What about some food? I don't know about you, but I'm starving. Hey, how about we go out and get something to eat? My treat."

"Mare, what's going on?"

"What did Watson tell you?"

"A lot. I just couldn't understand him."

Watson smiled at Mary who chuckled after he told her. "That's pretty funny," she said to him, and to Isabel, "He says he was trying out his French. Apparently, he's been learning from an app on a Kindle I didn't know he could access."

Isabel looked at them one after the other and laughed when they did. "I can never tell if you two are joking or not. But y'all sure are a hoot to hang with."

"We do our best, Belle. Now, let's go get our eatin' on."

"Yeah, nice try. Spill it, girl."

Mary thought to twist the truth, wring out a watered down version that would satisfy Isabel's curiosity but keep the depth of what she felt to herself. In the end, except for the most intimate moments, she ended up sharing her heart.

"Wow," Isabel said after listening. "I mean... Wow."

"I know, right? It's ama..." Mary said and then stopped. "Why are you looking at me like that?"

"Mare..." Isabel began but didn't know how to finish.

"What? Tell me."

"It's just..."

Mary looked to Watson, but he didn't offer any support.

"I thought you would be happy for me, Belle," she said, disappointed and feeling foolish.

"I am. Really. And I'm so glad you shared this with me. But I'm also a little, I don't know... Scared?"

"Why? I'm not the first girl to like a boy, you know," Mary said, irritated and wishing she'd kept her mouth shut.

"No, but it's the first time *you've* liked one."

"So? What's wrong with that? Why are you raining on my parade?"

"I don't mean to. Sorry. If you only liked him, or really liked him, or even really, really liked him... But you don't. What happens if..."

Isabel didn't want to tell her how painful love could be when it let you down and left you alone. And lonely.

Mary saw her fretfulness for what it was and nodded. "I've already factored heartbreak into the equation. In fact, I'm running a few experiments on this *Crazy Little Thing Called Love*, as Queen put it – like at *first sight, better to have than not, splendored thing, yada yada and etcetera*."

"So, you're not going to get hurt then if it all falls apart?"

"I don't know. A little, maybe," Mary said, deceptively. Despite acting cool and clinical, she already knew how she'd feel if that were to happen.

"Uh- huh. Well, my other concern is... How old is he? Because that *boy* looks more like a man to me."

Watson chimed in with a , *Yeah, that.*

"I don't know," she said, which was true because she'd never asked, because if he'd confirmed what she suspected, she wouldn't have gotten to know him. Or hug and kiss him. Or let herself fall so deep, so fast.

"I'd say he's twenty-one, twenty-two," Isabel alleged.

"You think so?" Mary asked, afraid her face looked as flushed as it felt because she thought Michael might be as old as twenty-four. And she *still* spent time with him.

"Does he know how old *you* are?"

"It never came up."

"I'll tell you this," Isabel said. "You look and act much older than you are, that's for sure. But even if he's nineteen or twenty, you are still just..."

"Sixteen. Yeah, I get it."

"Have you two . . ."

"No! Of course not," Mary said, hoping her indignation was taken as anger rather than an admission she'd given the same thing some thought.

Isabel tried not to grin, but Mary's discomfort made her want to kid around like she did sometimes.

"I can't wait to see Dax's face when I tell him you have a man for a boyfriend."

"Don't you dare!" Mary's tone was harsh and hard.

And unexpected.

"I'm sorry, Belle," she said. "I didn't mean to be mean."

"I was only teasing. Like you do with Dax and Tasha."

"I know, sorry. It's just that I'm not sure how to tell him. Or if I should."

"But if you're going to keep seeing this guy, you'll have to. Won't you?" Isabel asked, troubled she would even think to hide him from Dax.

"You're right," Mary said, attempting to buy some time. "But *I'll* do it, not you. And not you, either."

Watson said, "Qui moi?" with a look that made her grin.

"Yes, you."

"So why is he here? Where's he from? Why don't you have him over so Watson and I can *third-degree* him?"

Mary answered all questions thrown at her, some fully, some not. It was easy to talk about Michael with Isabel.

But with Dax, she feared it would not be.

~~

"You're braver than your new daughter, cause she told me, 'No way, Jose,' when I asked *her*," I said.

"Well, I married you so I'd have to be, wouldn't I?"

Tasha winked from the back of the small Cessna as we climbed to our destination in wide concentric circles, with me up front next to the pilot and beside the door.

"It's magnificent," she said staring out the window, and I agreed. The blue-green water was mesmerizing and vast compared to the island keys that grew increasingly smaller as we soared ever higher.

"Two minutes," the pilot said at ten-thousand feet.

The tandem instructor hooked himself to Tasha and gave her a thumbs up. She responded with one of her own, letting him know she was good to go. Her eyes were full of adventure, and I sent her a wink and a grin.

"Door," the pilot called out and I turned the handle.

The cool air refreshed, and the view stunned as I leaned over to locate the dropzone. I held up five fingers to indicate degrees and moved them right so the pilot could adjust our position relative to the landing area. After scanning the sky for other planes, I swung my legs out, grabbed hold of the wing support, stood on the step, slid to the right, and then hung from the strut as Tasha was waddled to the doorway.

Her enthusiasm was evident as she grinned at me and peered down. And, when the instructor yelled, 'Ready, set, go,' off we went.

I think most people liken jumping out of an airplane to stepping off a tall building, but it's not like that. Oh sure, you're zipping through the air at a hundred twenty miles an hour, but it feels more like flying than falling.

And let me tell you, it's exhilarating!

Tasha was all smiles as the wind whipped at her face, and she waved as we fell through the wisp of a nearby cloud. The instructor gave her another thumbs up, and she nodded at a GoPro camera attached to his now damp wrist.

At five-thousand feet, he waved me off and pulled the pin. They were 'yanked' up when their parachute opened, and I kept fly-falling till my altimeter read three-thousand.

One of the neat things about skydiving is the parts of its sum. There's the ride to altitude, which is fun. The exit and its *mind over matter* decision to jump from a perfectly good airplane, is interesting. The *hair on fire* descent challenges and excites the senses, followed by an awe-inspiring quiet as you glide in the air and view the unbridled beauty of it all.

And then there's the landing.

What should have been a graceful transition from air to earth wasn't because I flared my canopy too late, which forced me to slide across the ground on my bottom instead of running out the momentum on my feet.

I could attribute it to being rusty, since I hadn't jumped in years, but that would be misleading because it wasn't my first time. In fact and unfortunately, *it* happened enough to be called a *butt scootin' boogie*, an embarrassment given the number of dives I had under my belt.

Luckily, Tasha was too high in the sky to recognize my foible and wouldn't be able to mock me later.

And I'd appreciate y'all not telling her.

~

The sun turned palm trees into shadows that stretched across my lounge chair, marking a beautiful end to another perfect day that would only get better as the night bloomed.

"Thanks," I said when Tasha brought me an unsolicited Coke float from the beach bungalow and set it down.

She nodded and lifted her face to the sky.

"Are you still up there?" I asked.

"Yes."

"Pretty cool, isn't it?"

"And then some," she agreed.

"You should try it In the dark."

"Oh, I'd like that!"

Her eagerness, and the ice cream soda, confirmed what I'd been thinking – as wives went, I'd lucked out big time.

"On the way back," she said, "I kept thinking how odd it was to be doing something as normal as riding around in a car after jumping out of an airplane. It felt surreal."

"I know what you mean. Hell, I still feel that way."

"You know what else I thought?"

"That I was too sexy for my jumpsuit?"

Her grin gave a hint of what she thought about *that*.

"It occurred to me that Mary would've been orphaned if the plane had crashed or the parachutes hadn't opened."

"Some people might say that's morbid thinking," I said, "but not me. Don't worry, in the event of my untimely death she'll be set. I've already made arrangements."

"Yes, I guess you would have, considering . . . Do you think she'd mind my adopting her, too?"

"Hmm, would she like having a multi-millionaire mom? I don't know. That might be a tough sell," I teased.

"No, really," she said and sat on my lap.

"She'd love it, Tash. So would I. The sooner the better. Then I can start telling her, *'If it were up to me, sweetie – but your mother said no, so...'*"

"Yeah, well, I plan on spoiling her rotten, so we'll see who has to say *no*."

She kissed my lips and settled her head on my shoulder. The sun said *later* and left a multi-colored sky in its wake. When the stars began to shimmer their nightly shine, Tasha told me she was quitting her job. I nodded but said nothing.

"You don't seem surprised."

"I figured you might," I said.

"How? It's not about the money."

"I know."

"Then what?"

"After you came back, I figured one of three things would happen. You would throw me in jail but still love me. You'd let me go but leave and still love me. Or you would find a way to stay and still love me but wouldn't be able to live with being a hypocrite because of your integrity. If you quit, you might find the ethical concerns more manageable. Or so you'd hope."

"I could've just stopped loving you, you know. Did you consider *that*?"

"Would that you could, but you didn't cause you can't," I said and gave her a *know it all* grin.

"You think you're so smart, don't you?" she retorted.

"Well, I married you, so I'd have to be. Wouldn't I?"

Tasha grinned and nuzzled my neck. Then whispered, "What am I thinking now, clever boy?"

"How much you'd like me to carry you to the hammock and have my way with you?"

"Good guess. Except, I'll be doing the ravishing."

~~

After an unending bout of tossing, turning, and thinking about all possible outcomes, Mary reached an unavoidable conclusion – Dax was an impediment to her happiness. The man who found her, saved her, loved and raised her, was now an obstacle to overcome.

That kind of thinking was all kinds of wrong, she knew, and could only cause problems. It was also unfair.

Damn it, though. She loved that boy!

More than Dax?

No, of course not.

In the abstract, she'd choose Dax over him every time. But her feelings for Michael were different.

New, unexplored, separate from anything she had ever known or felt. How could she just stop seeing him?

Or have him taken away from her.

She considered going around Dax. Tasha might have a better understanding of the situation and could be helpful in bringing him around. And if Michael were only a couple years older, she would have gone that route. But based on what he said the day they met, and after Google told her how old you needed to be to visit a blues bar in Georgia, Michael had to be at least as old as Isabel thought.

Tasha might be okay with it, seeing as how Mary wasn't a *real* sixteen year old. And, though she had her doubts, Dax might be as well . . .

She'd like to tell him what was going on and talk about dating but was afraid he would say *no way*, plain and simple. And even if he let her, there could be restrictions that might irritate and cause resentment. Suddenly, the thought of his *letting* didn't sit too well. And that bothered her, too.

'Your judgement is impaired by emotion, you know,' she told herself but didn't care. And that made her angry.

Careful not to wake Watson, Mary rolled out of bed and closed the door behind her. She sat on the sofa to stew and noticed the blinking light on her phone.

Well, crap.

Michael sent a text hours earlier asking if she'd check their private nook for his ring.

'I can't seem to find it,' he said, and Mary felt his pain. It was the only thing left of his *father* and meant more to him than words could express. When he'd tried to explain by the stream, the crack in his voice made her reach out to him.

Not willing to risk someone finding the ring before her, Mary tied her tennis shoes and stepped outside. The shorts and shirt she'd worn to bed wouldn't be her first choice to leave the house in, but she didn't want to wake anyone – or listen to reasons why she shouldn't go.

Besides, it was after midnight and no one was in sight.

She jogged rather than walk, trying to alleviate tension that robbed her of sleep and replace it with fatigue. Lights over the sidewalks lit most of the way, but the path to the nook was mostly shadows as the moon struggled to slip through the hanging limbs and leaves.

The nearby stream's melody put her mind at ease, and she hummed a few verses of its song. Upon reaching *their spot*, she smiled and closed her eyes a moment, reminiscing. But when Mary felt for the phone in her back pocket to use as a flashlight, it wasn't there. Neither was the pocket.

What the heck?

She'd heard people in love were prone to stupidity or subject to fits of random absentmindedness. And with the disturbing realization she got down on all fours.

Some of what she touched was prickly. Some hard and jagged, some soft and squishy. But eventually she found the ring, giving her a glimpse at the flip side of the love coin. It might make you forgetful, but it also drove you to do things you wouldn't even consider, like feeling poop in the middle of the night – which now felt more stupid than splendorous.

Maybe she was doing love wrong?

Mary tied the ring to her shoelace for lack of a pocket and headed back. As the sidewalk streetlight got closer, she saw boys on a bench along the path. It sounded like they'd been drinking, and she prepared to give a pleasant hello and a wide berth.

"Well, looky here," the taller one said, standing as she approached. "Damn, if you aren't a sweet slice of pie."

"Thanks," she told him before he blocked her way.

"I'll bet you have all the boys begging for it."

Having *what-iffed* the scenario, she smiled graciously. "Y'all have a good night, now."

"Hold up, girly-Q," he said, grasping as she walked past. "How about giving us a little taste?"

Mary whirled and smashed his nose with her forehead then kneed him in the crotch, seized his wrist after he'd let go of hers, spun underneath his arm, drove a foot to the side of his ankle, and, when he buckled, kicked him in the face so hard he fell ass-backward.

And just that quickly, the threat was neutralized. Until the other one started to move.

"If you sit still, I won't have to break your friend's arm," she said.

He responded by pulling a knife.

Mary twisted and then yanked like she'd been taught, separating the broken arm from the shoulder to ensure the boy at her feet would be incapacitated if he came to. When his buddy stepped toward her, she could've run but didn't, preferring to hurt him before he hurt somebody else.

He waved the knife in an attempt to scare her, and she peeled off the Tee-shirt to use as a defense. His eyeballing, though unplanned, worked to her advantage as she rushed forward and caught him by surprise, deflecting a wayward swing of the blade and capturing his wrist with the twisted shirt long enough to drive her heel into his solar plexus.

He jerked himself free of the *Tee* and stepped backward to catch his breath, stabbing at her when she followed. Mary shifted sideways and slid the jersey up to his armpit, turned, shoved her back against his, leaned forward and then pulled him up and over her shoulder.

When he crashed to the ground, she stomped the back of his head once, twice. After he lay slack a few seconds, she slipped on her shirt and picked up his weapon.

"Son of a bitch."

Her anger flared and she sank the honed edge into the back of his meaty thigh, leaving the sharp blade imbedded after it broke at the hilt.

"There's your knife back."

Mary slid the butt of it in his hand to make a point and checked for a pulse. He was alive but out cold, same as his friend. And like her, neither had ID or a cell phone.

"Great."

After a deep breath, she noted the ring still laced to her shoe and left with every intention of calling the campus cops from Isabel's. On the way, however, she changed her mind.

The thought of being more fodder for the nightly news was, by itself, enough to give her pause. It was attention she didn't want and exposure she didn't need. How long would it be before some psycho *came-a-calling* because she'd been on television one too many times?

But more than that, there was Dax.

She'd broken her promise to stay safe by utilizing the swarm of students when *out and about*. And though not said specifically, it included solitary late night strolls and long walks to isolated places with boys he knew nothing about. Might he view her actions as a violation of his trust?

Would it color his thoughts about Michael?

Her decision to *wait and see* was self-serving but still within the boundaries of doing what she thought was right. And, unless it became necessary, Dax didn't need to know.

If they went to the police, she would come forward and take the heat, confident of the outcome. She'd been verbally molested as well as physically detained, and no one would think it unreasonable to defend herself from the possibility of being raped, given the circumstance. Her age, in *this* case, would factor favorably, ironically.

And if they didn't, she was sure justice had been served. Their *punishment* had the potential of being a more effective deterrent to future assaults than a monetary fine or time in jail. Assuming they'd even be charged . . . *I didn't touch her. She bumped into me and then went bat-shit crazy!*

The iffy part of letting things play out was also the most bothersome because they could've done this before. And by letting them go, she ran the risk that someone, somewhere, needed those two identified, arrested, or both.

chapter eighteen

Hale Bedford.
Dominic first met him nine months ago in the late early hours of New Year's Eve after being called to an incident at the Indian Pass raw bar. Dax had kept a woman from being attacked by three men, Bedford being one of them, and in doing so, shot and killed Hale's twin sister – after she'd hit him in the head with a crowbar from behind. The assaulted woman turned out to be Hale's wife and claimed she neither screamed for help nor needed saving, but a video refuted her denial and no charges were filed against Dax

Then, on the fourth of July, Hale's best friend Brett, one of the men waiting in line to rape his wife that New Year's night, was found dead on a lonely lane with a broken neck, wearing a hooded mask and holding a stun gun. It appeared he meant to attack someone but got himself killed instead.

Bedford blamed Dax, but he was playing a gig at the time of Brett's death. And now, Hale was dead, killed with the same gun as the man in the trunk.

Dom came to Georgia to find some answers and started with the detective who'd caught the case.

"Looks like a professional hit. One in the heart, one in the head. Must have used a suppressor. In and out without making a sound, according to the wife."

"Where was she when it happened?" Dominic asked.

"Upstairs. Said she and her husband were working out. But I don't think it was yoga, if you know what I mean."

"What do you mean?"

"The officer who took her statement found a drink on a stand near the Lazy-Boy and a *sex machine* in the middle of the room. It looked like he was watching a live peepshow."

"I see," Dominic said, trying not to let the image sink in. "Does she know when or why Hale went downstairs?"

"Said she didn't notice he'd left. Thinks it was at least a half-hour or more before she found him."

"Do you have any reason to suspect she's involved?"

"Not at the moment. She doesn't seem the type. Have you ever met her?"

Dominic nodded. "A couple times. When her sister-in-law was killed. And then their friend, Brett Vander. Do you know if they were involved in anything shady?"

"Well, rumor was they were into *swinging*, if you know what I mean," he said with a wink.

Dom nodded again, knowing *they* were into more than that based on what he'd seen on Brett's phone after finding him dead. "I meant was there any criminal activity."

"Some scrapes back in the day, but nothing since then. Your man in the trunk, though, had a pretty long sheet."

"Did Mr. Bedford know Terry Lamb?" Dominic asked.

"Hale didn't strike me as that kind of man, but who knows these days? I wouldn't have believed what I heard about his wife until a friend of a friend's uncle said he'd had her one night at their house. Hard to believe a woman that fine would give herself up like that. But, like I said, who knows these days?"

Dominic usually questioned the veracity of that kind of information, but the grapevine had it right this time. "Has Mrs. Bedford identified Mr. Lamb?"

"Haven't been out there yet to show her a photo."

"I'm heading there when I leave here. Mind if I do it?" Dominic asked. He didn't need permission, but it didn't cost anything to stay on the man's good side if possible.

"Go ahead. Just keep me informed if anything breaks."

"Will do. Thanks." Dominic stood and shook his hand. "One last thing. Did the officer ask about security cameras?"

"He did. They don't."

~

When she answered the door, Dominic saw remnants of her beauty still entwined in her worn and tattered weave.

"Mrs. Bedford? I'm Detective Greer, from Florida. May I come in?"

"I remember you."

"Yes, Ma'am."

"You want to talk about Hale?"

"Yes, Ma'am. If that's alright."

Barbara turned and left the door open for him to follow. When he closed it, she motioned him to the sofa.

"Would you like something to drink? Some lemonade or sweet tea, perhaps?"

"Yes, Ma'am. Sweet tea. If it's not too much trouble."

"It's no trouble, Detective. Excuse me."

Normally he would've passed but figured she might be less inclined to toss him out too quickly if he were more a guest than an intruder. Her southern sensibilities should give him a good fifteen-twenty minutes. He stood when she returned, took the tray from her, set it on the coffee table, handed her a glass, and then sat when she did.

"Thank you."

"Thank *you*," he said and raised his glass.

They sat quietly and drank their tea, neither in a hurry.

"You must give your mother my thanks."

"For what, Ma'am?"

"For raising her son to be such a courteous man."

Dominic didn't bother to tell her it was more his father but said *Thank you* and *I will*.

"Hale used to treat me that way, in the beginning . . ." she said, nearly to herself. "How can I help you, Detective."

After offering a preliminary, 'Sorry for your loss,' he got right to it. "Do you know if your husband was involved in anything that could have gotten him killed? In St. Vincent maybe? Or anywhere else, for that matter."

"You mean drugs or the like?"

"Yes, let's start there."

"I didn't know what all he was into and he didn't talk to me about business, so I couldn't say for sure. But no, I don't think so. We never used drugs or had it around the house. We drank, though." She tried to smile but failed miserably. "Why St. Vincent?"

"The gun that killed your husband was also used in a murder there. Have you heard of a man named Terry Lamb? Perhaps y'all knew him."

She didn't recall knowing him and shook her head.

"I have a picture," he said, and she looked at it.

His face was familiar to her, unlike most who were not. Hale had *loaned* her to him as if she were a pair of hedge clippers, and he'd used her in ways both loathed and loved. Barb might have blushed if she had any dignity left.

"I met him once."

"Where?"

"Here at the house. Hale had him over. He introduced himself as John Doe. I guess he thought he was funny."

"Was he?"

"Not really," she said, thinking of all he'd made her do.

"By any chance would you know when that was?"

Barbara knew exactly. It was the night before an orgy in early August where Hale made sure she was everyone's beginning, end, and depraved in between. But she wasn't going to tell him that and said it was sometime in late July.

"Terry Lamb was known to kill people for money, and I'm wondering if Hale might have hired him," Dominic said.

"Why would he do that?"

"Let me answer your question with another, and please forgive me for being blunt. Did Hale or Brett snatch women off the streets for sex?"

"Good heavens, no. They'd have no reason to."

"How can you be so sure?"

After looking him in the eye, she said what she knew to be true. "Because their needs were well met. Believe me."

"Then why did Brett have a mask and a stun gun?"

"Hale thought the guitar player put those there to cover his tracks after he'd killed him."

"Is that what *you* think?"

Dominic saw she didn't but waited for her to respond.

"I walked into the end of a conversation Hale and Brett were having the night he died. I didn't hear what was said, but they appeared conspiratorial. After meeting with you at the morgue, I suspected Hale knew something about what Brett was up to. When I asked, he said no, but..."

"What did you ask?"

"If they'd been trying to hurt that man's little girl."

"Why would you think that?"

"Palmer killed his sister, and Hale hated him. He would say things that made me afraid for him, but I didn't think he would do anything about it. Until Brett ended up dead. After that, Hale didn't say another word about Dax Palmer."

"Didn't you think that odd?" he asked.

"At the time, I was just glad to stop hearing his hate, but now that you mention it... Why would he do that?"

Dominic shrugged but had a thought he kept to himself. "Who knows, really."

Barb had her thoughts too but declined to share them. "Are Mr. Palmer and his daughter doing alright? I saw on the news that her and Detective Williams were held hostage the same night Hale was murdered."

"Yes. They're okay."

"That poor girl... As if she hasn't already been through enough. But she sure can take care of herself, can't she?"

"That she can," Dominic said and rose from the couch. "Thank you, Mrs. Bedford, for your time and hospitality. You've been most gracious, and I surely do appreciate it."

"There you go again, being respectful and polite," she said. "I surely appreciate *that*. And please, call me Barbara."

"Yes, Ma'am."

~~

Alexi stood at the door listening, not wanting to intrude as he had earlier when he walked in on Miko beating the shit out of the dummy. Every punch, kick, and elbow had landed heavily and would have made short work of anyone who'd been on the receiving end. He'd seen him work the *rubber man* before, but not so intensely. And while his quiet, controlled aggression was directed at the inanimate object, it made Alexi nervous all the same.

Perhaps he'd been upset over the District Court's ruling that froze eighty-seven million dollars pending a hearing, or because three subordinates were making noise about going into the trafficking business for themselves instead of lying low like they'd been instructed. It could also be a festering revenge for the man that killed his uncle. If the latter, Alexi might have something to help scratch that itch.

"Come in, Alexi," Miko said when he knocked.

"Palmer was scheduled to play at a honky-tonk outside of Thomasville the night Dimitri was killed. The manager said he got there sometime around midnight about two and a half hours late, apologized, and then said he was heading back home while his van was *functional*. He'd called earlier about other issues he was having with it."

Miko sat up straighter. "Interesting. It puts him in the area, but he'd have to haul ass to make it in time to kill them all and take the girls."

"Yes, but why would he? And how could he?"

"Let's take your last question first. He lied about the trouble he had with the van."

"Okay," Alexi said. "But . . ."

"You're about to ask another *why*. We'll circle back to that. As for the reason he'd kill Uncle Dimi, there are only three plausible explanations. One being to save those girls."

"Do you believe that? I mean, it seems far-fetched."

"I agree. Still, it's a possibility, though not as probable. Statistically or coincidentally."

"Coincidentally?"

"It was also the night Anthony sent his men to kill that detective, and the girl when she showed up. And as we saw on the news, Palmer is very fond of them and might not take their being threatened lying down. If he *is* the one, it makes more sense that's the *why*."

"But he was here in Georgia hours before that. You'd think that once he got the heads up from home, he would have hauled-ass in his lied-about vehicle earlier."

"Yes, it is a puzzle. That's why I want you to have our FBI spy get all the calls made to and from his cell phone that night, ASAP. If he tries to delay, remind him what's at stake."

"Yes, sir."

"Have him find out when those girls were dropped off in Wewahitchka, as well. That should help with the timeline. Maybe then we'll know, one way or the other."

Alexi nodded and said, "What's the third reason he'd go after your uncle? If he did."

"Palmer could be working for one of our competitors, perhaps under the FBI's radar. Or even with their support."

"And the circle back thing... Why lie about the van? How could he know he would need an alibi before he knew Anthony was involved or who he worked for?"

Miko tipped his head, giving him respect in the gesture. It was the classic *riddle, mystery, enigma* conundrum.

"Exactly, Alexi."

~~

Brian Murphy voiced his suspicions and confirmed Dax Palmer had played on the Saturday night before the murder.

"Alright then," Tim said. "Let's start with the leash."

"Coroner says the strangulation marks are consistent."

"But no one you've talked to remembers seeing one?"

"No," Brian said.

"And the leash you saw the day you talked to him at the beach was a..."

"Chain type, yes."

"Okay," Tim said. "Talk me through the timeline."

"He arrives at the Blue Moon after the lunchtime rush. The place is almost empty, and the waitress lets the canine in because it's hot out. She's a dog person."

"I'm more of a cat person myself," Tim mused. "They're anti-social and aloof. Kind of like you."

"Uh-huh. While he was eating, three of the *Biggie Blues* band members come in and begin to setup before the night's performance. Then they get a call from their guitar-playing frontman, he can't make it. Palmer overhears them freaking out, offers to help and *saves their asses,* they said."

"What time is this?"

"Around two, two-thirty," Brian said. "And they spend the rest of the day into evening practicing and bonding."

"He didn't leave the Moon all that time?"

"No. Not until just before showtime when Palmer and Watson went for a walk."

"Watson?" Tim asked.

"The dog."

"Now that's cute, what with Palmer being a *Moriarity*. How long were they gone?"

"Two of the *Biggie's* said around ten, fifteen minutes. The other was peeing and didn't have a clue," Brian said.

"So, he killed him before stopping in for lunch and then hung around to help out a few fellow musicians? Ballsy. Was the AC cranked up to throw off the TOD? Fingerprints"

"The temp was low but not too, and only Eddie's were on the thermostat. But he didn't clock out of work till after five, when Palmer and the boys were practicing."

"So he killed him on the way home after they closed the place down then."

Brian nodded and then shook his head.

"Except, as luck would have it, a *Biggie* pulled out of the parking lot after he did and saw him heading up the Tyndall bridge on *his* way home."

"Maybe Palmer waited until he wasn't being followed, and then doubled back?" Tim posed.

"I thought so, too. Until I checked footage from cameras that monitor the traffic on that bridge. I even considered his going home and coming back later in a different vehicle. But I didn't see any on the video that were registered to him."

Tim raised his eyebrows. "So let me get this straight; you're suggesting Palmer may have been on a recon mission and then casually took advantage of a chance encounter to create an opportunity to kill Johnson in less time than seems plausible, all on the spur of the moment?"

"I admit it sounds far-fetched."

"No shit, Sherlock," Tim said. "I assume you've walked to the house and back?"

"Yes. It's possible. Barely."

"Well, I suppose we could recanvass the area, pass his picture around, see if anyone recognizes him. Or his dog."

"It was very dark, and no one saw anything at the time, according to the report. And I'm afraid an identification now could be tainted because he's been seen on the TV recently. Might do more harm than good."

"What harm?"

"To the case," Brian answered. "And to Palmer."

"What do you care about him, if he's a serial killer?"

"*If* is what I'm trying to clarify. We can't willy-nilly this."

"Well, even *if* you could get a search warrant, which I doubt, if he's as smart as you say that leash is long gone. But your theory doesn't factor in evidence to the contrary."

"Such as?" Brian said, knowing what Tim would say.

"Eddie Johnson's table was set for two, with a potful of boiled shrimp on the stove, wine, glasses, silverware. Now, I suppose Palmer could've arranged the scene, but do you really think he had that kind of time?"

"No. Also, Eddie was killed five feet from his front door, facing away from it. Meaning our guy wasn't already inside. And here's the kicker – he had a gun in the waistband of his pants but tried to run instead of using it. How come?"

"Too afraid to deal, maybe? Did Palmer seem that kind of scary to you?" Tim asked.

"No, he was pleasant as could be. But remember when the camerawoman tried to get too close to his kid? His eyes were dead serious, and I don't doubt for a second he'd have shot her if she'd taken another step. Maybe Eddie saw that same look and bolted."

"So, he opens the door to the wrath of God and gets his Grandma killin' ass handed to him in a matter of seconds?"

"Something like that."

"I don't know, Murph. Makes more sense he turned his back on a dinner guest who had it in for him, cause this thing with Palmer is circumstantial at best, almost fantastical. I mean, I've seen you solve many a crime with a hunch and a smile, but this one seems, as you like to say, *most unlikely*. Maybe there is more meat on the bones of the other cases? Then you could toss this one in with those and . . ."

Brian heard without hearing as Tim continued to talk. He was right, of course. Other than his being nearby, there was nothing to link Palmer to Eddie Johnson.

Not a damned thing.

But despite Tim's valid skepticism, he didn't share it. In fact, Brian began to believe Dax pointed him at Eddie for this very reason – to dissuade him from looking any further.

How will you find proof somewhere else, if not here?

Palmer's voice in his head didn't sound cocky. Nor was there an implied challenge or air of superiority in its tone. He was 'Just the facts, Ma'am' telling it like it was.

"We'll have to see about that,' Brian told himself.

chapter nineteen

We met them at the crossroads tween here and home, exchanged hugs and handed out souvenirs – trinkets from Key West for the girls and Fiesta Key sausages for Watson.

When I asked about any strange or unusual happenings while we were gone, Isabel smiled and shook her head when Mary said a flying saucer landed on campus because an alien wife made her *I don't need a star map* husband pull over and ask for directions.

Isabel teared up as we said our goodbyes, and I told her to park her car and come home with us.

"I'll bring you back whenever you like."

"Thanks, but I'll be okay," she said. "I have studying to do and an early class in the morning. Maybe I'll come see y'all next week, if that's alright?"

"You are familia, Fluffy, and our casa es su casa," I said.

"Thanks. I might not speak French like some canines I know," she said with a grin, "but I *do* know some Spanish."

"Watson speaks French?"

The girls laughed at my confusion.

~

Mary listened as they talked about fishing, skydiving, scuba, the Keys, and their beach house in Marathon. It was obvious they missed her and wished she'd seen this or been there for that. Their affection wrapped her up safe and snug, and, for a moment, she thought it a perfect time to . . .

Watson nudged and said, *Go on, now,* but she shook her head, feeling estranged from them for the first time. Sensing her sadness and deeming it unnecessary, Watson told them about Michael, to her chagrin. But when Dax asked what he said, she told him a canard.

"He's thanking y'all for the sausages."

Tasha said he was more than welcome, and Mary gave Watson a sour look that came back with interest.

'What the heck are you doing?' he said with his eyes.

She turned to the window and asked the same thing. In less than a half hour, she had *thrice* evaded the truth, a word from an Easter story she remembered about Peter's denial of knowing Jesus three times.

Only here, it was much worse because it was Dax. And mincing words didn't change the fact she was dangerously close to lying to him. If she hadn't already.

But couldn't what she'd given as Watson's response be classified as a white lie, a no harm no foul sort of *wink-wink* kind of thing? Surely, Dax had done the same many times.

As for not mentioning Michael or the boys she'd beaten, those were more a fib of omission than an outright lie and didn't apply to their honesty pact. It was no different than Dax not telling her who, why, or how many he'd put down.

Right?

Her heart grew heavy as she tried to justify her deceit, knowing it was wrong but hard-pressed to see another way.

How about just telling him the truth?

Before it was too late.

~~

Ecstatic was the word that best described how Jeri felt. Finally a name could be given to one of the children pulled from Anatovich's ghoulish garden.

Thank God for dental records, she thought, wanting to share the good news with Tasha but not in the last hours of her honeymoon. She'd call later, maybe have her thank Dax for making it possible. If he hadn't saved those girls...

Jeri's grin reflected her silliness. She didn't believe he killed those men, but the idea he *might have* flitted around in her brain like a yellow-fly that wouldn't stop biting – even though she hadn't found anything in his background to lend credence to her mind's insistence. Hell, he hadn't even been issued so much as a parking ticket in all his live long days.

Dax was squeaky clean. Still, the fly persisted, irritated, and she wished for a swatter in the worst way.

murder in the light of day

Why not just ask, gauge his reaction? Then she'd know. Or would she?

Jeri didn't know him the way Tasha did, but one thing was certain – Dax didn't rattle. And she knew that because she tried to ruffle him every chance she got, just for the heck of it. He was too cool by half, and his *humble* arrogance made her want to knock him down a peg. So far, though . . . If he were the killer, she'd have her hands full finding out.

Tasha was easier to read. If *she* were a killer, or thought Dax might be, it would be written on her face. But then she wouldn't have married him if he were. That, Jeri knew.

Perhaps the most effective way to quash the buzzing in her head would be to show those rescued girls his picture, see *their* reaction.

Maybe she'd visit the red-haired cutie in Wewahitchka next time she went to Tasha's?

~~

The first thing Mary noticed after we brought our stuff in from the van was the door to my bedroom.

It was new. It was thick. It was soundproof.

As were the walls.

She grinned but didn't say anything, and Tasha blushed without meaning to.

"Mind if I give it a try?" Mary asked.

"Be my guest," I told her.

She followed Watson inside and shoved it shut.

"Why didn't you tell me?" Tasha said.

"It's a wedding present. The recording studio quality of quiet will allow us to do what we do without disturbing the *neighbors*. I thought of installing a chandelier for you to hang from on those really wild nights, but now I'm thinking stripper pole instead."

Tasha's hue deepened, not from embarrassment, or so I told myself, but from all the imagined sensualities to come.

"It must have cost a small fortune, Dax, because I don't hear a thing. Unless she's just whispering to be cute."

I opened the door to a screaming, barking cacophony of sound that included my headboard banging against the wall and shrill springs from a bed bounced like a trampoline.

183

"Well? Does it work?" Mary asked.

"Uh-huh," I said, enjoying her amusement. While the purchased quiet gave Tash and I a much needed privacy, its primary purpose was to save Mary from having to hear us.

"Thanks, " she said.

"What makes you think it's for you? Maybe it's because of all the racket you make in the morning that wakes me up."

"You mean when I'm making breakfast for you?" Her grinned widened and she winked at Tasha.

"Do you *have* to crack the eggs so hard?" I asked. "And why do you let the bacon sizzle so loudly? Geez-o-Pete."

"I might ask the same thing about the racket *you* make, what with the grunting and groaning, oohing and ahhing. Not to mention the directions."

Instead of the rock and a hard place, though applicable, I was caught between feeling awkward and alright. I didn't believe she had heard any of what she said because I'd been careful to keep that particular *sizzling* to a bare minimum.

"Directions?" I asked, too curious not to.

"'There. Oh, yes. That's good. Right there. Oohh... Yes.'"

I glanced at Tasha who was red as a beet but as cool as a cucumber.

"Honey, I'm afraid you misunderstood. We were just hanging a picture on the wall, and Dax needed help getting it straight before he pounded in the nail."

"Nail, huh?" Mary said. "Good one, Tash."

"Thanks."

"Well, the door's a twofer."

"How do you mean?" Tasha asked.

"It not only keeps y'all from being heard, but me, too."

I knew where she was going before her twinkle said so. Mary was a shit, for sure, but damned if I didn't like the hell out of her.

"Just so you know," I said, trying but failing to be deadly serious, "if that ever happens, somebody is likely to get shot. And it might not be *the boy* you try to sneak into your room."

"Why, Dax. Whatever..."

"Save it," I said, still amazed at how innocent she looked when wearing her *Who me* mask. "But you're right. I'll have to leave the door open to hear the house as we sleep."

"And how are you going to listen if you're asleep?"

"You know what I mean. Smartass."

Mary *Who me*'d me, again.

~

After dinner and doing the dishes, we relaxed by having an 'un-plugged' night of music, acoustic guitars only. The girls graciously sang my most requested song, *Summertime*, twice, and I kept my part of the bargain by keeping my solo's in check. An hour later, we finished with an old tune from a movie that starred George Clooney as a Soggy Bottom Boy. Watson was in rare voice as the *Dog of Constant Sorrow*, and we gave him props and treats.

I was closer to the table and grabbed Mary's cell when it rang, thinking it was from Isabel. Seeing it wasn't, I gave her the phone and she set it down, saying they'd leave a voicemail. Before I could ask, Tasha got a call of her own.

"Hi, Dom. Yeah, we made it back. Oh, it was great..."

"So who's Michelle?" I said to Mary before heading into the kitchen for some ice-cold soda cocktails.

"Someone I ran into on the FSU campus."

"Literally?"

"Figuratively," she replied.

"Is she nice? Funny? A friend?"

"Yes. I think so. Maybe."

"Come on in here and tell me about her. Michelle is one of my all-time favorite names for a girl. It can also be used for a boy. Did you know that? Except there's only one L, and it's pronounced *Mik-el*. And you have to be Italian, I think."

As the daughter of a contingency planner, Mary used *Michelle* as an alias for just this possibility, otherwise the jig might be up before she was ready to be... Jigged? She only meant to keep Michael hidden until the time was right, the moment most favorable.

What about now?

"Dax, there's something I..."

"Oh no," Tasha groaned. "Yes. I'll let him know. Thanks for calling, Dom. Yes, I'll see you tomorrow. Bye."

She glanced at Mary, and then called out to Dax.

"What is it?"

"It's the woman you saw. The one in the store with the bruises. She's dead."

"How? When?"

"Dax..."

"Just tell me."

"Last night. Her husband beat her to death."

~~

Miko took the thin folder from Alexi and motioned him to sit down. "From our FBI informer?"

"Yes, sir."

"And?"

"Palmer might be our guy."

"Lay it out for me," Miko said, leaning forward, elbows on his knees.

"Do you know about how cell-towers ping our phones? How they can be used to track someone?" Alexi said.

"Of course."

"Well, Palmer's pinging that night was intermittent."

"Explain."

"Basically, a phone will signal the nearest cell site every eight hours or so, unless you're on the move," Alexi said. "But the phone has to be on. If not..."

"He turned it off?"

"Repeatedly."

"Can we know when and where?"

Alexi nodded. "To a degree. The phone was shut off by his house before sundown, so it couldn't be tracked until a tower south of Blountstown got pinged when he called the blues bar and told the manager he had to change a flat tire. Then the cell shut off again."

"Maybe he left home with a low battery and didn't have a charger with him," Miko said.

"It's possible, but I haven't told you the interesting part. He calls an hour later some sixty miles away saying he's now having problems with his vehicle – won't start, won't stay running when it does. And it's another two hours before the phone is on again, five miles from the bar. He calls his kid, talks a few minutes, then stops to apologize to the manager and tells him he better 'get home while the getting's good.'"

"That's not very encouraging, Alex. Or very interesting. Unless..."

Alexi smiled and told him the rest.

"A few miles later, the phone is shut off for the last time. But he's not heading south to Florida. He's heading north."

"To my uncle's,' Miko said, rising to his feet.

"Yes. And the phone wasn't turned back on until he was almost to St. Vincent, down SR-71. Only a few miles from Wewahitchka where Dimitri's girls were dropped off."

Miko's grin was a malevolent sneer. He wanted it to be true, needed it to be. The pressure cooker of his rage began to whistle, and the doubts of Palmer's actual guilt gave way to murderous thoughts of revenge.

~~

Tasha's hand looked for him in the dark, but he wasn't there. She'd fallen asleep waiting for Dax to come to bed and was chased from a dream that left her unsettled.

Like an olde time town crier, the ceiling fan proclaimed that all was well, but she didn't believe it. Something felt out of sorts, and she turned it off. It was quiet, like the silence you'd hear inside a coffin or crypt. Then she remembered the room was newly soundproofed and her fingers searched the night stand for the control to the door.

"Dax and his remotes," she chuckled. When asked, he'd said, 'Why get out of a warm bed and walk eight feet when you can use your finger instead. It's more efficient, not lazy.'

After finding the right button, the door opened about a foot and she heard him sitting in his lounger – or rather its squeak from being rocked. The slow and steady rhythm was soothing, and she propped her head to listen.

He had been unusually quiet after hearing the news of Mrs. Turley, preferring to walk than talk. The colored lights from the alarms flashed inside the house as he journeyed up and down the driveway for over an hour before sitting on the back deck in the dark. Mary said she'd rarely seen him so withdrawn, and Tasha took her advice and left him alone, going to bed sometime after Mary and Watson.

But as the big chair rocked slowly back and forth, she recalled Mary telling how the cadence of its squeak led her to suspect Dax of planning to, 'mete out a needed justice.'

A queasy feeling came over her as she broke into a cold damp sweat, worried there might be murder on his mind.

He wouldn't do that. Not now, not after he'd promised. Still, Tasha got angry, thinking she'd leave him on the spot if he broke his word. Then, other thoughts followed.

What if the things he'd done wasn't an aberration of his character but an integral part of it? Could he come to resent her because of his promise? And by restricting his need to do what he believed right, however wrong she thought his methods were, was she inadvertently doing him harm?

Dax sometimes said right and wrong were relative, and for the first time she took those words to heart.

He didn't know Lisa Turley from Eve and yet took her death personally. Enough to do something serious about it. Except for the fact that *something* was homicidal, it gave rise to an incompatible perspective.

What if his actions served a purpose?

Yes, it was illegal, and she couldn't be a party to it. But there were undeniable silver linings to his dark cloud. Good people got to keep living – like herself, Mary, the three girls saved from appalling depravity. And bad people were kept from continuing to feed on the good.

Maybe he needed to do what he did?

And maybe she needed to let him go.

chapter twenty

Dominic's effort to multi-task didn't go as planned. His attempt to fill the cup from a thermos was successful, but his vision was fairly impaired as he held the doughnut with his teeth. So when Mary beeped as she drove by with her trailer in tow, he spilled coffee on his pants and bit down on the confection, which fell from his lips to the floor.

Dammit!

The good thing, the coffee was only mildly hot. The bad, the donut was now sandy from the floormat. As it was his last, and the one he'd wanted most, he dusted off the fritter as best he could and gingerly chewed while keeping an eye out some fifty yards ahead.

He glanced at his watch, careful to transfer the cup to the other hand first before spilling its contents on himself a second time. Feeling stupid, as well as clumsy, Dominic wondered what the heck he was doing there. Or more to the point, why he didn't just head up to their house and talk to them together, get this straightened out and done with?

But his cop's intuition said it was better to speak to Dax alone, without anything or anyone, like Tasha, interfering with his getting at the truth.

He'd rather not have to say her new husband might be a murderer until he had more to go on than an inkling. And questioning him would help his gut make up its mind – like it did a few weeks ago when Tasha had him come in for an interview after Hale Bedford blamed Dax for killing his friend. They'd only done it to *check* that box, and Dominic had no doubt at the time he was clean. He had a strong alibi.

And it was Dax.

But now something seemed to be *amiss*, as his favorite detective would say. And, while Dom lacked Holmes' keen perception, he could, on occasion, understand how two plus three sometimes equaled four.

'Or so you purport,' he told himself, pleased at using the toilet-papered *word of the day* in a sentence but unsure of its usefulness. Less pompous folk said, 'claim.' Or 'assert' if they were feeling fancy.

Anyway, with Bedford's hatred being *two*, and his dead acquaintance in the trunk a *three*, was Dax a four, or a five? And if a four, could Hale Bedford be right about Brett? That would add what, another four? Or five? So, two plus three would equal ten then. Or was it eight? Nine?

It was sad but true that Dominic did not have a head for numbers, and in rubbing a frowned brow he nearly missed seeing Tasha pull out of the driveway and turn toward town in the opposite direction from where he sat waiting.

"Hell's bells," he said and started the engine. "Let's go see where Dax fits into this confounded equation."

~

When the *Knocking on Heaven's Door* gate alarm sang, I pretended Tasha must have missed me terribly after only a few minutes apart, because that's how I rolled. I continued to Saran-wrap the leftover breakfast, wondering how to talk her into doing the dishes before she took off again.

Not that I minded doing them. In fact, I found a great deal of satisfaction in the act itself. But there was something about her standing at the sink with soapy, sudsy hands that made me want to stand behind her and *slowly* . . .

A knock at the door interrupted my makeshift fantasy before I could loosen the apron strings wrapped around her otherwise naked body. In retrospect, I should've gone *fastly*.

Dominic stood on the porch, waving a hand around to keep the biting gnats, or No-See-Ums, at bay.

"Hey, Dom. Come on in."

"Thanks. Damned critters. What the hell good're they?"

"I hear you. What's up? Tash just left, I'm afraid."

"Actually, I'd like to talk with *you*, if it's alright."

"Sure," I said. "Do you mind doing it in the kitchen?"

"No problem."

I asked if he was still hungry and got a stare in return.

murder in the light of day

"Why do you say that?" he said.

"That looks like doughnut residue in your moustache, and I have French toast, eggs, and bacon that needs eating."

"Well, as long as you're buying," Dom said, taking a seat.

"Coffee?" I asked.

"Please."

I poured a full cup and set it next to the maple syrup.

"Butter?"

He said he was watching his weight, and then poured a small pond of the sweet liquid over his toast.

"So what can I do you for?" I said in a down-homey way, scrubbing the iron skillet soaking in the sink. Whatever this was going to be, the dishes still needed doing.

"A lawyer for one of the Panama City TV stations spoke to the City Attorney about pressing charges. You vandalized one of their news vans?"

"I 'disabled' it to keep them from following Mary to FSU and us to the Keys. I first asked them nicely not to, but they declined. So . . ."

"That's what I figured when the captain asked about it. He understands. So does the C.A. And as long as you take care of this, that will be the end of it."

Dominic pulled an envelope from the inside pocket of his jacket and laid it on the table. I asked him what *this* was and rinsed the skillet in hot water before drying it.

"The bill."

I nodded. "Seems like a reasonable request. Is it?"

"A couple of valve stems, tow truck, half-a-day's pay for the crew, and their lunch."

"Where did they dine? Sunset Grill or Burger King?"

"They got a couple of pizzas out at the Trading Post."

"Good call. I love those. Especially the thin crust, meat lovers special."

"No argument there. It's a tasty snack, for sure."

I grinned at Dom calling a pizza a snack. He was a big man, pudgy but not fat by any means. But clearly one man's meal was another's entrée.

"Do you know a Terry Lamb?" he asked before shoving a forkful in his mouth.

"The name doesn't ring a bell. Who is he?"

"Our dead man in the trunk."

His *our* could have been a folksy idiom or a prelude to an interrogation. I took it as the latter and went with it

"And do we know if our guy had anything to do with what happened at Tash's?" I asked casually, as one would.

"I'm beginning to think not."

Dominic took a swallow from his cup and looked at me in what I'm sure he thought was an attempt to get a reaction or a response. I gave him a *Hmm...* and started to wash the silverware.

"I think he might have been here for you," he said.

"Me? Why?" My inflection leaned more toward curious than concern, striking a suitable balance between the two.

"Lamb served time on a murder-for-hire conviction a few years back, and Hale Bedford's wife says he was at their house a few days before turning up in the trunk. She also said Bedford hated your guts, but you probably knew that."

I considered what he said as one might and then replied accordingly, with one part surprise and two parts disbelief.

"He sent someone to kill me? That seems a bit extreme, don't you think? What did Hale say when you talked to him? And how'd his guy end up dead?"

I saw confusion in his eyes and mentally patted myself on the back for sowing it. It's not like I hadn't thought this all through.

"*Hale* was unavailable for questioning, because the gun that killed Lamb was used to kill *him* the night you went to Georgia to play your gig. And as for how his guy got himself dead, I was thinking you might be able to help me with that."

I almost smiled at his audacity in almost accusing me. However the show must go on, they say, so I played my part.

"I'm not sure what help I could . . ." After a moment's pause, I said, "Wait, you're not suggesting I had something to do with this, are you?"

"Did you?"

Dominic's eyes bore into me and this time I grinned, appreciating his directness. He liked to dot I's and cross T's. You have to respect a man like that.

And be careful how you tread around him.
"Uh, no, Dom. But I think you already know that."
"Do I?"

I gave a chuckle in response to his dour expression and took a seat at the table, drying my hands with the dishtowel.

"You know, I was kidding a while back when I said I was always available for questioning as a murder suspect after you and Tash asked me about Brett Vander. But you don't seem to be joking, so let me help put your mind at ease."

"Go ahead," he said with both elbows on the table, as serious as a clichéd heart attack.

"I'll start with the obvious – if someone came here to do me or Mary harm, I'd kill them. End of story. But it would be in self-defense. And I wouldn't haul their bloody body off my property, even if I knew their car was up the road. Why would I? That's the same bullshit Bedford told you when he accused me of killing his friend. But more to the point is the fact that I was gone to play a gig in Georgia, remember?"

"You could have killed him before you left."

"Why? How? His car wasn't there when I left."

"So you say." Dominic raised an offset eyebrow.

"Okay, let's say I'm lying," I said, which, in fact, was true. "Do you think I killed a man sitting in his vehicle because I thought he might be there to kill me, and then said, 'Shit, maybe I should have confirmed it first,' before shoving him in the trunk to cover my ass? Or perhaps I pulled over out of an abundance of caution to ask a total stranger minding his own business if he was there to murder me or mine."

While I'd said it to sound ridiculous, that was the gist of what actually happened.

Dominic stared at me with some scorn but shrugged his shoulders in a way that suggested my point was taken.

"Will you tell me," he said, pulling a small notebook and an even smaller pencil from his jacket, "everything you did that night? Starting with when you left the house."

It was all downhill after that, in my estimation, because I'd prepared for just such an encounter as this.

"Do you want more coffee? Or a soda?" I asked, getting up to grab one for myself.

"No, thanks."

I poured an Orange Crush into an ice-filled glass and sat down to spin my yarn. The secret to telling falsehoods was to present them honestly, being specific in some details but vague in others, mindful to address the salient points with a fair degree of sincerity. There was an art to it. And if not a Rembrandt, I was at least a Picasso.

After my alleged tale of automotive woe, Dom stopped taking notes and lifted his head. "Unbelievable."

"Tell me about it," I said and took his plate to the sink. "The van would run, then it wouldn't, then it would again. It was frustrating, believe me."

"I mean that's a lot of out of the blue problems the night Bedford was killed while you were up in Georgia. Don't you think that's kinda funny?"

Dominic wasn't talking about a *Ha-Ha* kind of hilarity, and while he seemed to be serious, I laughed it off.

"What's funny is you're implication. But what the hey," I said cordially. "Yes, I was in Georgia. So were millions of Georgians, some of whom might have wanted Bedford dead. But even if you thought I did too, my show was scheduled days before the hitman you think he sent sat in a vehicle you suggest I saw on my way out of town. Unless you're saying I just happened to run across him and figured *hell, why not kill two birds* – Bedford and the gig. You done with that cup?"

When he nodded, I washed it and set it in the dishrack. "So if that's the case, you figure what then? My van issues are fabrications intended to give me an alibi of sorts?"

I was teasing him with the truth in a light-hearted way.

"Something like that," he said. "I don't know, Dax. Why was Bedford's man here? And why aren't you more upset about my suspicions? That in itself is suspicious."

"There's nothing to be upset about. You have questions that need answers, and I have nothing to hide." I smiled, and then winked. "As far as you know."

"Funny," he said, reaching for a toothpick.

"If it helps, I took the van in to BJ's to get it fixed."

"It might. When was that?"

"The next day, I think. You can check with them."

"I will. Thanks."

I admired Dom's dedication and respected his instincts. Hopefully, I'd given him reason to overlook both.

"Is Mrs. Turley's husband in custody?" I asked, as much to change the subject as my need to know.

"Not yet. But we'll get him."

It wasn't clear from his expression if he was speaking *to* me, or *about* me. Either way, I nodded. I wasn't worried much about what he might think, only what he could prove.

Which was hardly anything.

~~

Tasha walked into the police station to the *hey* and *how 'bout it*'s from her peers, spending a few minutes telling about her honeymoon when asked by those who cared. The men teased where they could, and the women even more so as their questions centered mostly around, 'So, how was it?' And by *it* they meant, you know...

Cops were a lot like teenagers in that regard.

She strode to her desk, sat in her chair, and turned on her computer. While waiting for the Welcome screen, she glanced around and took it all in as if for the last time. But that was silly, because *that* would be two-weeks from now.

With the letter typed, read and reread, she sent it to the printer and shut down the laptop. She looked for Dominic but didn't see him and went on ahead to the captain's office. After a vocal response to her knock, she slipped inside and closed the door.

"Tasha. I didn't expect you in for another couple days. Not that I'm not glad to see you. How was your trip to the Keys? What's the fishing like down there?"

She filled him in on the particulars, agreed to feeling as happy and rested as she looked, and told him about the big one that got away.

"Damn, that must have been fun. And frustrating."

"Oh, it was. And it was!" She smiled along with him.

"What do you have there?" he asked about the paper in her hand.

Her smile disappeared and she handed the notice over. "My resignation, sir."

"What? No."

Tasha nodded and he asked her to take a seat.

"Why? What's wrong?"

"Nothing," she said, and nothing else.

"Would you mind elaborating?"

Everything she thought she'd say was easier said in her head. Out loud, not so much – because she loved her job and would rather not have to quit. But she'd made her decision to be with Dax, and her principles required yet another.

"It's for personal reasons, sir. Not departmental."

Whatever hope she had of leaving it at that was dashed when his expression didn't change from one waiting for an answer to his question. And the longer he stared, the more she knew she'd have to give him one. If for no other reason than out of respect.

"Well, it's simple, really. And selfish. I'm in love with my new family and I want to spend more time with them. Maybe travel a bit, see some sights, have new experiences. Like the skydiving."

"And then what?"

"Sir?"

"After you've had your fun, what then? You're a damn fine detective, Tasha. Dedicated, intelligent, capable. You get things done and make them better in doing so. And what you do makes a difference in people's lives. It matters."

Tasha was touched by his words and her resolve tested. "Do you give that speech to every officer who tries to quit?" she asked with a grin that kept the sadness in check.

Pappy Doyle's eyes softened, and his hands opened in a *maybe yes-maybe no* gesture. "I can't afford to let you go. You're one of my best detectives."

"Only one? Not *the*?" she asked when he smiled.

"You're about this close," Pappy said, holding his thumb and finger an inch apart. "If you stick around, maybe . . ."

They let the friendly moment linger like a foggy mist.

"Look, Tasha, I understand. But you don't have to leave to get what you want."

"I think I do," she said, knowing she did.

"I'm going to say something and ask that you keep it to yourself for now, even from Dominic."

"Alright."

"The chief is stepping down, and I've been asked to take his place."

"That's great, Captain. Congratulations."

"Thanks," Pappy said. "But the reason I'm telling you this is because I want *you* to be the Captain. Of course, you'll need to pass the exam, but I don't see that as a problem. The position comes with six weeks' vacation a year that I'll raise to eight, giving you more time for travel and adventure."

Captain Williams...

Tasha had to admit she liked the sound of it. "Why me?" she asked. "Armentrout has been here longer."

"It's not about seniority. It's about who can do it best. And you've proven to be adept and professional, thoughtful, openminded, tough but fair. You know how to treat people."

His praise, delivered in such an understated manner, meant a great deal to her. More than he'd know.

"Thank you, sir. That's kind of you to say. But..."

He raised his hand and asked her to consider his offer.

"Discuss it with your family and let me know what you decide. In the meantime," Pappy said, putting her letter in a desk drawer, "we'll table this for the time being. Alright?"

~~

When the gate alarm sounded again, I'd just finished an hour of playing only Van Halen songs. They weren't bluesy, but Eddie's guitar licks were straight-up badass. Whenever I'd learn a new one, I felt the sin of prideful accomplishment. He rocked in a way few others did and made it sound easy – which it was not. Thus my misguided vanity.

Now if I only had the talent to *create* those licks.

I met Tash at the porch, lifting her up and into my arms, kissing and carrying her inside like I had after our wedding day. It was fun; she thought so, too, and held on when I tried to let her go.

"Not yet," she said with a giggle in her hazel-green eyes. After long seconds of silence became even longer minutes, she smiled and told me to put her down.

"You're ugly and no one will ever love you."
"Ha- ha. I meant on the floor."
"Oh, right," I said, as if.
"How long this time?"
I looked at the wall clock and told her *seventeen*.
"Damn, Dax. You didn't even break a sweat. I wonder how long you could hold me if you had to."
"I guess we'll see as we go. But it will probably be more if I want to as opposed to *having* to. Although as it stands now, I have to *because* I want to."
"Aww, isn't that some sweet and sappy shit." She gave me the kiss I'd vied for and left me, as always, wanting more.
"So? How did it go?" I asked.
"Not entirely as planned."
"How so?"
"I tried to quit and got a promotion instead." She took pleasure in my confusion but pitied my perplexity. Again, I apologize for my excessive alliteration. Perhaps there's an AA type meeting I could attend, maybe get some help. *Huh.* Alcoholics Anonymous is also an alliteration.
". . . and that's how we left it," she said.
Fortunately for me, I'd more than half-listened while I pondered my propensity to . . . Never mind.
"Congrats and kudos, Tash. What an opportunity."
"Thanks. And yes. It is. But I can't take the job for the same reason I'm leaving the one I have."
I knew what she meant. Her career in law enforcement was over. Because of me. I was to blame.
"And before you say it's your fault, although yes, in part, it is, there's prescience in your saying opportunity."
"Prescience?" I asked.
"An insight or prophecy."
"Kind of a big word for a little lady, don't you think?"
"This from a man who'd rather use a five syllable word than one with two." Tasha grinned, because it was true.
"That sounds like caricaturing, to me. And about me."
"Hey, if the foo shits. Or shoe fits, if your dyslexically minded."

"Nice," I told her as we shared a chortle at my expense. "You were saying?"

"Being a Captain would be cool, if this were a Starship," she said, looking through her Star Trek rooted prism. "Here in St. Vincent, however, it'd be administration and politics. Things I have no real interest in. I'd prefer to be out on the street, explore strange new worlds. Seek out new life..."

"And new civilizations." I butted in and took a baton she hadn't passed. But I couldn't resist. "To boldly go where no MAN has..."

"Man, my ass!" she said.

"You're right. Those were words written in the sixties and we now live in a twenty-first century world. 'To boldly go where no man, my ass, has gone before.'"

Tasha laughed and slapped my arm.

"What?" I said. "We can say *ass* on TV now."

"It's *no one*, not *no man*, you twit. It's been updated to reflect gender equality."

"When did that happen?"

"I think when the first movie came out."

"No, I meant gender equality." I expected a punch but got a pinch instead.

"I hope it's always like this between us, Dax."

"I can't see why it wouldn't be."

"It's funny you say that, because it segues neatly to your *prophecy* of opportunity. Let me explain.'

She told me she knew I'd given thought to killing Turley but didn't tell me how. She conveyed her anger and fear and reiterated what she'd do if I betrayed her trust.

"I wouldn't do that, Tash."

"I believe you. I worry though, that you might come to hold your promise against me some day."

"I wouldn't do that, either."

"Maybe. You're in a tough spot, Dax. We both are. But we've made our bed and need to lie in it willingly. Lovingly. Without regret or resentment. To that end, I have an idea."

I tried to fathom how she knew what I'd been thinking last night and wondered if mind-reading was a female trait. Wouldn't that be something?

"Tell me," I said.

"We could do Private Detective-ing."

I smiled at her using a made-up word for my benefit. "I'd like to see that stenciled in gold-leaf on an office door. But you might have something, Tash. We could work cases, protect and serve where needed – like restraining orders. Hmm... How would you feel about me becoming a bounty hunter? I could track down bad guys and girls and bring their sorry asses in. That would be very satisfying."

"And why should you have all the fun? What about me?"

"I'm sure there will be plenty of typing that needs doin,' phones that need answerin,' coffee that needs makin'..."

"Say one more chauvinist thing," she said, "and there'll be a sorry ass *here* that needs kicking. Sorry, *kickin.*'"

The feisty spark in her eyes made me want to throw her over my shoulder and take her to my Neanderthal cave.

So I did.

chapter twenty-one

The first thing Dominic did after leaving Dax was to go to BJ's Automotive Repair, the second was to call the blues club to verify what he'd been told. Then he ordered three breakfast burritos at the McDonald's drive-through before finding a shady spot to reflect on what he'd learned.

There appeared to be a straight line from Bedford and Lamb, to Dax. The reasoning was sound but speculative.

And a little wobbly.

Dom wondered again if he would still suspect him if the hitman's car was on the other side of town instead of tenths of a mile from his house and admitted it might be less likely, taking other factors into account.

If Dax hadn't run across him on his way to Georgia, how else would he know where to find him? Or know he needed to? It was difficult to dispute the silliness of his stopping to ask a total stranger if they were there to kill him or his.

But what if that's exactly what happened?

It was obvious how much he loved Mary and not a leap to think he'd be curious or concerned about someone sitting in a car so close to where she was home alone. But if he *had* confronted the man and an altercation occurred resulting in his death, why didn't Dax call the police, claim self-defense? Any other citizen would have.

But that sort of citizen wasn't on television telling the world he'd kill them dead if they didn't steer clear of his kid. And that kind of man wouldn't let a Hale Bedford get away with that kind of shit. Or leave it to the cops to deal with.

So maybe it was him? And maybe that's why both men died by the same gun. It made a certain kind of sense.

It just didn't square with the available facts.

According to Dax, the trouble started after a semi-truck veered across the center line, making him swerve to avoid a collision and causing him to bounce violently on the uneven ground alongside a narrow shoulder.

BJ said between the corroded battery connectors, loose hoses and frayed wiring, it wasn't a mystery why the van got squirrely when it got jostled. And why Dax might have had some success after fiddling around in the dark. Because that threadbare wire controlled the fuel pump, and a bump or a jiggle could make or break the connection.

But even that was curious.

Only one wire was damaged out of a hundred wrapped with the same plastic zip-tie. He asked if it could've been cut, but BJ said it was mice, said he had seen it a thousand times. And that was that.

So after Dominic asked the club manager about phone calls, arrival time, and whether Dax's fingers were smudged from poking around the engine, his inclination was to move on and let it go.

And if not for what the guy said next, he might have.

'You know, you're the second detective this week to ask about Dax Palmer. Is he in some kind of trouble?'

Dominic chewed the rest of the last burrito with a slow deliberation and a furrowed brow.

What was he to make of that?

What would Tasha?

~~

"What about your Pomeranian girlfriend?" Mary asked. "She's practically a puppy,"

Watson felt her frustration, and her wish to deflect.

"First off, she is *not* my girlfriend. And comparing our difference in age is a false equivalent. Dog and human years are nowhere near the same."

"But you like her, don't you? A lot, right?"

"Yes. She's interesting. Funny. And easy on the eyes."

"You dog, you," she said with a grin and ruffled his head. "I didn't know you were such a player."

"I'm not. Bridget is way too petit for me, too yappy, too French. But sometimes the heart wants what it wants."

"Exactly!" Mary exclaimed. "I want Michael. Why can't I have him?"

Watson was glad to swing the conversation back to her. It took the focus off him and his feelings for that long-haired pooch. He said she was yappy, but her accent was music to his ears. "Who said you couldn't?"

"Dax will. When he finds out how old he is."

Watson shook his head because she had yet to ask his age, making her grumble pointless and premature.

"And what if he did? Would it be so wrong? Don't you trust his judgment anymore? Dax has been looking out for you a long while now. Michael just got here."

Mary was caught short and tried to hold onto her angst in spite of his blunt rebuke but failed.

"So you're saying the pissing and moaning part of the morning is over?" she said, giving a scratch behind his ears. Her fingers teased, and he didn't reply until she finished.

"I'm saying quit being a wuss. Find out how old that boy is, talk to Dax and accept your fate. Worst case, I'll have to put up with your moping around until you are an 'adult.'" Watson used his paws to make the air quotes.

"But that's more than a year away," she said, placing the back of her hand against the forehead of a southern belle. "How will I ever survive?"

"I don't know. Oh, woe is you?"

She laughed a little, put the truck in gear, and drove to the next lawn on the list. "You're right. It needs to be done."

"Good. How about today?" Watson said.

"I . . . uh . . . I don't know."

It was bad enough that he'd called her a wuss, but now he looked at her like she was a scaredy cat, a chicken, a . . .

"I'd rather ask in person than text or talk on the phone. Maybe I could wait till then?" Mary said, wishing to put it off a few days longer. Or forever, even.

And then her phone announced an incoming message. "Well, crap."

She'd heard fate could be fickle but didn't know it had a wry sense of timing.

"What is it?" he asked.

"Michael's coming through town later and he wants to know if we can get together."

Watson sympathized but tried to tickle her funny bone with some comic relief.

"Dun, dun, dunnnn."

~~

"Newman ready to rock and roll?" Miko asked, setting down the phone and pouring them a drink.

"Thanks. Yes," Alexi answered. "He's not happy about having to take those two screwups along. Thinks we should put a bullet in their heads and call it done."

"He's not wrong. And if they botch this like last time, it won't be a bullet but a chainsaw."

Alexi nodded and sipped his vodka. Miko's interest in the girl bordered on being obsessive, he thought. Why take her when there were so many other, younger girls to have?

~~

On the way home from Panama City, I was all smiles and life was all good. Watson rode shotgun and periodically stuck his head out the window because, that's what dogs do.

I couldn't wait to see the look on Mary's face. She didn't ask for much, and never for anything that cost real money. Which was why I liked to surprise her with an extravagance every now and then. I'd spent a few of my couple of bucks on a sound she had fallen in love with – the smooth tone of a Telecaster guitar.

Her preference was acoustic over electric, though she'd occasionally play one of my Strats – mostly to show me how it should be done. But the Tele in Otis Redding's classic had tickled her musical fancy, and I'd seen her literally sittin' on the dock of the St. Joseph Bay watching the tide roll as she listened to the timbre of that tone in song after song.

The vintage, blond-bombshell Fender was expensive, but she was a good girl and well worth it. She would see the dings and scratches as *character* instead of imperfection. And that was another in a long list of reasons that I liked her.

My last gift, other than the daily dose of wit and humor, was a pair of South Sea Cultured pearl earrings given when she'd agreed to let me adopt her. Although as a precaution, and unbeknownst, I'd recently swapped them for a modified facsimile that cost almost as much.

As we drove over the Tyndall hill and through its dell, tall pine shadows grew even taller across the stretch of road whilst the sun sunk lower in the sky. When we left the long treelined corridor of the Air Force base, the city of Mexico Beach welcomed us with sunsetting arms and vibrant hues. A picture perfect postcard.

I called Tash to say we'd be home soon and asked if she needed anything.

"Just some more of your sweet lovin'," she said.

"So, you like me-Tarzan you-Jane?"

"Ooh-ooh-ooh, ah-ah-ah."

I grinned at her monkey mime and gave one in return, but it sounded more *Tool-Time* Tim Allen than chimpanzee.

"How's your wine?" I asked.

"I'm fine."

"Yes, you are. And then some. But do you need wine?"

"I'm good," she said.

"Again, yes you are. And yes, you were. All three times, as I recall."

"Four, actually. But you stepped out of the bedroom, so I had to take care of it myself."

Tasha was funny. Titillating. And mine.

"Did you get what you went for?" she asked.

"Yes. The guitar looks great and plays even better."

"I'm sure she'll love it. Maybe not as much as the fishing boat I'm thinking of giving her as *my* adoption present."

Her chuckle said we'd have lots of fun over the coming years trying to buy, or at least rent, Mary's affections.

"I assume she's not within earshot, lest the cat is out."

"The cat's still in, but Mary isn't. She took your truck to meet up with someone. Did you know she had a new friend? Her name is Michelle," Tasha said.

"She mentioned it last night, but then Dom called about Lisa Turley. Sorry I didn't tell you. It just slipped my mind."

"Nothing to be sorry about. How far are you away?"

"Forty minutes or so, depending," I told her, refraining from beeping at the car of rubbernecking tourists in front of me, because the scenery was too beautiful to blame them.

"Well if you hurry and beat Mary home, I'll do that thing you like so much," she said in her sultry, sexy voice.

"Oh, baby. Now you're talking. You haven't baked me a pineapple upside-down cake in, like, forever."

Tasha laughed, said *Good one*, and then hung up.

Yeah, she's a keeper.

I tapped *Mary Jane,* but she didn't answer her ringtone. Tasha did.

"What, you again?"

"Sorry. I tried to call Mare, see if she wanted anything, but must have tapped you instead,"

"No, you tapped right. Looks like she forgot her phone."

"Huh," I said, and meant it. Mary didn't do that. It's always tucked in her back pocket when she leaves. Isn't it?

"What do you mean, huh?" Tasha asked

A silly supposition manifested out of thin air. Did she leave it at home on purpose?

"Oh, nothing," I said, not sure it was. Did Mary know about the tracking app I'd installed? It began to bother me that I didn't give as much thought to the possibility of her forgetfulness as I did to...

"You sure? It sounded like something," Tasha replied.

I was not invading her privacy, just so you know. Yes, it could be construed that way, but it's for her own protection. And unless pervs have tried to rape, kill, or kidnap *your* kid, you're in no position to judge me.

"No" I said. "It's just..."

If she were out killing, or worse, dating, then not taking her phone would make sense – if she knew about the app. But *that* wasn't an issue in this case because she was out with a friend. A girl friend. Not some handsy teenage boy.

Somewhere in the recess of my brain a voice called me a *grandpa* and told me to get with the times.

Relationships were not just boy-girl, girl-boy anymore. They're also boy-boy and girl-girl.

While I hadn't seen any such inclination, I'd be fine with whatever floated her potential new boat as long as she were happy and treated with respect. And then I wondered, but wished I hadn't, if the teenage girls Mary might want to date would be as horny as their male counterparts?

And what if my daughter was the handsy teen?

"What did she smell like? Clean? Perfumed?" I asked.

"Smell? What? You're breaking up."

"I said, how did she . . ."

When the call dropped, I asked Watson about Michelle, and he looked at me like he didn't have a clue who she was.

"Mary's friend. The girl she met while y'all were at FSU. Is she nice?"

It wasn't what he said, but what he didn't.

Which was nothing.

Yet, the silence spoke volumes.

Alright, that's a tad melodramatic and a bit of a stretch, but his failure to answer me did pique my curiosity.

And Mary's phone wasn't the only thing I'd LoJacked.

~~

One of the things Mary liked about Michael was the lack of awkward pauses. He seemed content to sit quietly on the over-sized beach towel as the sun set, and she didn't feel the need to talk even though things needed to be said.

And asked.

Despite Watson's concern, she'd already decided not to defy Dax if he refused to let her see Michael. She might get hurt, or even angry, but she would not go behind his back. Watson was right; Dax was her foundation.

And Michael?

When the stars began to appear, he laid back to watch them twinkle, and she lay on her side to gaze at him. Not for the first time did she think he was handsome as all get out. Or wonder what *it* would be like . . .

Mary opened her mouth to finally ask his age but kissed him instead, with meaning – while she could still tell herself she didn't know for sure how old he really was.

At the risk of being thought of as a tart but wanting to experience some of the *wonder*, if only for a moment, she sat astride him. His affection was clearly evident, and a sensual discourse ensued. The slow, rhythmic motion of her hips induced a groan that pricked and stoked her desire. His kiss deepened during their discussion as he rolled on top and continued the conversation, making her writhe and ache.

He stood to remove his clothes, and what she wrought soon glistened in the faint moonlight. A powerful yearning consumed rational thought and left her vulnerable. What would she do if he reached for her?

What would she do if he didn't?

Michael smiled at her and winked.

"Come on," he said and turned toward the Gulf.

Without a second thought, Mary stood up and began to slip the sundress from her shoulders.

~~

My van didn't have four-wheel drive, so parking by the sandy entrance would have to do.

I looked around and saw the empty vehicles down the beach but didn't have a clue to Mary's whereabouts until someone stood up in the middle of a brush-covered dune. My imagination didn't have time to adequately prepare me as I watched her stand and start to strip so she could follow a naked boy into the water. The steering wheel cracked as I pushed on it, and I felt all the emotions you'd expect. And some you might not.

To my credit, I didn't step out of the van. Instead, I kept her from undressing by laying on the horn. Even after being assaulted by a torrent of emotions, and her angry glare, I felt god-awful about embarrassing her.

But, if she didn't hop in the truck and get her ass home, and I mean right NOW...

chapter twenty-two

In the span of two weeks, Newman had been a private investigator, a detective, and now, an FBI agent. The week before, he'd murdered the family of a man who ran afoul of Miko by failing to do what he'd been told. After apologizing for his lapse in judgment and begging for his life, Newman then killed and gutted the man, feeding him to his Mastiff-Pitbulls, who were far more hungry than loyal.

"Pull in front of the house," he said to the *broken*-ass. "When we're inside, go park where I told you and then cover the back. Try not to screw it up."

When the car stopped, Newman reminded the *lame*-ass to keep his mouth shut and follow him.

The door opened after a second knock and a man with a shotgun stepped forward.

"Who the hell are you? What do you want?"

"Paul, be nice," a woman said from inside.

"Mr. Taylor? I'm Special Agent Procter, this is Special Agent Gamble. May we come in, sir?"

"What the heck for? Kinda late for an FBI visit, ain't it?"

"Yes sir. I'm sorry, but our plane was delayed for hours and we just got into town."

"Procter and Gamble, huh?' Paul asked. "Sounds hinky. How do I know you are who you say?"

"Yes sir. We get that a lot. May I show you my ID?"

Paul kept his finger steady and nodded. "Careful now."

"Yes, sir. I understand," Newman said, and then took a wallet from his jacket and showed him his credentials. "Do you need to see agent Gamble's as well?"

"No. That won't be necessary. Is this about my Leigha?"

"Yes sir. We need to show her a few pictures and ask a couple of questions."

"Can't this wait till the morning? She's just settled in."

"Yes, I suppose so," Newman said, knowing it would be easier to force his way in and get what he wanted. "But it will only take ten, fifteen minutes at the most. Then we'll be out of your hair, sir."

~

Leigha listened near her bedroom door and thought he sounded like the man she heard laughing with the monster who had kept her locked up and made her do terrible things. What if it *was* him?

What if he came to take her back?

She sat on the corner of her bed and trembled.

~~

"Hey, hon. Did you have fun?" Tasha asked when Mary came through the door. But she didn't look happy, and she'd stormed in rather than strolled. "What's wrong?"

She heard the van door slam shut followed by Watson's footsteps on the porch, and then Dax's.

He didn't look happy, either.

"What's going on?" Tasha asked after quiet seconds of nothing being said.

I was still trying to wrap my head around what I'd seen, and my feelings were a murky mess and not to be trusted. So when she glared at me, I raised my palms and shrugged. Mary, however, found her calm before I could and spoke.

"Dax, I'm sorry. I should have said something earlier. I wanted to, but... I was going to tell you tonight."

Maybe it was the confusion, the anger, fear of losing her – I don't know. But for the first time I didn't think I believed her. And by the wet shimmer in her eyes, I think she knew.

"I don't *care* what you think," she said furiously. "It's none of your damned business what I do! You're not my..."

Thank goodness she quit before sticking it all the way in, but Mary's point was made. She wanted to hurt me back. And she did.

"Mary!" Tasha exclaimed. "That's enough."

Mary turned and marched to her room, throwing the door closed after Watson stepped inside.

"Well, it's official," I said sardonically. "We're a family."

"Geez, Dax. What happened?"

I told her what I knew, and some of what I felt.

Tasha slipped an arm around and tried to comfort me with affectionate pats and rubs. And like Watson, I took any and all scratching I could get.

"Maybe she's right; what she does isn't my business. It's her life, after all, and I'm just..."

"You can stop right there, mister. Mary is damned lucky to have you. And any life she has is not only your business, it wouldn't *exist* if not for you. Why that little pissant doesn't know how good she's got it."

I started laughing and didn't stop until it ran its course.

"Thanks, Tash. I needed that. *Pissant*. Nice."

She gave me a hug and a kiss on the cheek.

"You're welcome. By the way, what made you look on the beach?"

"Huh?" I said, realizing I had not planned for this. Not that it was a big deal, but I'd rather not be accused of spying on my daughter so soon after keeping tabs on her.

"How did you know where to find her?"

"I, uh..."

Fate was sometimes fortuitus, I thought, as it was now. Not only did it save me by the bell of an incoming text, but Mary opened her door a split second later and literally ran into my arms and buried her head in my chest.

"I'm sorry. I'm so sorry. I had no business saying that. To speaking to you that way. Please forgive me. Please..."

"It's alright, hon." I kissed the top of her head and lifted a tear-stained face. "Of course I do."

I stroked her hair and glanced at Tasha, who had a tear working herself. Me too, but I hid it better because I'm a big, strong, man. Tash's grin begged to differ, however.

"I'd like to talk to you both," Mary said. "If that's okay."

"Sure, sweetie," I said. "Anyone else like some wine?"

They looked at me funny because I hardly ever had any. But if there was ever a time when a ten to thirteen percent alcoholic beverage was needed, hearing my little girl might be sexually active had to be right up there.

"I'll get it," Mary said with a twinkle in her eye, back to her old self again. It could have been the healing properties of forgiveness. Or Kendall-Jackson's.

I took a deep breath and raised my eyebrows at Tasha, hoping for the best but preparing for the worst. She patted the spot beside her on the couch and I moved to sit and then remembered getting a text.

"Hmm..."

"What is it?"

I was still looking at the message when Mary came back with an opened bottle of chardonnay in one hand and three stemmed glasses hanging from the fingers of the other. The clink and clanging had a Christmas-time feel to it.

I'm not sure why...

"Dax?"

I handed Tash the phone, wondering who might've sent such a text. Only one person made any sense at all.

"*'Help?'* What does it mean? Who's it from?" she said.

"I'm not sure. I don't recognize the number."

Mary set bottle and crystal down on the coffee table.

"Let me see." After a glance she said it might be the red-haired girl from Wewahitchka.

"What? Why would you think that?" Tasha asked.

"Who else could it be?" she said, parroting my thoughts.

"I don't understand. She doesn't know who Dax is, so why text him? And if she *were* in some kind of trouble, why not call the police? Or me? She has my number."

"Unless someone is pulling a prank," I said, "or sent the text to me by mistake, Leigha is the only one that comes to mind. As for her knowing, she saw me at the Pig once getting chicken when you were out in Oklahoma. Maybe she got my name from the news, then found my number. And if it *is* her, it makes sense she'd contact me and not you or the police."

"And why is that?"

Tasha looked somewhat indignant, but it was a fair ask.

"Because she's seen what I'll do to protect her."

I hadn't meant to sound ominous, but I did.

"Where are you going?" Tash said when I took my keys.

"I think I'll drive out and see if everything is alright."

"And how are you going to do that? Knock on the door? Do her parents know who you are, what you did?"

"I don't know. I'll just take a quick look around, peek in a window, satisfy my curiosity."

"Dax, that's silly. And you could be arrested if someone sees you and calls the cops. Then how will you explain your being there? Do you want the world to know why?"

"Of course not. I'll be careful," I said, reaching into the top end-table drawer. "Don't worry. It's probably nothing."

"Then why are you taking a gun?"

"In case it's something." I smiled to make it better, but Tasha left the couch and got between me and the door.

"We should have the police drive over and check it out. There's no reason for you to go."

"I have to know if she's okay, Tash."

"You don't even know it's her. Why not call the number and find out before you risk the exposure?"

"What if that message was all she had time to send? If I text or call back, it puts her and her family in more danger."

"You're assuming a lot you can't possibly know."

"I agree. That's why I have to go."

"I'm coming with you," Mary declared.

"No," Tasha said. "You and your dad stay here. I'll go."

"Tash, I'd rather you and Mary . . ."

"I'm the detective here. Remember?"

"Look, I'll be back before you . . ."

"Bullshit," Mary spat at me. "The last time you went off by yourself, you got shot in the chest on a dark country road. That's not going to happen again. I'm coming."

"No, I want you to stay put. I mean it, Mare."

"Okay. And as soon as you go, I'll be right behind you."

Her defiance was unsettling and didn't mix well with her behavior on the beach. I think she pissed me off.

"So you're not going to listen to me anymore then?'

"Of course I am. But if you didn't want a girl who would think for herself and do what needs doing, you should have raised me differently."

"She's got you there, Dax. And she's right. Either we all go, or none of us do."

213

"Tasha, I . . ."

"I'm not asking," she said as hard as a tack.

The trouble with strong-willed women is that they are just that – fierce, independent, stubborn.

And I wouldn't have them any other way.

"Mare, dress for night operations – dark clothes, shoes. Get your gun, an extra clip, a suppressor, and your vest. We leave in two minutes."

"Dax, she'll be in the truck. Why does she need all that?"

I glanced at Mary and nodded toward Tasha. "Tell her number three."

"*It's better to be armed and not need it, than to need it and not be armed.*"

"What is that?" Tasha asked her.

"Dax has a list of twelve do's and don'ts." Mary grinned. "I call them the Dirty Dozen of *Daxioms*."

"Time's a tickin' girl," I told her and off she went. "And don't forget your phone." I almost said *this time* but didn't want to get into it if she'd left it at home on purpose earlier. I could have been wrong about that.

"I still think I should go by myself," Tasha said.

"I know. But like Mary, I'd follow anyway once you left."

"You two are two peas."

I nodded, pleased but worried we were too much so.

"Guess you're coming too, huh?" I said to Watson.

His expression said stupid is as stupid asks.

We agreed to take Tasha's truck but when I tried to get into the driver's seat, she looked at me and said 'Please.' Not in a *Mother, may I* way, but a *You gotta be effing kidding me.* And as it turned out, she was effing right – because we got there a hell of a lot quicker than I thought possible.

Faster even than I would have.

~~

Newman went through the pretense of an investigation by showing the barely fourteen-year old girl photos of men the 'FBI' suspected of sexual criminal conduct. Some of the men worked for Dimitri Anatovich but most of the pictures were randomly pulled off the internet. Except for two.

As he scrolled through the pics on his phone, he'd ask if she recognized them and if so, had they'd *hurt* her – a gentle euphemism for having sex with her.

Newman had been surprised to learn that Miko's uncle, though notoriously known to be selfish with his money, was downright generous with his little *Princesses*. Four of the six men killed along with Dimitri had had the pleasure of her company, and he could understand why.

She was a tasty treat.

Her fate was sealed, however, after she'd identified the first of the two men he was there for. Miko didn't know if she'd seen him or not, but if she had his instructions were clear – tie up any loose ends.

And when Palmer's face appeared on the touchscreen a few pics later she hesitated, and her *no* was an obvious lie. It wasn't until he pulled his gun and pointed it at her father that she told him who he was and what he'd done.

But instead of killing them instantly and all at once, he opted for the traditional home invasion and its ever popular sadistic twist – raping the wife while the husband watched. Newman thought it cliché but still a classic.

After the man was duct-taped to a kitchen chair, he was dragged to their room to watch his wife tied to the bedposts.

"Take the girl out back and give her to Joey," Newman said quietly so the parents couldn't hear. "Tell him to toss her in the trunk and wait for my call. Then come back here and do the mother."

"I'd rather do the kid."

"Later. When we're done here. And try not to get your dumbasses kicked this time. Now, move it."

Newman didn't mind the noise the girl's parents made after she'd been taken out. Their house was too far away from the nearest neighbor to be heard. But when a call from Miko came in, he told them to shut the hell up. Or else.

"Go," he said into the phone. "Yeah, she saw you. I'm taking care of it. Yeah, it was him. You were right."

His brow lifted more from curiosity than concern.

"Really? Good. Yes. No, they won't be a problem."

He hung up and reached inside his jacket for the gun to check the magazine, but it was gone. Then he remembered.

"If you'll excuse me, I left something in the living room," Newman said, pouring salt of civility on their open wound. "Y'all don't go anywhere now."

~~

We parked down the road a piece and made our way to Leigha's on foot. Rather than have Mary become a potential duck sitting in the truck, I had her and Watson find cover in the south woods that bordered the one-story farmhouse.

From there she could scope out the terrain, protect our flank, and practice being ultra-quiet with wind at your back. But mainly, she'd be safe from harm should any be found.

As Tasha and I looked around, I persuaded her to let me have a look-see before taking any *official* action. I did so by whispering, "I'll be right back," before running to the house from the large tree we were hiding behind.

The first window I glanced in yielded nothing. Neither did the second and third. I looked at Tasha, shook my head, and then raised a hand when she made a move to join me.

My index finger told her to *wait a second*, and I shifted from the side of the house to the front. There were two bay windows facing out, and small panes on either side of a red door. Curtains were drawn on the bay nearest me, and I crawled under its sill until I reached the porch and stepped quietly toward the entrance.

I took a breath then a quick look through the rectangle. Nothing. No one.

Well, not nothing.

In addition to the standard living room accoutrement, a shotgun leaned against the couch. But that didn't give me pause, nor did the handgun laying on top of the coffee table.

It was the roll of duct tape.

If it had been any other room, I probably wouldn't have given it a second thought. I stole another peek.

I put an ear to the door and then turned the knob to see if it was locked, just in case. It was not. But I didn't push it open because there wasn't as yet a good enough reason to.

And an alarm might sound.

A vehicle sat in the driveway, and it was too early to be in bed, so where was everyone? Why was it so quiet inside? And what is it about the duct tape that made me antsy? Too many movies, maybe, with too many villains using it in ways unintended by the manufacturer.

Footsteps sounded on a wooden floor, and I leaned just enough to see. An official looking man dressed in black suit and tie strolled down the hallway. And if my hand weren't holding a half-twisted doorknob, I'd have filled it with a gun – because he was also wearing latex gloves.

Just like I used to.

When he entered the front room, I opened the door and stepped inside. His reaction told me what I needed to know.

"Guess I should have locked the door," he said, as cool as could be. "But no matter. You're here now."

Instead of going for the Glock on the table, he casually reached behind his back. So I closed the gap between us in hurried steps – just in time to keep from being stabbed by grasping his wrist and forearm with both hands.

He yanked the hair at the back of my head with his free hand, and I drove an elbow to his jaw to create space - then stuck my thumb into the socket to gouge out his eye. When he let loose, but before he grabbed my fingers, I smashed my fist into the crook of the arm holding the knife.

When it folded, I used the momentum to force the blade into his chest, pounding three times until it was buried.

I gave the knife a hard twist to make a hole in his heart, so he would bleed out. He no longer looked as cocky as he had ten seconds ago, but I'd been lucky. And I knew it.

After he fell to the floor, I saw Tasha just inside with her gun raised and pointed at me.

"Police. Don't move!" she yelled.

I thought she'd shoot me dead if I so much as twitched, but when she looked past me, I dropped to the floor. Bullets whistled overhead from the front and behind. Then another man in a suit and latex gloves fell beside me.

"Thanks, Tash. I . . . Are you alright?"

She was up against the wall with one hand underneath the bulletproof vest, rubbing and nodding.

"Yes. Got the wind knocked out of me, but I'm okay."

I nodded and turned as muffled sounds suddenly arose. I affixed a suppressor to my gun and put one each in the heads of the suits before I left to investigate.

"Don't . . ." she said, trying to stop me, or so I thought, but that wasn't going to happen.

"They're done," I told her and walked away

"Dax, wait . . ." she said, but I felt an urgency and didn't have time to delay.

The back door in the kitchen stood wide open, probably from when the other suit came in to shoot me in the back. I stepped softly down a hall and stopped next to a closed door where the noise came from. I stood to the side, flung it open, and, when no one fired, glanced inside.

Jesus!

Talk about getting there in the nick of time. I asked the man taped to the chair if they were alone by putting a finger to my lips and pointing to the wall closet. When he shook his head, I stepped in and removed the tape from his mouth.

"How many?" I asked.

"Two. Said they were FBI," he said,

"Where's Leigha?"

"I don't know. One of them took her out. Who're you?"

"A friend. I'm here with Detective Williams," I said and retrieved my knife from an ankle strap. "Do you know her? She came after Leigha was brought home."

"Yes, we . . ."

I heard two rapid shots from outside and a sound that could have been a yelp in between.

"Stay in the house with Miss Williams," I said, handing him the knife after freeing his hand. "I'll find Leigha."

I ran from the room and called out before leaving.

"Tash, her parents are in the bedroom. They're alright. I'm going out back to look for Leigha."

I checked at the door to guard against being ambushed, and then crept along the back of the house in the direction of the gunfire. My anxiety might have contributed to my carelessness because instead of visually clearing a path first, I turned the corner of the house and got run over.

When she saw who I was, relief replaced the fear in her eyes. "Ah rue rewed kum."

I felt her face and peeled the duct tape from her lips.

"I knew you'd come." Leigha hugged me by leaning into me. "Are mom and dad okay?"

"Yes. They're with Detective Williams. Are *you* okay?"

"Yes. But I was so scared."

"What happened? I heard gunshots," I said and looked her over to be sure she hadn't been injured.

"A man with a cast was pulling me through the plowed field, but he stopped when we heard the commotion from the house. I was afraid for my parents and kicked him hard in the shin. When he let go, I lit out as fast as I could run. He must have shot at me. But he missed."

"Thank God for that," I said and rubbed her arm. "Did you hear a dog bark when the man was shooting?"

"No. I just heard the gun. And my breathing. It's hard to run with your hands taped behind your back."

"I can imagine. You go on in now and let your mom and dad know you're alright, okay? They'll cut you free."

"Aren't you coming too?"

"I have to look for the man who took you. Will you tell Miss Williams I'll be right back?"

"Yes. Thanks for coming to help me," Leigha said.

When she left, I looked and saw the plowed field in the distance. The stars were out in full bloom, but the light they gave was minimal. It helped keep me from being spotted, but it did the same for the man who'd shot at Leigha.

How many others were there? Why were they here?

My head was on a slow swivel, my ears keen to hear as I moved quietly, glancing at the woods and willing Mary to stay put until I came for her. The footprints in the field were easy to follow, but I didn't rush.

A shape appeared in front of me, a large something sprawled on the ground. As I got closer, the mound turned into two and I tamped down on the fear that began in the Taylor's bedroom. I looked around before moving forward, desperately afraid of what I'd find. One of the lumps was the man who'd taken Leigha. He was dead.

219

Watson was alive, but unconscious. And bleeding.

"Hang in there, boy," I said and scratched him behind the ear, as if that would make everything alright. "Where's Mary? Huh?"

I knew she'd killed the man by the shot pattern – bullets to the arms and legs in case of a vest, and two in the head. But where the hell was she? A glint on the grass a few yards away caught my eye. It was her gun.

Panic started to assert itself and I pushed back, needing to stay calm but fighting a losing battle. I looked for signs of a struggle but didn't find any. Nor did I see any blood.

The first thing that came to mind was she'd somehow been disabled and carried away, so I told Watson I'd be back and hurried into the woods. Calling out for her might seem like the thing to do, but if she were still nearby, the man or men who took her would be alerted.

It made sense she'd be taken to a vehicle because they hadn't killed her outright, so I went through the trees to the street. A faint snap in the distance could've been someone stepping on a twig or branch, and I hustled to find out. A minute later, I heard a door close and an engine turn over.

No longer concerned about making noise, I ran full out, reaching the road in time to see taillights vanish in the night. I grabbed my phone and punched the app icon. She was on the move, or at least her cell was, and I raced to Tash's truck.

I checked on the *fail-safe* signal, confirming Mary was heading north, and then hurried to get to Watson. I found something to wrap him up in and carried him as quickly as I could. My plan was to leave him with Tasha and go after Mary, but that all changed after I pulled in the driveway and knocked on the door. When it opened, I was aghast

"Tasha!"

Mrs. Taylor looked up at me from the floor with teary eyes as she pressed a bloody towel on Tasha's stomach.

"What..." I asked and knelt beside her.

But I could see what had happened. The vest stopped one bullet, but another found its mark a few inches lower. Probably when her arms were lifted as she raised her gun.

"We found her slumped against the door..."

"Tasha. Tash!" I shouted, but she didn't respond. "How long has she been out?"

"Fifteen minutes. Maybe more."

I reached underneath her but didn't feel an exit wound.

"Leigha, would you get a new towel please? Mr. Taylor, could you hand me the roll on the coffee table?"

After removing the vest and raising her blouse, I placed the fresh towel on the wound and, with Mrs. Taylor's help, wrapped the duct tape tightly around Tasha's body to stem the flow of blood.

"Thank you," I told Leigha's mom and lifted Tash up and into my arms. "I have to get her to the hospital. Do y'all have somewhere you can go? I don't think they'll come back, but it would be better if you weren't here if they did."

"I already called the police. They should be here soon," Paul said. "Leigha told us who you are, Mr. Dax. We want to thank you for saving our little copper-top."

"She's a brave young lady Mr. Taylor. You should be very proud of her."

They followed me out to the truck and helped get Tasha inside on the back bench seat. Leigha gasped when she saw Watson lying on the floor and asked if he were mine. I said *no*, not wanting to upset her any more than she already was. "I found him in the field. That man must have shot him. I'll get him fixed up, don't worry." Before leaving, I asked Paul why those guys were there.

"He showed me pictures of men who might've hurt me," Leigha said. "Then he showed me yours..."

chapter twenty-three

It could only be by the grace of a god I didn't believe in that I was able to keep it together in order to think clearly.

I was wracked with guilt for not putting my foot down, but really, what else could I have done? Order them to stay home? Tasha was a grown-ass woman who'd do what she damned well pleased, and Mary...

My wild imagination wrestled with my reason, proving to be a worthy, if bothersome, adversary. The tracking app supported the probability she was still alive, otherwise why transport a dead body?

'Unless they took her cell for some odd reason and left her dead or dying out in the woods,' Imagination said. 'She could be out there, bleeding out, waiting for you to find her.'

"Shut up," I said, and told logic to punch that asshole in his glass half-empty mouth. "She's alive."

She has to be...

'She is,' Reason assured me wiping its bloody knuckles. 'How can you continue to function otherwise?'

Indeed.

"Tash?" I reached behind to feel her face, see if she was still breathing. When she groaned, I teared up from relief.

We were barreling down the road over ninety-miles an hour, and I turned off the screaming siren to make a call.

"This is Murphy."

"Detective. Dax Palmer, here. I'd like to ask a favor."

"Palmer? How did you..."

"I need you to call Bay Medical and have them send EMS to the CVS on the corner of 22 and 98. ASAP. My wife and a friend have been shot, both unconscious. I'll be there in ten."

"What the..."

"Thank you," I said, hung up, and made another call.

The men at Leigha's were there because of me, one way or the other, and her *friends* could also be at risk. Talking to Jeri would expose me to scrutiny but it couldn't be helped. Safeguarding those girls took precedent.

"Dax-a-million," Jeri said when she answered. "How be you and that fine, friend of mine?"

"Jeri, listen. I'm going to give you a lot of information. Please don't interrupt till I'm done. Do you have something to write with?"

"Hang on. Okay, go ahead."

Her voice was measured, professional. And afraid.

I asked if she could track Mary's location, and then told her why. Jeri was patient and I was brief, giving a summary more than a report. When finished, her question mirrored my own.

"Is Tasha going to die?"

"I don't . . . Oh, shit!" I said and floored the gas pedal. A buck, and then a doe ran across the road.

But it was the inevitable Johnny-cross-lately deer that had me reenacting a scene from a Tom Cruise movie where he plows blindly into a ribbon of smoke caused by a multiple racecar accident. I clipped the tail of the doe with the driver side mirror and just missed killing her fawn with the back bumper on the passenger-side.

"Dax! What's wrong? Dax!!"

"We're good. It's alright," I said, but it clearly wasn't. For the second time tonight, I'd almost gotten Tasha killed – though it still remained to be seen if she'd survive the first.

"Sorry. A deer in the road. Jeri, she's lost a lot of blood, but I have to believe she'll be okay . . ."

I faltered and clamped down on my runaway feelings.

"Dax, I don't understand. Why did Leigha text you?"

"You'll call Angel and Emily? Make sure they're safe?"

"Of course, but you didn't answer my question. How do you know Leigha? Why does she know you?" Jeri asked, but I didn't answer. Well, not directly.

"Is Anatovich's business still operational?"

"What? No. It's shut down. And his assets are frozen."

"Anyone in the organization who might take issue with those girls being rescued? Someone wanting retribution?"

"I don't know. But... What are you saying? Dax?"

"I have to go."

"Dax, wait..."

As I hung up, her words spun around in my head like a top. That was the last thing Tasha said to me. At the time, I thought she was trying to keep me from going to look for Leigha, but maybe she was saying something else? Like she needed me – because she'd been shot.

And I left her suffering and alone.

Damn it! Recrimination was for later.

I switched the siren back on to clear the way. And help drown out the howling terror of my imagination.

~~

Jeri held the phone against her ear even after the dull tone said Dax was gone, stunned by the implication of what he'd said. For a moment she forgot about Tasha and thought of what his questions hinted at.

Seeking revenge for stealing stolen girls? No, she didn't think so. But for killing Anatovich and six of his men? Yeah, that made all kinds of sense. If Dax was *the man*.

"Good Lord Almighty," she said. Could it really be true?

Why else would that little redhead reach out to him? And if he *did* murder those men?

There were too many questions following that one, and she didn't have the time to pose them. Jeri set Tasha aside a little longer and got busy making phone calls – starting with the two girls Dax seemed to care for and was worried about, one of whom *the man* caressed with affection when he took them from Anatovich's house.

~~

Two emergency vehicles were waiting in the drugstore parking lot when I arrived. Along with one detective.

The EMT's took Tasha from the truck, laid her down on the collapsible gurney, and then wheeled her away. I lifted Watson off the floor after feeling for a pulse and carried him to the ambulance she was shoved into.

225

"We can only take one," the EMT said without looking, slipping a blood pressure cuff on Tasha's arm.

When I moved to the other van, the medical technician stood in front of the back door but didn't open it.

"Sorry, this is for people only. We can't take the dog."

"Yes. You can.," I said. "And you better."

He opened his mouth to reply but must have changed his mind after gazing into the black hole of my intent. When the young man glanced at Murphy, I saw the detective's nod at the edge of my periphery.

"He's my friend," I told the tech after laying Watson on the inside gurney. "If he dies cause someone at the hospital dicked around about his being a dog, I'm gonna be pissed."

I hopped out the vehicle, told Murphy *thanks*, and kept on walking.

"Where you going?" he said, laying a hand on my arm.

I bristled and turned, prepared to knock him down if he tried to detain me. But his eyes said otherwise. Where mine was full of foreboding, his were tempered with compassion. Not at all what I would expect from someone dealing with a suspected serial killer.

"The people who tried to kill Tash and Watson took my daughter. I'm tracking her phone and need to leave."

"Can I help?"

"You already have, Brian," I said and ran to the truck. After making short work of the rubberneckers in my way by flashing the police lights and squawking the siren, I got back on FL-22 and headed east to Wewahitchka and SR-71 north.

I pulled up an app that let me track multiple signals and saw they were still in sync some fifty plus miles away. But I was eating up the road, and whoever took Mary had to drive relative to the speed limit in order to keep from being pulled over. Once they hit the interstate however, my advantage would be mitigated by their ability to drive seventy-eighty.

Mary was only thirty-six miles in front of me when they came to the SR-71, I-10 junction, and I threw caution to the wind in a reckless attempt to prevent them from getting too far down the highway.

226

After nearly running a semi-truck into the median upon entering the I-10 East entrance ramp, I glanced at my phone. The green dots denoting the different tracks were offset and no longer precisely overlaid one on top of the other.

It was then, as the speedometer reached a hundred and thirteen, that I realized the display feature on the phone was on maximum zoom *out*. Imagine having to weave in and out of traffic with one hand on the wheel while the other held a cellphone by thumb and ring-pinky fingers as the index and middle digits *zoomed* the touchscreen for a closer look.

Oh, shit!

The next exit was ten miles further on, and I took it and doubled-back due west to follow the *fail-safe* signal heading north-northeast on 286 toward Sneads. I'd have to leave it to Jeri to find Mary's phone rolling down Interstate 10.

I was going after her earrings.

chapter twenty-four

In every reincarnation of her reoccurring dream, the guy with the cast shot Watson before Mary could shoot *him*. Every time...

She'd hidden behind a wide pine, listening and looking with Watson by her side. A sound too faint to be definitively recognized as gunfire came from the red-haired girl's house, downwind of their position. She glanced at Watson, but he hadn't heard anything. It seemed he'd smelled something though, because his nose lifted in the air.

Mary saw movement in a field near the backside of the yard and Watson took off in that direction. She ran after him and soon discovered why he'd bolted. A man was pointing a gun at a girl running away, and, when Watson growled to get his attention, the man turned the weapon on him.

She stopped and took aim, but he fired before she did. Watson's yelp tore at her heart, and she peppered the man with bullets, even as he fell to the ground.

But he wasn't a man, as it turned out. He was one of the boys who attacked her at FSU. Why was *he* here? She didn't understand or care to hear an explanation. It didn't matter. He tried to kill her best friend.

She put a bullet in a skull and crossbones drawn on the cast of his broken arm and another couple in his head. On her way to help Watson, a sledgehammer slammed into her back and she crashed to the ground, followed by a sharp and constant pain that made her pass out.

Then, the repetitive nightmare would start over again. Only this time it was different.

Mary couldn't say where she was, but in *this* dream her mind was sluggish, her body beat. It was all she could do to keep her eyes open.

Her worry for Watson, however, was still as strong.

"Is he alright, Michael?" she garbled.

"Who?" he asked as he laid her down on the bed.

"Watson."

"I don't know."

"What about Dax? And Tasha?"

"Don't know that, either. There's aspirin if you need it."

Mary thought it sweet when he put a shiny new bracelet on her wrist. Maybe it meant they were going steady now.

"I think I love you, Michael."

"I think so too," he said with a twisted, lopsided grin.

Then he vanished – and she was back at the farmhouse trying to save Watson from being shot.

~~

After flying like a bat out of hell in Florida, I was forced to slow my roll at the state line to keep from being pulled over by the Georgia police and possibly detained. I switched off siren and lights and crawled along at posted speed limits. It was agonizing and kept me from gaining lost ground. To make matters worse, the signal stopped transmitting, only giving her last known position just north of Bainbridge.

Pounding on the dashboard beat back the despair, but it didn't last. I started to beg for her to be okay.

Can you read my mind, sweetie? Hang on. I'm coming.

It was another forty-two minutes before I arrived at the still blinking dot and drove down an obscure road between a hill and tree landscape.

"I'm here, honey," I said, and pulled the truck into the woods to hide it from view. After a deep breath, my anxiety was squashed like a car from a junkyard compactor, leaving only steel resolve.

I carefully worked my way toward a house tucked away in the forest. The hilly up and down terrain made the trek difficult, but the adrenaline more than compensated. When I reached the summit of a modest knoll, I laid on my stomach and took stock of the lighted dwelling and its surroundings. No guards patrolled the grounds, which made me hopeful.

What if she's not here?

She had to be, or at least she *was* because the last signal said so. I resisted every urge to charge inside like a bull in a china shop and kill anything that stood in my way because, unlike the movies when the hero battles a horde of bad guys and finds the antagonist with a pistol to the heroine's head, real life was different. Once my presence was known, the smart thing would be to kill Mary and then capture or kill me when I lingered over her dead body.

Unless she was important to them, somehow.

An unexpected opportunity arose when a man traipsed across the manicured lawn into the trees. His stride looked familiar, but I didn't know why. I did, however, know that strolling into the dark woods was a strange thing to do.

~~

"Are you sure you're okay?" Mary asked as they settled in on the upper branch of the tallest tree after flying around for what felt like an hour. But you know how dreams can be, and it could have easily been only a few seconds.

Watson nodded. "The bullets missed the vital organs, so I'll be good to go after you get back. When's that going to be, by the way? And where the heck are you?"

"Don't know. But I guess I'll find out soon enough. Do you know if Dax and Tash are alright?"

"No, but I feel they are. Don't you?"

"Yes," Mary said and woke up worried about Dax. He must be frantic; his worst nightmare come true.

She looked around and assessed her situation. She was lying on a bed in what looked like a storage container, with her left wrist handcuffed to a metal ring bolted onto a steel plate. She wasn't afraid, however. In fact, she was peaceful. Maybe it was because of her training, or Watson being alive, or because of all the things she'd already been through.

Regardless of the reason, she was the calm in the storm Dax had taught her to be and readied herself for *whatever*. So when the metal door squeaked opened at the far end, she was mentally and emotionally prepared.

Or thought she was.

"You're awake. Good," he said.

Mary's first thought was that it was another dream, but the searing pain when she tried to sit against the wall at the head of the bed told her otherwise, and the answer to *that* question lay in the bulletproof vest lying on the floor.

"You shot me in the back?"

Michael nodded and said. "Stun-gunned you, too."

"Why?" she asked, reeling from the initial shock.

He lifted the bottle he'd left for her and spilled out three ibuprofen. When she popped them in her mouth, he poured a glass of water. "It was the easiest way to deal with you. Drink."

"I mean, *why?*" Mary said after swallowing.

"Did I take you? Simple, lust and revenge." He pulled a folding chair to the bed and a knife from his back. "In case you do something stupid," he said, and then sat.

"I don't understand, Michael. Is that even your name?"

"It's the American equivalent of my given one. Miko."

Mary shook her head, trying to clear a muddled mind. "I don't get it. Why kidnap me? It must have been obvious how much I liked you. I thought you liked me, too."

"Oh, I do. And I will. Don't you worry about that."

His smile was lecherous and lacked any of the warmth she felt on the college campus in their private nook. And the realization that it had all been a lie crushed her spirit. She was a stupid little girl who let herself be fooled into love.

Mary choked back a tear, along with the hurt. Her skin crawled thinking of how she'd rubbed up against him on the beach, and with the thought came a cold, hard anger. She'd been toyed with, played for a sucker, and the affection she had for Michael became a revulsion for Miko.

"And the revenge?" she said dispassionately.

"Well, so you know, I was satisfied with just taking you. You're quite the little vixen, but you know that. Your father certainly did and I'm looking forward to hearing all about it. As for the revenge . . ."

Mary listened as he told it – how he'd wanted her after seeing her on television, had those boys try to snatch her at school, followed her to Leigha's, and played a hide and seek game with her cellphone. But after he went on a rant about what Dax did to his *poor Uncle Dimi*, she'd had enough.

"For crying out loud, your uncle was a pedophile and a murderer who deserved to die. But that's not why he's dead. He sent men to kill Dax's fiancé! Me too, if I'd let them. You think he's supposed to put up with that? No, your uncle is responsible. He fucked up, plain and simple. End of story."

Miko leaned forward and poked the side of her breast with the tip of his blade. He thought of killing her for sass, but it would only be a moment's pleasure compared to the countless others to come. He couldn't wait to violate her *six ways to Sunday* and break her like a wild pony. He might try to tame her without drugs or restraints. It could be dicey, though. She was lethal, dangerous even, and he'd have to be careful. But just the thought of her thrashing and fighting like hell as he held her down gave him an erection.

"I wouldn't count my chickens yet," Mary said, ignoring the confusion in his eyes. She could've grabbed for the knife, but then what? He'd just move, and the handcuff prevented her from going after him. She needed to be patient and wait for the optimal time to strike, like her Nerf-knife training. In the meantime, she kept him close by keeping him engaged.

"You should let me go. Now, before Dax finds you."

"Did you hear what I said? Newman was expecting him. Your dad is dead. They all are."

"I doubt it," she said. "Can't say the same for *your* men."

Miko brought the knife to her neck and grinned.

"You're a cocky little bitch, aren't you? Alright, let's say they are. So what? The guy you knifed at FSU doesn't know shit, and Newman wouldn't *say* shit, no matter what."

"I'm sure your uncle thought the same of *his* tough guys when he had them go to my mom's house. But, so you know, Lucas gave me Anthony and your uncle's name after a little *persuasion.* And I, in turn, gave them to Dax. It's sort of like the circle of life, don't you think? Only in reverse."

Miko pressed on the blade to replace her sass with fear, but she looked at him in a matter of fact, go-ahead way. He'd never seen such nerve in someone so young.

And never in a girl.

"Your best bet is to call it all a wash, Dax and your uncle. I suggest you let me go and leave us be. If you do, I'll ask him to leave you alone and let you *live*. I'll even beg, if I have to."

"That won't be necessary," I said and stepped inside the metal box contained inside an overgrown hill. The back of a seated man obscured her face, but I heard her fine.

"Dax, wait..."

I didn't understand why she'd said it until he stood and turned. Geezo-Pete, the man was nothing but a boy.

"Yeah, Dax. Wait," he said, holding a blade against her throat. I would have killed him right off if not for its location – the carotid artery. If I shot him in the head, gravity would be all it would take to cut her neck as his body fell.

"Drop it, or she dies. Now," he said with a sneer.

I looked at Mary, raised the hand supporting my gun in surrender, and let the one holding it lower slightly so I could shoot the boy's elbow. It was the best chance to get the knife off her neck before wiping the smirk from his face for good.

It was risky, but what choice did I have? You never give up your gun in a hostage situation. If you do, everyone dies. Just as I was about to pull the trigger, my head exploded.

"Kill him," Miko told Alexi.

Mary didn't waste a millisecond pleading or yelling but did the only thing she could – sink her teeth into Michael's forearm. And when the knife fell to her lap, she picked it up by the blade and threw it at the man with his arm raised to bash Dax's brains in with a broken branch in his hand.

The sound satisfied as the sharp point entered his neck, and, if he had left it there, he might have survived. But like most people would, he pulled it out...

She moved quickly while Michael was still within reach, rolling to her side and kicking him where most vulnerable. As he doubled over, she wrapped the crook of a leg around the back of his neck and brought him closer. Her handcuffed wrist and arm cried out in pain, but she held on tight so her legs could link. And though he hollered, punched, scratched and bit, she didn't let go till the life was squeezed out of him.

~

Mary listened to her Aunt Jeri tell Dax they'd found her phone in the bed of a stranger's truck, Leigha's friends were safe and sound, and that she was on her way to the hospital and would talk to him when she got there. Her tone changed when she said *Anatovich* and it made Mary nervous for him. Something was different, but she couldn't think about that.

As they wrapped up their speakerphone conversation, she faced the window and let the tears fall.

Thank God, Tasha was okay! Watson, too. But she'd be lying if she said all her tears were for them.

Mary chastised herself for still loving the boy who had made her laugh, talked mathematics, and thought Seinfeld was a comedic genius. Dax didn't know who Michael was or what he'd meant to her, having only heard the latter part of what they said to each other. All he knew was Miko wanted to even the score, and she hadn't told him anything else.

Not yet. Not tonight. Tomorrow. Maybe.

She did her best to wipe her face without appearing to, feeling guilty for wasting lovelorn tears on an illusion.

Or more accurately, a delusion.

"A penny for your thoughts," I said after we crossed the Florida border. I hadn't meant to intrude but did so anyway, needing to know if Mary was doing alright. She'd been quiet since we left the storage container.

"Did you know that saying is over five-hundred years old? I often wonder what that *penny* is worth nowadays."

"Do you now?" I asked with some skepticism.

She gave a short-lived grin and a thanks for saving her.

"I can't take much credit for that. In fact, you saved me."

"Are you sure?" she said facetiously. "Didn't you violate your own rule in order to create a diversion?"

"Uh..."

"The one that says never get into a conversation with a bad guy when your rear-end is exposed? I must say, the way you suckered that man inside was brilliant. And letting him crack you over the head was a nice touch. Very believable."

"Alright, you. In my defense, I was focused on how to keep you alive. And for the record, I said four or five words, tops. That's hardly a conversation."

"Uh-huh," she offered.

"That was a hell of a throw with that knife, hon," I said. "Couldn't have done it better myself."

"Thanks. I was aiming for his chest."

I started to laugh, but her eyes said she wasn't kidding. *Holy moly...*

"How did you find me, by the way?" she asked.

"Your earrings."

"Oh, really? So you didn't give me real pearls?"

"I did, but they're home in the safe. I swapped them out after the incident at Tasha's. Please, don't be mad," I said.

"I'm not. It seems like too many people are out to get me. And you just don't want to lose your little girl."

"Exactly. Damn, I'm so glad you understand. You know, what I'd really like to do is get you Microchipped. Like those identification implants that let you keep track of a dog."

"Are you saying I'm more like a pet to you?"

I don't think she really thought that, but her expression was priceless. "Of course not, Kitten. But that reminds me, your litter box needs cleaning when we get home."

She smiled and said, "Okay, sure. I will if you will."

"Will what?"

"Get chipped. Then I'll know when you sneak up on me. Like you did tonight on the beach."

"Mare, I was not sneaking... And who was that boy?"

Her smile wavered and she reached over and flipped on the siren. Guess she didn't want to talk about that right now.

"Are you alright?" Mary shouted to me over the noise.

"Yeah," I said, rubbing the back of my neck. "I'm good."

chapter twenty-five

The receptionist in the hospital lobby gave me the floor and room numbers, along with a funny look when the doors to the elevator closed – a look she must have call-forwarded, because the lady at the nurse's desk gave me the same one.

"Please wait while I page the doctor, Mr. Palmer," she said, but Mary couldn't and left to go find Watson.

"Miss?"

"Please, Ellen," I said, after glancing at her nameplate. "It's been a heck of a night, and she needs to see her brother. I hope you understand."

Ellen nodded, though a bit oddly, and called for Dr. Kim.

"I want to thank y'all for taking such good care of him. It's really appreciated," I told her.

"You can thank Detective Murphy," she said, gesturing down the hallway. "He was very insistent."

"I will. Thanks."

"Dr. Kim? This is Mr. Palmer, Miss Williams' husband and Watson's... Father?" she said, smiling for the first time.

"Friend," I corrected and shook the doctor's hand. She gave me the details of their respective surgeries, but it was what she said last that threw me for a loop.

"Your wife lost a lot of blood and will need bed rest for a few days. But she'll be fine. So will the baby."

Baby?

"Thank you, Doctor," was all I could say, and she patted my arm and walked away.

What baby?

"Mr. Palmer?" Detective Murphy said. "I know you want to see your wife and I'm sorry to ask, but could we talk for a few minutes first?"

He led me to a quiet niche that offered some privacy.

"I see you found your daughter. Thank God. Y'all had one hell of a night. Three dead in Wewahitchka ... I assume there are others?"

"Two more in Georgia," I told him. Why not? It would be all over the news first thing in the morning.

"Well, I'm sure they had it coming."

He looked at me in earnest and I answered accordingly.

"Yes, they did. What's on your mind, Detective?"

"My serial killer. Some new information came up and I was hoping to run it by you."

"And why would you want to do that?" I asked, knowing full well the reason. I could have begged off; said I was tired and wanted to see Tasha. But he'd show up at another time, another place. Besides, speaking to him was the least I could do to repay the kindness he'd shown me tonight.

"I have respect for how you think, Mr. Palmer," he said. "Your insight could be helpful."

Yeah, right.

His flattery, though wasted on me, was subtle. Efficient. I was sure many had fallen victim to it, based on my internet investigation. Murphy's conviction rate of those he arrested was higher than every detective in the county, combined.

"Well, I don't know how much help I can be, but I'll try. And call me Dax."

"Thanks. Dax, there was a man murdered about a year ago in Destin. Maybe you heard about it – he was stabbed multiple times in the chest and then shot in the head."

"Parked in front of his ex-wife's home, as I recall."

"Yes. Mrs. Dobson is her name."

"How is Elisabeth doing? Is she well?" I seemed to have surprised him, but he bounced back quickly enough.

"How well do you know her?"

"I don't. Not really. I met her once in the hospital."

"Why was that?" he said, but I thought he already knew. It was clear he had spoken to her and that's why he'd asked.

"I saw her story on the news and my heart went out. Since I was in town for a gig, I decided to visit and give what little comfort I could. She'd been beaten, you know. And not for the first time."

"I see," Murphy said. "When was that?"

"I'm not sure. Perhaps you could remind me?" I had every belief that Elisabeth Dobson hadn't given him what he needed to arrest me. But, like a dog with a bone, he was not going to let it go. And he let me know it.

"It was nine hours before her ex-husband was killed."

"Interesting," I said, and it was. Not the murder, but his attempt to indirectly pin the tail on me. "Why was he there, I wonder?"

"What do you mean?" Murphy asked.

"Why would someone the police thought put her in the hospital, a man who had a restraining order against him, be allowed to be in front of her house in the first place?"

I told him just as indirectly why that man needed to die.

"Had you ever seen or met Mr. Dobson?" he said.

"No. Can't say as I have." That was a lie.

"Are you sure? At one of your performances, maybe?"

"Nope. I'm sure," I said. Lie number two. I could've said I didn't recollect, a legal ploy to protect me from perjury, but I went with *nope* instead.

"Well, that might be a problem. You see, I spoke to the manager of the Hog's Breath Saloon, and he said you were playing the night Mr. Dobson was killed."

"That sounds about right," I said calmly, patiently. "But how is that a problem? Did he complain about my playing?" *Ha-ha.*

"He said Dobson was there the same time you were."

"Really?" I told him, more a deflection of the truth. Let's call it a half-lie.

"Said he was up by the stage, sitting in front of you."

"You're kidding. Huh." Another half-lie, but now a truth. "Wait, did he have like ten empty beer bottles on his table?" It was actually twelve, but who's counting?

Detective Murphy looked a little annoyed, but that was his problem. Mine was staying out of jail.

"You're saying you didn't know who he was?" he asked. His inflection betrayed the truth of what he believed.

"Yes." That's four lies if you add the halves, for those of you keeping score.

"So, you come into town, visit Mrs. Dobson, see her ex, leave the bar minutes after he does, then he ends up dead? That's one hell of a coincidence, Mr. Palmer."

"I agree."

"I don't believe in coincidences," Brian said and stared. Maybe he thought I'd crack under the light of his glare.

"Well, just because you don't believe in them doesn't mean they don't exist, Detective. Else why go to the trouble of creating such a lengthy word to explain its occurrence?"

I stood to take my leave and chose to give him his due. "So. You think I'm the guy?"

His grin confirmed my suspicion. A smart detective like Murphy would most likely watch the smartest detective on television – Adrian Monk. And in every episode, Monk said *He's the guy* to let you know he knew who did it.

"Yes, I do," Murphy said, with conviction

"I see. Is there anything I can say to change your mind?"

"I don't think so."

I then asked him something a bit more personal. "What do you think about that new theme song they sprang on us?"

His grin became a smile, and I shared it with him.

"It's alright. You can't go wrong with Randy Newman. But I prefer the old one. It fit better; I think."

"Me, too," I said and extended my hand. "Thank you for looking after my family. I owe you."

"You're welcome, Dax. I'll see you again," he said.

"Take care, Brian," I told him and left for Tasha's room.

Between Murphy, Dominic, and Jeri, there was a whole lot of challenges comin' round that mountain when it comes. Including any other potential Anatovich assholes who might crawl out from under the muck.

The knot at the back of my head had a heartbeat all its own, and I considered asking for something to ease the pain. But the music of their mirth beckoned like Pied Piper's flute.

I gazed at them in fascination from the doorway.

One was shot, the other stolen. Both could have died. But here they were, laughing, having fun. Looking ahead to better days rather than dwell on what was behind.

Damn, I love those girls.

"What's so funny?" I asked and walked into the room.

"You are," Tasha said. "Mary says you've been demoted pending a review, on account of her having to step in and save the day. Said there's a new Dax in town, and she's it."

"So the student has now become the master?" I asked a pleased-with-herself, grinning-from-ear-to-ear, little girl.

"Hai," she said, hardly able to contain her glee.

"Well, scooch over Miss Miyagi and let me give Mama-san a kiss and a look-see."

Mary made room, and I touched my forehead to Tash's. It was our way of connecting. Her eyes were filled with love. She didn't blame me for what happened or despise me for leaving her to die alone.

I teared up for some reason and rather than let it spill on her cheek or, God forbid, let Mary see me close to crying, I said something to take the spotlight off of me.

"The doctor says you're pregnant?"

"What? Really?" Mary squealed.

"Yes. I just found out myself."

"That's great, Tash!! What is it?" she said.

"I don't know." Tasha looked at me.

"Me either," I told her, and then said, "Congratulations."

"Thanks," she said with eyes full of sparkle and light.

"Who's the father?" I asked with the straightest of faces, one we'd laugh about for years to come. Tasha couldn't wait and started in right away, trying to slap at me but unable to because of the tube in her hand.

"Mary, will you please smack your Dad for me?"

"Sure," she said and socked him in the arm. Or tried to. But he was lightning quick for an old man and side-stepped her attempt. He *did* trip and fall backwards against the wall, which turned out to be funnier than if she had hit him. They laughed until they were crying and continued as he lay still on the floor to milk every last guffaw from them.

"Stop," Tasha wailed. "Your killing me!"

"Alright, you had your fun," Mary said. "And so did we. You can get up now." She kicked his foot, but he didn't move. "Come on, Dax. Quit it..."

Panic masked the pain when her knees hit the floor. "Dax, wake up! Stop... Please!! Don't... Daaadd!!!"

chapter twenty-six

2:37AM.

That was when a tectonic shift in Mary's being caused a crack in the foundation of who she was. They were both inconsolable. The only difference was Tasha cried for three days straight, and Mary did not.

She couldn't.

Tasha needed her. Watson, too. And if she gave in to despair, Mary knew it would destroy her. So she pretended to be a stoic and kept herself together, even though she was irrevocably broken.

The doctor said he died from a ruptured aneurism that must have developed between the thin tissues of his brain after he'd been hit in the head with a crowbar by the woman from the Indian Pass Raw Bar.

Mary asked if it could've burst from his falling against the wall when he tried to avoid being socked in the hospital, and the doctor told her *no*. It was the thick branch he'd been struck with, he said, and she was not responsible.

He might have been lying to protect her, but she needed it to be true more than she needed the truth. So she grabbed hold of his words and held on to them tightly in desperation, like a drowning person clinging to a life preserver.

~

They scattered his ashes on the water near Bird Island.

"He loved it here," Tasha said. "It'll be a nice place to come and spend time with him."

Mary didn't disagree but wished she could've given Dax what he really wanted by tossing his body into the water so he could feed the fish, as they'd fed him. And if she hadn't been caught trying to sneak him out of the hospital morgue, she would have.

The wishes of the dead, however, were less important than those of the living.

Especially if it was her pregnant, grieving mother.

An impromptu wake occurred when some people came by the house to bring food and give condolences. Mary kept her eye on Tash, Jeri, and Isabel, and followed their example by being cordial. But it was difficult.

It didn't help that she hadn't slept since the hospital, and, when a one too many well-meaning person asked how she was doing, Mary almost said, 'How the hell do you think? My dad is fucking dead!'

She had to leave. Now.

Mary took Isabel by the hand and led her outside.

"I have to get away from the house for a while," she told her. "Go for a ride."

"Can I come with you?" Isabel said, hoping she'd say *yes*.

"No. I need to be alone. Will you let Tash and Watson know when I'm gone? Look after them till I get back?"

Isabel nodded and threw her arms around Mary.

"I'm so sorry, Mare."

Mary patted and rubbed her back, rubbed and patted. "I know, Belle. I know. Me, too."

She sent her back inside, climbed into Dax's pick-up, pulled out of the garage, maneuvered around the visiting vehicles, and drove down the driveway.

~

She couldn't remember driving to the Indian Pass boat launch, but it didn't matter. Not really. Not anymore.

After leaving the keys above the visor, she got out of the truck and decided to take a walk along the beach, ignoring others by keeping her eyes glued to the sand.

Her mind was scattered, undisciplined. One minute she thought about everything all at once, and then there would be periods of emptiness. Time had no meaning and served no purpose as she kept her head down and put one foot in front of the other until feet became yards, then miles.

Only once did she look up, when the sun was about to blink out for the night.

Dax told her stories he'd heard others tell of a bright green light that flashed the moment the sun slipped past the horizon. And though he'd looked for years, decades, he saw it only one time. A few weeks ago, in fact.

She wanted to see it, as well. To share it with him, feel their bond, know he was still there.

But there was nothing. No light, no connection.

No Dax.

Her phone began to ring more persistently as the night settled in, and she reached into her back pocket to throw it into the water out of irritation. But she turned it off instead.

It wasn't their fault. They were just worried about her. She was, too.

When she neared the tip of the peninsula, a part of her said she'd travelled over twenty miles. Another part asked if she were trying to walk herself to death. She didn't think so, hadn't planned to, at least, but...

She fell to her knees, just as she had in the hospital days ago and felt her heart pounding against the wall of her chest. She took a deep breath. And then another, deeper still.

Mary closed her eyes, and then lay on her back after the pain began to ebb. The sound of water lapping on the shore made her want to cry, and, when she looked up, it reminded her of the night he found her in the woods.

She would give everything to have him back.

When an errant star shot across the sky, she wished on it harder that she'd ever wished for anything.

~

Mary didn't realize she had fallen asleep until she found herself perched on a low-hanging cumulus cloud with no interest or desire to fly. Her heart was heavy, melancholy.

And her thoughts were of...

"Dax," she whispered.

He knew how she felt about him. Still, she wished she'd told him more often. Maybe thrown in a hundred more hugs to go with those occasional punches to his arm.

But the longer she thought about him, the madder she got. If it weren't for rotten bastards like her father and other like-minded sons of bitches in the world, Dax would still be alive. They had no right to live. None.

"I'm going to kill them. All of them."

"Hold up, Buttercup," he said and sat down next to her. "I'm wondering if we can't find another way. A better way."

Dax!!

"I was just thinking the other day..." His voice soothed her troubled spirit, and she slipped an arm in his, leaned up against him and listened.

After he was done, she told him all about Michael and apologized for lying. He cautioned about hardening herself against love, said her deception was within the tolerances of their honesty pact, and told her they were *good*.

The burden of her worry fell away after hearing that.

They spoke of casual things, fun things, and later sat in quiet comfort, lazily moving their feet back and forth as they dangled over the edge of the cloud.

"I miss you," she said.

"There's no need. I'm here, sweetie. And I'll always be. Whenever you'd like. For as long as you like."

"No. You're not. This is just a dream. It's not real."

"Have you forgotten what happens if you build it?"

With a wave of his hand, the *Field of Dreams* ballfield appeared before them. Mary's eyes lit in wonder, and Dax marched down the bleacher steps toward the first-base line.

"You know, I was a darn good ball player in high school. Could've gone pro, I think. If I'd applied myself."

"Uh-huh."

"No, really," he said and stepped over the chalked stripe to the infield, transforming into his seventeen year-old self and wearing a baseball uniform with maroon lettering.

"Romulus? Where's that?" she asked.

"Michigan," he said, swinging the long bat in his hands. "Man, that feels good. It's been a long time."

"You were kinda cute back in the day, Dax."

"Thanks, hon."

"What the heck happened?" she asked, grateful for the opportunity to tease him again.

"Uh-huh," he said, with a now boyish grin. "Well, see ya later, alligator." When he turned to leave, she wanted him to hear what he already knew, to say what she needed to say.

"I love you, Dad."

"Me too, kiddo."

"Which is it?" she said. "You love you too? Or me, too?"

She grinned when he chuckled, smiled while he jogged into the outfield, and cracked up as he disappeared into the Iowa cornstalks miming, "I'm melting. I'm melting!"

The tears on her face could have been from laughter or sorrow but either way, she jumped up off the bleacher seat and ran out across the field.

"Wait up," Mary hollered, not ready to let him go.

Not sure if she would ever be.

thanks for reading

I was having trouble finding the right thing to say after killing off a beloved character and turned to a colleague.
"I don't know . . . Beloved? Really?" was her response. She's a funny lady. Also, a writer. And my best friend.
The truth is, I didn't want Dax to die. But sometimes, what an author wants isn't always what they get. And so . . . I'm curious about what happens next.
Maybe you are, as well.

As always, I want to thank you for spending time with me. Perhaps we'll meet again.

larehalebooks@gmail.com

Made in the USA
Columbia, SC
15 March 2022